THE VALLEY OF THE GOD OF YOUR CHOICE, INC.

WILDSIDE BOOKS BY DAMIEN BRODERICK

Adrift in the Noösphere: Science Fiction Stories
Building New Worlds: New Worlds *Science Fiction. The Carnell Era, Volume One* [with John Boston]
Chained to the Alien: The Best of ASFR: Australian SF Review (Second Series) [Editor]
Climbing Mount Implausible: The Evolution of a Science Fiction Writer
Embarrass My Dog: The Way We Were, the Things We Thought
Ferocious Minds: Polymathy and the New Enlightenment
Human's Burden: A Science Fiction Novel (with Rory Barnes)
I'm Dying Here: A Comedy of Bad Manners (with Rory Barnes)
New Worlds: *Before the New Wave. The Carnell Era, Volume Two* [with John Boston]
Post Mortal Syndrome: A Science Fiction Novel (with Barbara Lamar)
Skiffy and Mimesis: More Best of ASFR: Australian SF Review (Second Series) [Editor]
Unleashing the Strange: Twenty-First Century Science Fiction Literature
Warriors of the Tao: The Best of Science Fiction: A Review of Speculative Literature [Editor with Van Ikin]
Strange Highways: Reading Science Fantasy [with John Boston]
Xeno Fiction: More Best of Science Fiction, *A Review of Speculative Literature* [Editor with Van Ikin]
x, y, z, t: Dimensions of Science Fiction
The Valley of the God of Our Choice, Inc (with Rory Barnes)
Zones: A Science Fiction Novel (with Rory Barnes)

OTHER WILDSIDE BOOKS BY RORY BARNES

The Bomb-Monger's Daughter
The Dragon Raft: A Young Adult Novel
Space Junk: A Science Fiction Novel

THE VALLEY OF THE GOD OF YOUR CHOICE, INC.

DAMIEN BRODERICK
AND RORY BARNES

WILDSIDE PRESS

To the memory of the Good Doctor,
Isaac Asimov,
and all his Alternates

INTRODUCTION

I blame Dr. Isaac Asimov. It's all his vault.

Forty percent of my lifetime ago, when the Good Doctor was four years younger than I am now, he published a book with the curious title *The Alternate Asimovs*. It was not about his parents, his wives or his children (two of each), nor did it detail the scientific and science fictional adventures of alternative Isaacs in far-flung parallel worlds. No, these were earlier and unpublished versions of two novels and one story by Asimov—later developed, or in one case editorially deformed, into well-known items in his extensive catalogue. They had been retrieved from a special vault in the Boston University Library dedicated to his work.

"Grow Old Along With Me" was the 163 page nascent version of Asimov's first stand alone novel, *Pebble in the Sky*. By the standards of the 1950s and 1960s, this short novel of some 49,000 words was almost long enough to be released as a paperback, but in 1949 it had to be extended to 70,000 words to sell to Doubleday. (These days it would have to become a trilogy, or at least bloat out to 170,000 words.)

The significant time-travel novel *The End of Eternity* from 1955 (now often regarded by critics as one of Asimov's best and most ingenious, despite a certain clunkiness) was first sketched in a 90 page novella under the same title. Completed in early 1954, it had been sent to Horace Gold, the famous editor of the then new magazine *Galaxy*. Gold had already serialized *The Caves of Steel*, destined to become perhaps the best known of Asimov's famous robot novels. But he rejected "The End of Eternity," and a year later Asimov expanded it to its published form as a novel.

Finally, *The Alternate Asimovs* revived the original version of a 50 page story, "Belief," about a man who found to his chagrin that he could levitate. Only after the last third of the tale was recast into more upbeat form would editor John W. Campbell allow it in 1953 into the hallowed pages of *Astounding* magazine.

In 1986, I read this unusual gathering of what might be considered half-baked stories, fascinated by the opportunity it offered to look into the hidden past and trace the development of a science fiction writer through the sometimes agonizing process of revision, addition, excision.

And Asimov's boldness in allowing these works to be plucked from his vault and displayed encouraged me to do something similar. (Yes, yes, I know I'm not worthy to touch the hem of the Good Doctor's sandal, but allow me some rhetorical leeway here.) I've never had the gall to imagine a book titled *The Alternate Brodericks*, but I have published versions of stories and indeed whole novels that I later expanded, revised, bent, spun and mutated. *The Black Grail* was a longer and greatly improved version of my first-published novel, which rejoiced in the horrid publisher-imposed title *Sorcerer's World* (the original title was *The Gate Between the Worlds*, also not my own but at least not as coarse and misleading,).

I rejigged my mainstream novel *Transmitters*—a postmodern collage that appropriated chunks from an unpublished novel by my frequent co-author Rory Barnes, with his permission—as *Quipu* (E-Reads 2009) in its US release. Another collaboration, YA Singularity novel *Stuck in Fast Forward* (HarperCollins Australia 1999), was morphed into the much more adult and elaborate *The Hunger of Time* (E-Reads 2004). And some stories have appeared in both raw and cooked forms: "The Sea's Furthest End," published in 1964 when I was 20, grew into the long novella "The Game of Stars and Souls" in my collection *Uncle Bones* (Fantastic Books 2009).

* * * *

This time, though, Rory Barnes and I are offering something rather different: the unpublished short novel that subsequently evolved into the prize-winning *Transcension* (Tor Books 2002). Asimov mentioned in an Afterword to "Grow Old Along with Me" that his book might be regarded as "a kind of teaching exercise on 'How to Revise'…" while noting that "there may even be some who will get a certain pleasure" from the original version and not bother to search out the revision. That could be the case here, too, since the reception of *Transcension*, which is a consciously challenging read, included puzzlement, head-shaking and some finger-wagging.

On the enthusiastic side, critic Lisa DuMond wrote: "Along with the serious questions to ponder in *Transcension*, there is also action, danger, romance, and humor. So much of the dialogue in the Valley of the God of One's Choice is tempting to share, but that would spoil it for you. And if Broderick's work is about anything, it's about temptation, so give in to it. Go ahead." She added: "One of the slickest tricks in *Transcension* is the subtle growth of the adolescent characters, maturing in their thoughts and speech with every page turned. Even some of the 'adult' characters manage to surprise with bursts of growth just when none seemed possible."

But these markers of steps toward maturation in our character Amanda annoyed at least one Amazon patron:

> …the narrative of Amanda (one of the two main characters) is told almost entirely in her deferred-teenage slang, the salient feature of which is the omission of virtually all articles and prepositions, so that it resembles a sort of literally-translated Russian, only worse. I found it very, very wearing to read.

It's not hard to see why some fans of traditional sf might feel that way. Here's a sample of Amanda's voice from early in *Transcension*:

> Feet touched curved metal, shoes gripped. Hanger still dim, empty. Stood there few beautiful seconds. Solid bulk freighter beneath feet didn't vibrate, hum. Right now quiet as tomb—but could feel supersonic power of thing. One day would ride it. Breathed deeply, extended both arms in welcoming gesture to team Stodes bursting into hanger, yelling instructions: get down, stay where are, put hands on head.

And another:

> Started sob, quite loudly. Couldn't help. Chest shook, hands shook as well, even though locked together against waist. Said nothing. Sour taste in mouth got worse, like vomit.

Long-time science fiction readers might be reminded of the somewhat Russianized voice of Manny, narrator of Robert Heinlein's *The Moon is a Harsh Mistress* (1966), or of the even more abbreviated, clipped diction of the brilliant child Candy Smith-Foster, in David R. Palmer's *Emergence* (1984). It takes some time to acclimatize yourself to this speeded-up vernacular. But that's a thing about the future, and about adolescents, isn't it? They speak differently from their parents and other adults.

Still, let's acknowledge that it can be a strain. The original version, presented in this volume, is only half the length of *Transcension*, and Amanda and her peer group speak pretty much like kids on TV today. Perhaps this makes it easier to sink into her world, to enter into imaginative empathy with her frustrations, adventurous spirit, dangerous recklessness, and slowly developing bond with Mathewmark, a young man from the Valley of the God of Our Choice, Inc. At any rate, Rory and I decided that it's worth giving readers the chance to look through clearer glass into these alternative societies of the future. In the Afterword to this book, we'll describe how we two writers created this book, and I then wrought its more demanding descendent.

And then, annoyingly, lost the original after two separate backup systems crashed, and the file vanished from two computers in two countries separated by almost half the planet. And a decade later we found it, on one 3.5 inch diskette buried in a pile of old computer garbage neither of us could read any longer. And then discovered a legacy machine, in a library, that could open the lost file. Phew. So here it is again, safe and sound and found.

And as they used to say in the pulp magazines:
Now read on...

—Damien Broderick,
January 2014

1: MATHEWMARK

Old man Grout kicked up a splendid fuss when the metro tunneled under our valley. He prayed like a madman in church, yelling to the lord his god. Yelling to the lord our god. Yelling to every god in the Valley, although some of them are goddesses and some of them Gaia and a few of them stranger gods still. We all believe, in the Valley, one way or another. Although, secretly, some of us believe that our neighbors believe a bit too much.

Old Grout was something to see. He was something to hear. His wild white hair stood on end. It must have been the electrical activity in his brain. Old man Grout gave the god of his choice orders in a booming voice: strike down the works of polluters, pour boiling oil on the tunnelers, send plagues, send scorpions, send the hounds of Hell.

We got the message all right—sitting there in church, trying not to giggle. But it was a bit hard to tell if old Grout's god got the message. And there was no way of knowing if the tunnelers got the message. Were they down there, drowning in boiling oil, leaping about like scalded cats, scratching at their hideous rashes, fending off the hounds from hell in the darkness of their infernal world? There was no way of knowing because the tunnel started hundreds of kilometers from our valley and it finished on the coast, fifty kilometers in the other direction.

The people in our Valley never leave our Valley. The only way you could know the tunnelers were down below us was to lie on the ground with your ear pressed hard against a rock. Then you heard them—faintly. You heard their machines, you heard noises like mice in a granary, sometimes you heard the distant rumble of explosives.

Old man Grout was furious. He'd stand in the yard of the church of his choice and wave his great bible in his hand.

"The Lord will not condone this wickedness," I heard him thunder one Wednesday morning, the sacred day of his sect. "Hearken to the word of revelation!" His yellow old beard was getting spittle-flecked. "Attend to the voice of the Psalmist, for it is said in Psalm 20, verse, um, er, seven: 'Some boast of chariots, and some of horses; but we boast of the name of the LORD our God.' Do you see, those who have eyes to see and ears to hear? The chariots of Man may thunder their way at the speed of a harnessed horse, but no faster, for list to the Psalmist: 'They will collapse and fall; but we shall rise and stand upright'."

There wasn't much to be said to gainsay that, it seemed to me, but on the other hand the argument wasn't *absolutely* persuasive. After all, in the days of the Hebrew prophets they didn't even *have* tunnels deep in the bowels of the earth—unless they were the ones driven by the fiends. Even more arguments were pronounced, though, which convinced the rest of the Valley. Old man Legrand stood in his own righteous kirk and quoted from the same bible.

"It saith in the Book of Isaiah the Prophet, book 35, verses eight and nine: 'A highway shall be there, and it shall be called the Holy Way; the unclean shall not pass over it, and fools shall not err therein'! The unclean polluters shall not pass over it, and by the God of our Choice the polluters shall not pass *under* it, either!"

All this talk of Holy Ways and chariots and horses gave me a powerful interest in the subject, I have to admit. I found myself dreaming of the old automobile in the Museum that used to be driven for mockery at Halloween, and wondered if it could go faster than a running horse back in the days when we still had a supply of gasoline in the Valley.

"Yea verily I tell you," old man Legrand was fuming, "in the vile days of the last century men of wicked ways did have mighty engines of two thousand horsepower under the bonnet, fuelled with the black oil of Egypt. But hear what Isaiah says in chapter 36 about that: 'I will give you two thousand horses, if you are able on your part to set riders upon them. How then can you repulse a single captain among the least of my master's servants, when you rely on Egypt for chariots and horsemen? The Lord said to me, go up against this land and destroy it'." There were moans aplenty, believe me, and many good folk made the sign o'god and bowed their heads in terror.

I never really understood why the authority even bothered to ask the Valley elders for permission to build their tunnel. They could have gone ahead and built the thing without telling anyone—nobody would have twigged. If anybody had heard the mice in the granary, they would have thought it was just that: little rodents, scratching about in their burrows, putting aside stolen grain for the winter. As it was, the tunnelers formally asked for permission, and then, when the elders split into warring factions and couldn't come to a collective decision, they made a secret deal and went ahead with the project anyway. I didn't know that at the time, of course, none of us did. It would have been a mighty scandal. If you ask me, though, there never was any real choice—the tunnelers were just going through the motions. I reckon their city slicker lawyers had told them to cover their backsides—consultation with the rural community, or their representatives, and the fewer of them the better.

Old man Grout used to spend half the day lying on the ground. You'd see him in his sorghum patch, his mules grazing unattended and eating the sorghum. Ear pressed against the earth, old man Grout listened to the sounds of depravity and corruption. Then he'd be up on his knees, yelling curses into the ground, shouting so loud you thought that maybe the tunnelers actually could hear him. A moment later he'd be standing up, his head thrown back, yelling at the god of his choice.

One day I was driving our cart past his sorghum patch. Ebeeneezer, our mule, is plodding along and suddenly he stops. There's old man Grout's mules just wandering about, blocking the track and there's old man Grout in the far corner of the patch. Only this time he's not prone on the ground, he's not listening, he's digging. He's digging like a madman. He's digging with a crowbar and shovel. The hole is a meter deep, all you can see is old man Grout's top half. And he's throwing dirt up into the air like a volcano. I got down off our cart and left it standing in the track. Ebeeneezer was standing nose to nose with one of old man Grout's mules. Perhaps they were talking to each other in some sort of mulish way. I walked over to old man Grout. I had to dodge a few clods of flying dirt. I stood on the edge of his hole and said, "They're bound to be hundreds of meters down, Uncle. You'll never reach them."

"God gave me muscles to dig with, boy," said old man Grout. "And what God gives, God wants used. He don't abide no slacking. I'll get there. I'll break through the roof of their godless tunnel and the glory of the Lord's wrath shall pour down like as unto the waters of Babylon, yea and the angel of the Lord shall not rest until the wicked...."

Old man Grout raved on, leaning on his shovel, staring up at me like some wild beast fallen into a trap. When I could get a word in, I said, "Another meter down and you're going to hit solid rock, Uncle. It will be rock all the way."

"Cleft for me!" yelled old man Grout into the hole. "Rock of ages! God helps those who help themselves. You need faith, boy, faith. If I get the thing started, the Almighty will pitch in too. The pair of us are unstoppable. Me and the Lord, we'll get there, we'll smite the heathen tunnelers, we'll smite them good!"

I left him to it. I climbed back onto our cart and went down the track to the McWeezles' place. I helped Auntie McWeezle load half a dozen sacks of turnips onto the back of the cart and then she asked me in for scones and buttermilk. As I was drinking the buttermilk I said, "Old man Grout's digging down to the tunnel. Him and the Lord are going to smite the tunnelers."

"Don't be disrespectful, Mathewmark," Auntie McWeezle said. "Uncle Grout walks in the eyes of the Lady."

"He told me himself," I said. "He's going to dig the first couple of meters all on his own, and then the Lord is going to lend a hand, do a bit of clefting."

"And the Lady just might, Mathewmark," Auntie McWeezle said, passing me another scone. "Faith moves mountains."

"I don't know that it digs shafts," I said. "That tunnel is surely a hundred meters down, if not five hundred."

"And a wicked, Gaia-hating thing it is," Auntie McWeezle said.

"It won't worry us," I said. "We won't even know it's there."

"Don't tell me those trains won't carry no polluters and gene-twisters," Auntie said. "Them trains will carry gamblers, idolaters, money lenders, fornicators, blasphemers, eaters of unclean foods, mockers of the word of the goddess and every kind of wickedness. The ground we walk on will be the roof of hell. The crops will wither. Strange mutant apples will turn to wormwood in the mouths of goddess-fearing folk..."

"You sound like old man Grout," I said.

"Uncle Grout may get a bit carried away at Sacred Service," Auntie said, "but..."

"He may get carried away in his hole," I said. "Carried away by the grim reaper. It looks to me like he's working on a heart attack, the way he was digging this morning."

Auntie McWeezle made the sign o'god in the air with her index finger. She's a good old soul, Auntie McW. Many's the time, when I've wanted someone to talk to, when I've wanted to get away from my parents and my kid brother—many's the time I've run to Auntie McWeezle's kitchen for sympathy and buttermilk.

"Don't say such a thing, Mathewmark," Auntie said now. "Don't tempt fate."

"It's old man Grout who's tempting fate," I said. "I'll bet you he's dead before planting time."

Auntie McWeezle shooed me out of the house. I climbed up on the cart and turned Ebeeneezer in the direction of our Village. I spent the rest of the day fetching and carrying for the good people of the Valley. It was almost night when I turned for home and let Ebeeneezer have his head. He'd need no more urging from me, he knew where we were going. As we were passing old man Grout's sorghum patch I noticed the last of the sun's rays glinting on his spade. It had been tossed out of the hole and left to lie where it had fallen. Old man Grout's mules were still milling around, trampling the sorghum. I jumped down from the cart and told

Ebeeneezer to continue on home by himself. I walked over to the hole. I knew exactly what I would find.

* * * *

There was a terrible irony about the hole that killed old man Grout, but we didn't know this until a week after his funeral. The tunnelers needed an air shaft, which had been negotiated during the endless legal battles at the Gatehouse. They had been clawing their way up towards the surface for several weeks, their machines grinding away, letting the broken rock fall to the tunnel below to be carried away five hundred kilometers to the coast. The air shaft came up out of the earth less than a meter from old man Grout's hole, so he hadn't been so crazy when he said he could hear them at their polluters' work. If he'd lived he would have met them on his way down. Him and his punishing Lord, and Mother Gaia, and all the other gods of our choice.

2: AMANDA

Mom had me grounded after our trial tube burn, and Vikram's parents did the same to him. Really annoying. I could flick my eyes up to the left as much as I liked and try to toggle my phone implant on, but the damned thing was dead as a doornail, and so was my vee access. I could use the monitored hard phone downstairs to call out and take incoming, I could e anyone in the world as long as the NannyWatch listened in like the robotic pest it is, I could go down the mall and hang with my friends—if I stayed inside burb bounds and came straight home by dinner time.

"Vik's my best friend, Mom," I whined. "This is cruel and unnatural punishment." I kept on in this vein until even I was sick of the sound of my own. Eventually, with an extremely bored glance from her piercing, glazed eyes, she looked up at me from her legal monitor. Mom was preparing some brief for the metro-to-coast Deep Maglev rail consortium. She and Dad had been battling the bigots of God's Bloody Valley for the last four and a half years, trying to establish their corporation's right to tunnel under the loonies' machine-free utopia. It was funny, really, in a gruesome way, because if my parents hadn't been so devoted to this particular law case I'd never have got the cool idea of riding the rods in the underground tubes.

Which is, I have to say modestly, one of the truly great ideas of my life.

"Amanda, darling," my mother said in a bright, chilly voice, "do you really want me to switch off your speech centers?"

I opened my mouth again, ready with a hot and angry answer, then shut it and swallowed hard. They'd done that to me once before, when I was about ten and unbearable. I'd been speechless for a whole day. Talk about cruel and unnatural! You stand there getting red in the face, moving your mouth, flapping your tongue, and nothing happens in your throat because your brain has been short-circuited. You know what you want to say, or think you do, but nothing comes out. Infuriating! I'd tried to get back at them by grabbing a spraygel and marking spiteful graffiti messages all over the living room vidwall, but somehow I couldn't make my arm turn the bright blue and red squiggles into words. All I managed to do was cover the wallscreen and myself with blobs of luminous gel. I felt like a tongue-tied baby, and ended up running into my room and squeezing the door and howling my eyes out.

So I knew what she was threatening me with. Worse, I knew she meant every word.

I swallowed again, hard.

"No."

"No, what, Amanda?"

No point arguing, I thought. No point demanding my fair and just rights as a senior child. No sense doing anything except knuckle under and wait for the next eight months and seventeen days to creep past one day at a time until I was legally an adult of 16 and could kick off out of this creep hole and maybe set up with Vikram and some other cool guyz in a flop.

"No, Mom, I don't want to force you and Daddy into imposing any more penalties on me for my own good."

"Fine. Now, darling, I still have rather a lot of work to finish before the council meeting this afternoon, so why don't you go to your room like a good girl and practice your violin?"

I stomped off to my soundproof room and sawed my way through a Mozart divertimento. It didn't divert me for long. I wondered if I could trap a wasp-ad and use it to send a message to Vikram. The mood I was in, we might as well both break curfew and scoot back to the freight hangars and try find some other way to hitch a supersonic ride through the bowels of the earth.

That's one of the benefits of having olds who are contracted to handle the legal tangles of the metro Maglev deep rail project. Vik and I had hacked the household Lawman program and downloaded about a million pages of AI jargon and engineering plans, then used a couple of smart ferrets to plough through the data and find us a way into the tunnels.

The first one we'd tried was too easy, too obvious, and a burn bust when the automatics found us all kitted out in blackgear and grappling nets trying to drop in through the maintenance hangar ceiling. Twenty minutes later we were standing in front of the city's Magistrate, Mr. Abdel-Malek, looking sheepishly at our feet. I knew it was only a matter of time before the olds arrived and coldly tore horrible bleeding strips off us. I was quite relieved when he sentenced us to a night's detention and remanded our hearing to the following morning.

And was I ever right about Mom and Dad's reaction.

"You disappoint us, Amanda," my Dad said, looking more furious than disappointed. "What a remarkably stupid thing to do."

"You do know that the freighters go supersonic once they enter the main conduit?" Mom asked, in a frighteningly relaxed voice. I couldn't tell if she was hiding the fright I'd put into her, or was genuinely unmoved. Maybe it was sufficient that I'd interrupted her routine. Both of them were dressed in evening clothes and had been fetched to the lock-up in a discreetly unmarked police autoglide from the opera, where no doubt they'd been sitting with some nauseating heavies from the tube project. I was supposed to be safely tucked up at home, racting a vee in my bedroom. Well, I'd certainly left them with that clear impression, meanwhile planning to sneak out the back way the moment they were driven off to the opera house.

"We had buckynets," I said in a surly voice, still looking at the tips of my toes, which were clad in grippo carbon sneakers. I don't know if Mom even knew that buckynets are the safest safety device in the world, made out of incredibly strong and reliable carbon tubes that lock together in a way that makes steel seem about as strong as brown paper. "We had mag grapples. We weren't taking any risks."

Mom made an alarming snort through her nose, and shook her head, once to the right, once to the left. It just killed me. It was so much worse than shouting, or smacking me, or for that matter turning me back over to the Magistrate. Her gaze shifted, then, and she smiled with a kind of awful cool beauty. Vikram's father had entered the chamber and was bearing down on us. Vikram's father is a big man, bigger than Dad, way bigger than Mom. I know which one of them I'm most afraid of.

"Dr. Singh," my father said, extending his hand. " Not the happiest occasion."

"Mr. Kolby, Legal McAllister, good evening." He was gruff, and his eyes were dark and angry under his crisp white turban. "I believe it is time to separate these children of ours."

"That is certainly my intention," Mom told him. "Until recently my daughter has had a unblemished record." This was untrue, of course, but it's not as if I've ever been charged with arson or murder or mutating household pets or anything. "I do not wish her to remain in danger of further—"

Dr. Singh rose to his full height, glaring down at my mother. She regarded him without the slightest fear, baring her perfect white teeth.

"I hope you are not suggesting that my son is a..."

"Not at all," said Dad hastily, looking a little flustered. "These are the pranks of adolescence, nothing more." He twitched his eyes in my direction, winked ever so slightly with the one out of the line of sight of the other two adults. In the face of this new threat to the whole family, his anger had come and gone, and even his disappointment at my stupidity. "I look forward to having them off our hands at Maturity."

"Well, that's as may be," Dr. Singh grumbled. "For the time being, I suggest you—" He paused, cleared his throat. Mother had gone absolutely lethal, even though she hadn't moved a muscle. "We had best all look to our charges. Speaking of which, have formal charges been laid?"

"The kids have been bound over in custodial detention for the evening," Dad told him. "No vee privileges, no phones. I think they'll be quite safe and comfortable. Hearing in the Magistrate's court at 10 am tomorrow. Will you or Mrs. Singh be in court?"

"I have a ballistic flight booked for Chicago at seven," Dr. Singh said. "My wife is in Delhi at the moment attending a family wedding, and my son and I were to join her in the afternoon. This little mess has ruined everything." He looked around him, hailing a peace officer imperiously. "So, no—I'm afraid young Vikram is going to have to face the music alone. Sir," he told the young night duty officer, "I'd like my boy brought out now, if you please."

"You wish us to keep an eye on the lad during your absence?" my father asked.

Dr. Singh sent a look of suppressed distaste over his shoulder. "On the contrary. I intend my son to have no further dealings with any member of your family. Good evening to you both." He swept off toward the holding area.

In a quiet, pleasant voice, my mother said, "You stupid, stupid girl. Do you see what you've done?" She took Dad's arm and turned him toward the exit desk. "Stew in your own juice, Amanda. And don't expect any privileges for at least three months, once they let you come home."

* * * *

I felt the usual blend of anger and sinking, stomach chewing loss. Why am I such a disappointment to my parents? But anyway, why should I care? All they ever think about is themselves and their damned careers and climbing the social ladder. Dr. Singh and his wife were rather higher up the social hierarchy than my family had yet managed to reach, even if Mom was the legal for one of the major new sub-surface construction projects. The Singhs were stockholders, not mere functionaries. I'd really blown it. Well, Vikram and I had blown it together, but he was the golden boy so I didn't suppose he would suffer any long term consequences. Damn-all chance *he'd* have his vee access cut off for a whole night. Good grief, what was I going to do? Stare at the ceiling of my cell? Scribble on the walls? Read a book?

It was a depressing and truly boring way to spend the night, but the next day in court was worse. Mr. Abdel-Malek, the principal Magistrate for our metro enclave, is a very calm gentleman with a soft and sinister tone to his voice. I've heard that society ladies find it quite sexy, in the right context. Plainly they've never heard him speaking to a miscreant who has threatened the freighter system by attempting to tie her webbed body to a maglev train due to thunder through the new metro-to-coast tube at the speed of sound. Actually I dispute that we put anyone or anything in danger. Vik and I did extensive sims of the air flow, the vector changes, the stresses we'd experience in our protective webbing, all that. Piece of cake. Well, not really a piece of cake, or it wouldn't be worth doing. But nothing lethal. Just really, really glumpzoid. We'd be the talk of the Mall. We'd be Mall gods.

Or would have been, if we'd even got as far as the freighters themselves. As it was, everything came unstuck and unraveled when we entered the loading hangars. It was baffling. I spent much of the night unable to sleep, staring at the blank ceiling, wondering about this. There had to be another way in to the tube, somewhere the automatics weren't watching every square micrometer.

* * * *

Standing next to head hanging Vikram Singh watching Mr. Abdel-Malek enter the adjudication room and take his place behind a large, plain desk top, a jolt went through me. It wasn't fright, although I was certainly worried that the adults had got together and devised some awful punishment, like forbidding us to visit the Mall until we were 30 or something. Instant social death. Better they should cut our heads off and freeze us down and be done with it. No, what sent an electric spark through my bones was a moment of truth. I knew how to get in to ride the freighter!

"Vik," I hissed.

"Not now, Mand," he muttered back. He was avoiding my eyes. His Dad must have torn a strip off him.

"Listen, I've just thought of a—"

"All be seated," an auto voice told us. Mr. Abdel-Malek had already lowered his elegantly trousered backside onto an ergonomic support and was accessing a summary of our crimes and misdemeanors—you could tell by the way his eyes were slightly raised and directed at the ceiling, the sure sign that his brain was downloading a compressed data file. After a moment he glanced back down and looked at us both. I quailed, despite myself.

"You know why you're here," he told us. No time wasting formalities for the Magistrate. "You have had eleven hours in detention to consider the gravity of your offence. Do you have anything to say in mitigation?"

Neither of us spoke.

"Amanda?"

"Uh, sir, there was really no danger, you know, we had taken every—"

His voice was soft and calm and send a shudder through me. "I do not wish to listen to your self-serving excuses and rationalizations, Ms. Kolby-McAllister. I have read your confession of fault. You clearly understand the seriousness of what you tried to do. Is there anything you would care to add that might explain what you and this young man did? I am not interested in hearing you attempt to duck your responsibility."

Just youthful high spirits, I thought. Blame it on hormones, I thought. We were bored shitless, I thought, what's *wrong* with you people? Of course I didn't say any of that, I'm not completely self-destructive, rumors to the contrary notwithstanding.

"No, sir. I'm very sorry."

"Vikram Singh, anything to add? I see that your previous record is not quite so murky as that of your co-defendant."

"I'm also very sorry, sir," Vik told him, and sounded as if he meant it. The boy was altogether too law-abiding by nature, if you ask me. I was burning with eagerness to tell him the great new idea I'd had, the terrific way we could side-step the automatics and get on the freighters after all for a major fun run through the depths.

The Magistrate sighed and steepled his fingers. "Both of you are on the verge of Maturity, so I will not speak to you as if you were still children. You are certainly old enough to know right from wrong, lawful from lawless, sensible from recklessly stupid. You plainly both knew that what you attempted would be dangerous both to yourselves and to the safe operation of a very expensive transportation system. Ms. Kolby-McAllister, you are especially culpable in this regard, since your parents are closely involved in the maglev project and they testify that you gained access to the project by cracking their encrypted data files."

He looked from me to Vikram and back, and I felt a little bit sick with anxiety. I'd felt the same entering the hangars, webbed with carbon fiber nets, ready and poised to grapple on to a freighter that would take me screaming at the speed of sound through a tunnel bored into the rock under the earth. In other words, to be honest, I was half buzzed by it all, and while I was scared of what the Magistrate might do to us, of the privileges he might decide to deny us, I was kind of getting off on it at the same time. Maybe that's one reason criminals never change their spots unless the psyches get in and rewire their brains.

"For one month," he declared in the same soft, distinct tone, "both of you will have your phone links removed. You will remain within your parents' quarters after the hour of five in the afternoon and until you leave for school or authorized outing in the morning. You will not enter or attempt to enter the property of the Maglev Freighter Corporation, or any of its subsidiaries, and the security systems of their hangar complex will be permitted to list you as registered offenders until the day of your Maturity, from which point criminal penalties will attend any further infractions. Do you understand me?"

"Yes, sir," I mumbled.

"Speak up clearly, Amanda," Mr. Abdel-Malek said. "Say it with some conviction."

I think there was an intentional pun in that last word. My heart accelerated, and I nodded emphatically.

"Yes, sir, I do understand. No further entry into the Maglev hangars. I give you my solemn word on that." That was okay, I had a better way in.

"Very well. You are released into the custody of your parents, Ms. Kolby-McAllister. Mr. Singh, you will remain in detention until one of your parents returns from business and collects you. Next case."

Dad was waiting outside for me, and they led Vikram off to a side room, so I didn't have a chance to tell him my great new idea. Besides, it probably wasn't the right psychological moment for it. But I knew that once I had a chance to talk that boy into it, I'd wind him around my little finger. We'd get to ride the rods without going anywhere near the hangars.

See, I'd remembered something from that legal case Mom had been tied up with, on and off, since I was about twelve. The loonies of God's Valley. And the vent shaft the corp had just punched up through two hundred meters of rock.

Now all I had to do was find some way into the most ferociously independent and paranoid territory left in the country, maybe the entire world, and work out a way to override the vent shaft safety codes. I wished they hadn't cut off our phone implants. I would have dialed up Vik right away and told him about it. It'd be dread. It'd be megadread. We'd be Mall gods after all.

3: MATHEWMARK

The good people of the Valley weren't too thrilled about the ventilation shaft. It appeared overnight. It was only a day or two after we'd filled in old man Grout's hole that we awoke to find a conspicuous metallic column sticking out of the ground in almost exactly the same place. It was about a meter and a half in diameter and, say, four meters high. Maybe it wasn't steel but some kind of polluters' invented stuff. Painted green, but the paint wouldn't chip off. Cut into the side at ground level, in luminous red, were the words *Metro Maglev Deep Rail Authority, Ventilation shaft 26B*. And then, in yellow, *It would be very much in your own interests not to enter or drop anything down this shaft*. We don't have very many warning notices in the Valley, but when we do, we write things like *Repent!; Keep Out; Light no Fires; Danger!* Just simple, plain language that tells people what they need to know. There was something really menacing about the long-winded, mild-mannered drivel about our own interests.

Me and Mom and Dad and my brother, Lukenjon, were among the first to see the thing sticking up out of the ground in the early morning light. We walked down the hill to old man Grout's patch and just stood and looked. We were soon joined by our near neighbors and then others from further afield. We don't have telephones or other works of the devil in the Valley, but news travels fast. Very fast indeed, faster than a man can run, faster than a mule can gallop—faster even than a horse can go. My Dad sometimes says that the speed at which news travels is the strongest argument there is for the existence of God. He's only half joking. Frankly I don't know what other arguments there are—in the Valley we don't argue about the existence of the God of our choice, we know he, she or it exists. Full stop.

When there were about three dozen people and a dozen mules standing in a circle around the ventilation shaft, Old biddy Smeeth picked up a broken harrow tooth and walked right up to the thing. She swung the harrow tooth in an arc, smashing it into the side of the column. Clang. It was hollow. We were left in no doubt about that. And it extended deep into the ground. We could hear the reverberations, almost feel them through our feet. We looked up at the top of the column, a dark exclamation mark against the blue sky. The stuff about our "own interests" seemed a bit silly as well as menacing. You couldn't "drop" anything down the shaft, you'd be pushing it to climb to the top without a ladder, giving each other a leg up.

Old biddy Smeeth turned round and addressed the rest of us. "This is an abomination in the eyes of Kali, it is an outhouse vent in the temple of the gods. We must cast it out!"

"How?" I said.

"How?" old biddy Smeeth said, "How? Mathewmark. Are you so lacking in wisdom that you needs must ask how?"

Old biddy Smeeth has never been my favorite neighbor. She's always finding fault, always letting you know that she personally finds considerably more favor in the eyes of Kali than you do. Still, it doesn't do to talk back to an Elder, not in front of a gathering.

"I only seek your wisdom, Auntie Smeeth," I said.

"Pray!" cried old biddy Smeeth. "Everybody pray!"

There was a bit of foot shuffling. A couple of people found they had urgent things to do to the harness of their mules. But old biddy Smeeth would not be denied.

"Let us pray, brethren," she cried. "Let us pray to the God of our choice that this abomination be blasted from the surface of the earth. Let the might of Kali drive it back down into the infernal regions from which it sprang!"

Old biddy Smeeth fell to her knees in the trampled sorghum patch. She raised two hands to the heavens and closed her eyes. Then she opened them again for a quick look around to see if everybody else was joining her. She cried to the goddess. People started kneeling, some more quickly than others. More and more voices joined in prayer. There was no coherence, voice battled with voice. Beside me Lukenjon was on his knees, getting into the spirit of the thing, yelling something about "Tower of Babel, tower of sin, tower of outrage, tower of tin." Lukenjon is much more pious than I am, but he also writes lots of crappy poetry, real doggerel. Sometimes his devotion to the lord and his soppy versifying get a bit mixed up.

I must admit I was about the last person to get down on my knees. But I did. And I prayed. I didn't pray out loud, I just had a quiet word with the lord. Actually, if the lord could hear me above the voices of all the rest, then I reckon that's another powerful argument for the existence of God. Although, I suppose, the argument is circular or something. A lot of truths about the lord are a bit circular when you come to think about it. Anyway, what I said to the lord was: you do what you think right, Lord. Ignore old biddy Smeeth if she's on the wrong track.

Then, not suddenly, but slowly, a slow moan rose above the sound of prayer. It was a deep, rolling, sighing, mournful sound. And it came from the heavens above. It grew louder. Many people fell silent. One or two fainted. "Kali the destroyer is made manifest!" Old biddy Smeeth cried. "She is amongst us!" You could tell she was taking the credit.

In our Valley the god or goddess make themselves manifest fairly often, they're part of our lives, working the odd miracle or two. But this moaning, sighing sound was something new. Beside me Lukenjon was hard at it. "Voice of the lord. Voice of the sword! Sword of the tin slayer! Slice it up, lord, layer by layer!"

"Shut up, Luken," I said quietly. "I want to hear this thing."

It didn't take long for me to work out where the sound was coming from. It was coming out of the mouth of the ventilation shaft several meters above our heads. It was the moaning of wind rushing out of a pipe. Any number of musical instruments work that way. The shaft was just a huge tin whistle. Once I'd worked that out, I also knew what was forcing the air out of the shaft: there was a train down there, bowling along towards us, pushing the air in front of it. Old biddy Smeeth had got it terribly wrong, we weren't listening to the voice of Kali or any other god. If anything, we were listening to the voice of the devil.

* * * *

The next day there was a meeting of Elders at the temple. I wasn't there, of course, but Mom and Dad were. Apparently old biddy Smeeth and a few of her mates couldn't be convinced that they hadn't heard the voice of God. The Smeeth group claimed the moaning was a sign that divine punishment was going to strike down the ventilation shaft at Kali's earliest convenience. Someone asked why it hadn't already been struck down—the thing had been there for at least thirty-six hours. Old biddy Smeeth said she wasn't listening to such blasphemy, and mentioned working in mysterious ways. The God of our Choice would get around to striking the thing down in his or her own good time and it wasn't for mere mortals to call the sacred time-table into question. Old biddy Smeeth knew this, because Kali had told her. The more important debate at the meeting of Elders concerned the question of permission.

The people of the Valley don't have much contact with the outside world . Outsiders aren't allowed in through the Gatehouse at the Valley entrance. And the good people of the Valley never leave. Or if they do, they leave and never come back. But sometimes it is necessary for the Elders to engage in business with outsiders. Then there is a meeting in the Gatehouse. The Elders chosen to bargain with the Outsiders enter the Gatehouse through the Valley door and sit on one side of a wide table.

The Outsiders enter the Gatehouse by the Door of the Damned and sit on the other side of the table. That's as close as anybody from the Valley gets to the outside world. Recently there had been quite a few meetings in the Gatehouse. The lawyers for the Maglev Rail Authority and Freighter Corporation had wanted to speak to certain Elders. And certain Elders, it turned out, had struck certain deals.

Ructions! There hadn't been such turmoil in the Valley since the great pan-krishna-rainbow serpent dust-up in 1977. That was way before I was born, of course. But there were still some ancient Elders around who could remember those days. The reason our religion is so strong is that it incorporates all the truths known to all the little itsy-bitsy religions like Christianity and Judaism and Buddhism and Islam and so forth. We've got the lot. Or rather we've got bits and pieces of the lot. And sometimes you get disputes about what to put in and what to leave out. That happened back in the days of the pan-krishna-rainbow serpent dispute. Families were torn asunder. Wife (or wives) wouldn't speak to husband. Brother wouldn't speak to sister. An alternative temple was built right across the track from the Great Temple itself. The two congregations used to praise the lord at the tops of their voices, trying to drown each other out. After a really good Sunday of gospel dueling hardly anybody in the Valley could speak, their vocal cords were so shot. It all died down in the end, of course, the dispute was using up too much energy, the crops were starting to fail. Finally the Alternative Temple was hit by a lightning bolt. That did it, it was a sign from on high. But, while life might have returned to normal, people still talk of those days, even though hardly anyone is old enough to remember them directly.

And now it was happening all over again. Only this time the Valley was split on the question of permission. Why had the bargaining Elders told the Maglev people they could put their ventilation shaft in our Valley? What secret deals had been done? It must have been the devil himself who scrambled the Elders' minds. Or so it was said. But it was also said that liar bees had been seen in the Valley. I've always tried to keep an open mind on the question of liar bees. Some people think they are real, think they are all over the place, buzzing around the fields, hiding in the woods, perching on the cradles of new-born infants the better to corrupt their innocent little minds. Auntie McWeezle reckons they exist. She's seen them, she's heard them.

"They are as real as you are, Mathewmark," she said when I brought up the subject. "There's all sorts of wickedness in the Outside. And wickedness can't abide goodness and peace. The wicked know our Valley is steeped in innocence and it riles them. They plot and scheme, the wicked.

And the liar bees are their agents. They come in on the north wind. Like a plague of locusts. Moral locusts!"

"Come on, Auntie," I said. "Why would anybody on the Outside want to send funny little talking insects into our Valley? How would it profit them?"

"Wickedness is its own reward," Auntie said and poured me more buttermilk. "Besides, the Valley is prime real estate."

"Real estate?" I said. "No one from the Outside can buy real estate in our Valley. It's forbidden."

"And while the good people of the Valley remain stout of heart and pure of spirit it will remain forbidden, Mathewmark."

"Well, there you are," I said.

"But if the moral contagion gets a grip," Auntie said. "then all will be lost, the Law will wither and die and people will be so depraved that they'll barter their heritage for the pleasures of the fleshpots."

"And this is what the bees are telling people," I said.

"Indeed it is, Mathewmark. The liar bees have been whispering in the Elders' ears. Offering sweet blandishments. How else do you explain the granting of permission?"

You can never tell with Auntie McWeezle. Sometimes I think she believes everything she tells you, and sometimes I think she exaggerates for the pleasure of it. She's as old as the hills and her face is lined with wrinkles and she hardly has any teeth, but her eyes sparkle sometimes, and they were sparkling now. Maybe because she was pulling my leg. Maybe because she really believed the liar bees were buzzing around us, looking for our weaknesses. I still had half a dozen loads to fetch and carry, so I thanked Auntie for her buttermilk and set off on the cart.

The devil tempted me, I confess it freely. Auntie's words niggled at the back of mind as I made my deliveries. I'd never seen a liar bee, and neither had any of other young people I knew. Jed Cawthorne was five years older than me, and he'd been a bit of a hell-tearer, I'd heard tell. So as we lugged a load of corn together I decided to put the question to him.

He guffawed in my face. He laughed so hard he sprayed spit. I wiped it off my face with a sleeve and scowled.

"Don't believe ever'thing you hear, young Mathewmark," he said finally, shouldering the sack he'd dropped in his hilarity.

"Never said I believed it," I grunted.

He squeezed one eye shut and tapped his nose knowingly.

"It's the demon dogs you need to worry about," he told me, "they'll come down in the night and bear you off to hell's teeth for a chewing." Then he was chortling again at his own wit. He might be older than me but I'm bigger, from all the lifting and toting, and I had a moment there when I wanted to clock him one. Lay him out on the ground. But that's wickedness, too, fighting with your kin and kith. I just scowled and fell silent.

Jed wasn't finished with me, though. Just before I jumped back up on the cart he came close and leaned into my ear.

"If'n you really want to hear the whispering naughty promises of the liar bee," he said, his sour breath in my nostrils, "you have to invite them down politely. Call them to you, young Mathewmark."

"What do you mean?" I said, jerking away. "Why would you need to call the Tempter? He's supposed to call you."

"Nope, it's the rules of hell. They can't come in to the Valley unless you invite them."

I cleared my throat in disgust and spat into the gnawed grass where Ebeeneezer had been chewing it. "You don't know anything, cousin Jed. Everyone'll tell you it's vampires and the walking dead you have to invite past your door."

"Suit yourself," he said, and rolled the last barrel toward his store. "See you next week."

I rode away chewing my lip. He could have invited *me* in for a bite of lunch and cool draught of spring water, but we were both too annoyed with each. Well, Jed probably wasn't annoyed. He'd be tickled pink at the way he'd pulled my leg and got a rise out of me. I let my good old mule Ebeeneezer take us out of the yard and down the dirt track, teased by the ridiculous doubt that maybe Jed was right after all. After all, he was older than me and he'd seen a bit more of life. More than a bit more, if the rumors were right.

I opened my mouth, gazed up at the blue sky, thought better of it and closed my mouth again. But nobody was within ear-shot. Over in a distant field two kids were bent down clearing weeds, and they waved as we passed them, but they wouldn't hear me tempt the devil. Still, I waited until we'd left them behind, then I said softly, "Show yourself, tool of Satan. Let me hear your blandishments."

Nothing happened, of course. I felt like a fool. I raised my voice and shouted in a sarcastic way, "Come down from the devil's palace, liar bees! I dare you to test my faith, for I am a man who may not be bent from the path of righteousness."

Dust puffed up from the mule's plodding hooves. The wheels turned with a squeak. No flying insect of temptation fell from the skies to put my soul in peril. It wasn't as if I'd really expected it to.

* * * *

There's a patch of wooded country between Jed Cawthorne's place and old man Legrand's log cabin. At that time of year quite a few of the tree varieties are in flower. That stretch of track was alive with insects, their hum and drone like a distant, old, familiar tune. The day was drowsy with the heat of early summer and the scent of flowers. Ebeeneezer knew where we were going. There wasn't much for me to do. I was half asleep on the cart, the reins slack in my hands.

"You rang?" a voice said in my ear.

I woke up with a start. I looked around.

"What?"

There was no-one near. I must have been dreaming. A large bee of a sort I'd never seen before buzzed once around my head and disappeared into the trees. I shivered, even through the day was warm. I told myself not to be a fool. Suggestion, that's what it was, the result of suggestion. Spend half an hour yarning with Auntie McWeezle and of course you'd dream of liar bees or something similar.

"Nothing ventured, nothing gained," the voice rasped. The humming grew louder. I pulled out my big handkerchief and folded it lengthwise so I could swat the devilish thing if it tried its wiles on me again. The bee zoomed in and sat on my right shoulder.

"Hey kid," it said in a buzzing little voice, "listen up."

I still couldn't believe my ears. Must be dreaming. "Are you addressing me?" I blurted.

"If you're the one who invited me, kiddo, and I know you are, you're the one and only. And hey, Valley boy," it said in a small, self-satisfied, irritating voice, "have I got a deal for you!"

4: AMANDA

The Sacred Sanctuary of the God of Our Choice, Inc., had been set up, according to Mom's legal beagle, in 1934. Back then it was just called the Coburg Valley, a name that homesick early German immigrants had given it prior to World War One. During some other war in Vietnam or China or something there'd been a big influx of young people called "hippies" or "draft excluders" who didn't want to be sent off to fight and die in some part of the world a long way from home, and who can blame them? That had led to the rise of what looked to me like a phony religion that some of these guys and their girl friends had got themselves ordained in, so they were "ministers of religion" and no longer eligible to be packed off to get shot at and bombed and suffer the slings and arrows and agent orange sprayings of outrageous fortune.

But like our sociology instructor says, it's a short step from a cult to a culture. The Valley people experimented with faith and drugs in equal proportion, and they tried out what they called "free love" (sexing without a permit) and that led to babies, and before you knew it the place was turning into a genuine community.

I got a lot of this off the web archives, using a boring and slow keyboard and screen because my implant connect had been disabled by the court. Mom's legal beagle search agent, which I'd hacked years ago, only provided stacks of dry-as-dust records and databases and gigabytes of precedents and arguments before the beak about local ordinance infractions and the rights or supposed rights of the faithful in respect of getting their asses shot off, and so on, all very dull unless you needed to find a legal loophole in about a century's worth of accumulated judicial drivel. Which I did. I wanted a loophole you could drive a couple of grounded kids through. I needed to get into the Valley physically, evading its crusty old loony guards who stood watch at the pass between the hills, not to mention its laser beam detectors on this side which had been set up to protect the faithful from the foul pollution of modern thought.

Amazing stuff! These crackpots thought science was a curse. They reckoned it was sinful to stick a phone in your head. They told their kids that the rest of the world was having a high old time consuming and fornicating and ignoring the word of the Lord of Their Choice. Well, fair enough. Can't say they were wrong about that. I just can't see why they got so worked up about it? What's wrong with a bit of consuming and fornicating, as long as you get your immune implants at 12 like civilized people?

Anyway, by this stage the Valley community had got all ingrown and weirder than shit. They wouldn't come out and we couldn't go in. I mean, we could go in, of course, any time we wanted, just by brushing them aside, but that's not polite. They had water-tight legal title to the Valley, even if it was prime mouth-watering real estate. High powered Legals like Mom had been scouring the sub-clauses of the municipal and regional development Acts for years now, with full artificial intelligence support from the likes of her legal beagle program, and they couldn't budge the mad old things. The only legitimate access to the Valley loonies was if they specifically invited you in, which they never did, or if one of them ventured outside into the real world.

Or, I suddenly saw with a burst of excitement, if you could talk one of them into leaving of her own free will. How would you pull off this impossible trick? You couldn't get in and show one of them everything she or he was missing. You couldn't dangle a VR inside their brains and send them on a magical mystery tour of the imagination, because they had no VR chips in their brains, poor things. The law was very firmly of the opinion that flying in and kidnapping one of the dopes and bearing them off to the pleasures and enticements of the outside world was simply not done (Penalty: 25 years freezing and $1,000,000 instant fine).

Ah, but nobody said you couldn't divert a wasp ad over the tops of the hills and through the trees and whisper a little come-on in their ears.

This had been tested in the courts, and found to be perfectly legal— and therefore hushed up at once. I only learned of it because Mom and her team had used the method shamelessly to persuade one of the Elders to come on board and grant them permission to drive up the vent shaft in an empty paddock.

I sat back and stared in disbelief at the screen. The first person who'd tried to inveigle the faithful had been Sam Sam the Roadster Man. He'd hired a team of industrial psychologists to rewire an entire hive of wasps, and sent them in on a north wind seventeen years ago. The commercials they spouted were so completely, stupidly wrong for the market they hit that the whole idea was discredited for a generation. I watched a stereo video feed that several of these bugged bugs had radioed back to Sam Sam's hired guns.

Wasp: Psst.

Startled believer: Huh? Is that you sneaking around behind me, MaryLou Atkins?

Wasp: Wanna buy a roadster that flies like the wind? Wanna get your mitts on a dynamite unit that tears up the way like a bat outta hell?

Indignant believer: Hell, you say? Step forth, tool of the devil and show thy grizzled features that the Lord might smite thee mightily!

Wasp: Only 500 down and 200 a month for a limited time interval. Voice signature legally binding.

Shocked believer: Take that, minion of chaos!

<whack whack splat>

Wasp: ZZZZzzzzssssphht.

The campaign was a dud. This was marketing in the dark, salesmanship without preliminary focus groups and polls, this was rank incompetence and stupidity from the look of it. I hit Menu and tracked the rest of this sorry tale. A year or so later, a Science Education Foundation tried the same trick, using bees wired for Darwinism and evolutionary psychology. (Don't ask me, I haven't got to that stage in my education. Something to do with how we are all descended from apes, I gather. Sounds as silly to me as what the Valley loons believe, but hey, I'm only 15 and majoring in violin.) The success rate was not particularly improved.

Bee: Young lady, let us reason together.

Terrified girl in bonnet: Help! Help! Auntie Hazel, it's one of those demons in pleasing garments!

Aunt: Slacker girl! You can't take me in so easily! Back to your sweeping!

Bee: Madame, perhaps I can interest you in a dialogue concerning the two great world systems?

Aunt: <shriek>

Justified girl: See, Auntie, I told you. It's a limb of Satan. A winged limb.

Aunt: Get the whisk, you foolish child! Give the bugger a whack! Send it back to Hell's Teeth!

<bang crump whine>

Bee: *ZZZbuzzzssss pooffff.*

And so on, year after year. You'd think they'd learn. You'd imagine that people would get the point. The Valley loons built up a whole mythology about the tempting creatures of Satan, which is one way to look at wasp ads and their fellow pests, I suppose. The advertisers tired of failed campaigns to sell uplift bras and microwave ovens to devoted retro primitives. The government maintained a low-level presence, inviting the more adventurous to sample the delights of big city fun. Sometimes they had a success. Mostly they lost their bugs.

From my point of view, the best news was that this remains a legal method for corrupting the minds of the loonies, but only if they give some clear indication of their interest in being contacted.

I sent in a low-level artificial intelligence searcher to find out if anyone had expressed interest in the outside world lately. I thought it was more likely than not, since the arrival of the vent must have set off a lot of talk, discussion and public dispute. Surely some bad kid with a bit of spirit had said something along the lines of an invite. I left the software agent to search all the automatic monitor records from the past day.

And it didn't take me long to track down a store of moth-balled ad buzzers, grab control of their tiny brains, program up a few simple code controls, and send a pair winging off and over the pass.

I wanted a spy in the sky. I needed to take in the lie of the land. If Vikram and I were to get our ride on the bullet train, as I intended, we were going to need all the info we could scrape together.

Bees are easy to drive, it turns out. I piloted the two spies into the Valley on the third afternoon of my imprisonment in my own room, which luckily was a non-school Wednesday, and mapped a threedee of boring fields, creeks, dirt roads, farms, the smallest, dingiest town you've ever seen. Off to one side, sticking out of the false color imager like a silver finger caught by the sun, I found a vent shaft rising from the rocky soil of an empty field.

I set down one of the bees to the top of the vent and let it crawl about, sussing out the control system. The other bee I sent lofting on the air currents while I waited for the search engine to find me a stooge.

<I have located an utterance that might be construed within legal limits as an invitation> the program told me.

<Let me hear it> I ordered.

This boy's recorded voice, slightly distorted by his distance from the nearest monitor, called out a request for a tool of Satan. Close enough, I thought, grinning. That should stand up in court, if we ever get back there, worse luck.

<Find that person for me in real-time> I instructed the search engine. The machine locked into the bee I still had roaming around in the sky.

<I have contact> the AI told me.

<Display visual>

Yes indeedy. Here came this incredibly old-fashioned device, a flat dray with huge wonky wooden wheels, pulled along by one poor four-footed critter in a leather harness. A guy was leaning back with his eyes shut, it looked like, sucking on a stalk. I zoomed on down. Thick yellow unwashed hair, nice face, a slight, light shadow of beard. Hideous clothes, looked like they'd been stitched together by hand if you can believe such a thing. His own right hand, strong and nicely shaped I thought, holding the reins loosely. The animal seemed to be driving itself while the master snoozed. Perfect.

I dropped the bee down next to his ear. Let's give this system a bit of a trial run.

"You rang?" I had the bee say.

He sat up with a jolt.

"What?" he blurted.

Didn't seem the finest candidate for a spot of espionage and double-dealing, but I didn't really have a big pool of candidates. "Nothing ventured, nothing gained," I muttered to myself, and switched on the bee's auto ad routine.

"Hey kid," the bee shouted at my new pal "listen up."

I sat back to see how he'd take it. I was grinning hard enough to crack the dragon stencil off my face. I decided we were in. Yep, Vikram and I were surely in. All I had to do was persuade this dummy, then persuade Vik, then get out of the house, into the Valley, down the vent. What were a few simple obstacles when the thrill ride of a lifetime awaited?

The guy was swatting at me—well, at the bee—with a nasty looking rag. I danced away. I'd have him eating out of my hand.

5: MATHEWMARK

So they existed. I was a believer now: liar bees were out and about and doing the devil's work. It just went to show that you had to take old biddies like Auntie McWeezle seriously. They'd lived a long time, they knew a thing or two. I was wide awake now and I was approaching old man Legrand's place with even more turmoil of the heart than I normally do.

Old man Legrand is Sweetcharity's grandfather. And since the dark night when her parents were carried away in the floods, the beautiful Sweetcharity has lived there with him. He takes his grandfatherly responsibilities very seriously, old man Legrand. There isn't a girl in the Valley who is more closely supervised than the orphan Sweetcharity Legrand. Which makes being in love with her a bit difficult. But at least I get to see her sometimes—my carting duties mean I've got a good reason to visit the cabin occasionally. Any other boy in the Valley who just turned up on spec—and a few have—would be sent on his way pretty damn sharpish. Old man Legrand is not above waving a long handled bill-hook at folks he doesn't like the look of. And it's no good going on about the fact that the God of His Choice is meant to be a pacifist. Where his grand-daughter is concerned, old man Legrand is a warrior of old.

"Morning, Uncle," I said when Ebeeneezer ground to a halt outside the cabin.

"Afternoon, boy," Legrand said.

We both looked at the sun. Perhaps it was past mid-day, perhaps it wasn't. I didn't really care. But old man Legrand did.

"How much past, boy?" he said.

I took a guess, "Now you call my attention to it, uncle," I said, "I reckon it's approximately in the vicinity of about half past noon at the very least."

"Five past, young Mathewmark. The lord didn't make the sun go round the Earth just so young slackers could reckon that things are approximately in the vicinity."

"I reckon he didn't, Uncle," I said. There was no point in arguing with Legrand, what I wanted to do was catch a glimpse of his grand-daughter. We started unloading Jed Cawthorne's seed corn. As we did so I surreptitiously looked around the place. The cabin door stood open, but I could see no one inside. Nor could I hear any sound from any of the sheds and barns. No one was milking, no one was hanging out the washing. Old man Legrand had sent Sweetcharity on some errand. Or he'd sent her down to the bottom of the field, given her weeding duties among the cabbages. I wasn't going to be able to exchange loving glances, I wasn't going to be able to brush against her accidentally when I entered the cabin doorway. Sweetcharity would have no chance to kiss me quickly on the cheek when we were suddenly hidden from view as we loaded firewood onto the cart.

Which was all right by me. Sweetcharity would have a chance to meet me on the track when I drove away.

So we unloaded the seed corn. And loaded the firewood. And old man Legrand said, "Reckon you must be thirsty after all that, young Mathewmark. Have a draft of rain water."

"Right neighborly of you, uncle," I said.

The sun in its orbit round the Earth could go hang. My stomach was telling me exactly what time it was—it was lunch time. And here was old man Legrand offering me a drink of water. Still, there was no point complaining. I took the tin mug I was offered and filled it from the barrel beside the cabin door. I drank and climbed up onto the cart.

"So long, uncle," I said.

"May the Lord ride with you," old man Legrand said, "Careful with them logs."

I drove off. Careful with them logs! What did the old skinflint think his precious firewood was—baskets of eggs? I forgot about him, it was his grand-daughter who occupied my thoughts. As Ebeeneezer plodded along I scanned the track ahead. To my right were open fields of corn and barley. To my left were woods: tall, dark trees growing among thick undergrowth: lots of hiding places and small secret trails.

"Psst!"

I turned my head quickly, expecting to see Sweetcharity hidden in the foliage. But it was a liar bee, a meter distant and hovering.

"Bugger off!" I said. And then I made the sign o'god, partly to ward off the evil bee, and partly to cleanse my soul of the stain of foul language. I don't normally swear, but the bee had unnerved me.

"Oh, pardon me," said the liar bee. "I thought this was meant to be a free country."

"This is the Valley of the God of One's Choice, Inc—there's nothing here for you," I said. "Begone! Insect of Satan!"

"Look," said the bee, "We can do a deal!"

"No we can't," I said. "Hie thee off!"

"Bye bye for now," said the bee and disappeared into the woods. I drove on, flicking the reins to encourage Ebeeneezer.

"Psst!"

I didn't turn my head.

"Psst! Mathewmark, you deaf or something?"

I turned my head quickly. Sweetcharity stood well back from the track. She was almost completely hidden by the darkness of the woods. But I could see her smile, see the dappled light dancing on her hair. I brought Ebeeneezer to a halt and vaulted from the cart. I'd have to leave my mule and his load unattended, but there was nothing I could do about that. I ran into the woods. Sweetcharity turned and ran herself, going deeper into the gloom. The trail was narrow, something that might have been made by wild animals, low to the ground. I had to hold my arm in front of my face to ward off branches and brambles. Sweetcharity had disappeared. Then I saw the flash of her dress—a brilliant white in the gloom as she ducked behind a tree. When I located the tree, she was already behind another. I caught her behind the third. She laughed in my arms.

"Why, if it isn't young Mathewmark," she said. "What on earth brings you to this secluded spot?"

Sweetcharity was still breathing quickly from the chase. Her waist was slim in my encircling arms. Her breasts were against my chest.

"Kiss me," I said.

"What a suggestion," she said.

"Sweetcharity, don't tease," I said.

"Physical intimacy is a sacrament," she said, very prim and proper. "Any young gentleman knows that."

I put my lips to hers. We swayed together, with no more need for banter. There was a crashing sound in the undergrowth nearby. Sweetcharity sank quickly to her knees, dragging me down with her. Her eyes were startled, full of fear.

"Grandfather," she whispered. "He'll whip me."

We lay in a heap, trying to sink into the leafmold, into the very earth itself. The sounds of Legrand crashing about in the undergrowth came closer and closer. He was casting around. He didn't know exactly where we hid, but he knew we were close by. Peering out from where we lay, through the tangle of undergrowth, I saw him. He was wild with rage and exertion. The whip was no figure of speech, Legrand had one in his hand. It was all coiled up, but it must have been five meters long. A bullock driver's whip, something to make the air crack over the head of the leading beast. Hell's teeth! The man was crazed. He was wild of eye and breathing hard. And it wasn't only Sweetcharity who was at risk.

"I know thee for the lecher you are, you hell-spawn, Mathewmark!"

We were both doomed. The pair of us shrank deeper to the ground. Legrand blundered about. He hadn't seen us, but it was only a matter of time.

"Yah, yah, yah! Monkey look for peanuts!" a voice said.

"Oh, Kali-be-kind," I whispered to Sweetcharity, "the bee."

"Motheaten old fart! Couldn't hit a flea, couldn't hit me!"

"You, hell-fiend!" yelled Legrand. "Show thy scurvy visage!"

"Poop, butt, wee. I'm behind a tree!"

"I'll smite thee, I'll smite thee down, ye fiend!" Legrand shouted.

And he commenced smiting, flailing around with his whip. But the thing was too long. Far too long. It wrapped itself around branches, it got caught in bushes. Legrand tugged it free, using language not heard in Wednesday sermons, nor Saturday nor Sunday either.

"Stupid old goat!"

"I'll flail your sinful hide."

"Get stuffed, shit for brains."

We could no longer see Legrand. The bee was leading him away. Taunting him all the time. Legrand was blundering after it, yelling curses, far gone in his rage, howling and shrieking. Finally the sounds disappeared into the depths of the woods.

"Well, that's a relief," I said to Sweetcharity.

But she was sitting up, looking at me, almost as wild-eyed as her grandfather.

"It.. it... was a liar bee," she gasped.

"Yeah, I know," I said. "It was buzzing around me earlier."

"It saved us," Sweetcharity said with wild-eyed alarm. "Oh God of our Choice, we've been saved by a liar bee!"

"Maybe we should give thanks," I said. "A little prayer..."

"Thanks! A prayer! Are you mad, Mathewmark! That was a liar bee. We can't thank a liar bee. We're in league with the devil if we thank a liar bee."

"It seems to have drawn that madman away."

"Don't you call my grandfather a madman! How dare you?"

"Hell's teeth, Sweetcharity, the man's demented."

"Don't blaspheme! Don't you dare mention the infernal region and Grandpa's name in the same breath!"

Sweetcharity was pulling herself away from me, standing up, brushing randomly at her clothes. There were leaves in her hair. Her eyes flashed.

"You're in league, Mathewmark," she said. "You're in league with the prince of darkness."

"Sweetcharity, darling," I said imploringly.

"Don't darling me!"

I'd never seen her so pretty. I'd never wanted to know her body as I wanted to know her now. Carnal lust!

"Please, Sweetcharity," I said, standing up and stepping towards her. Reaching for her.

"Don't touch me!"

"Sweetcharity..."

"The Prince. You're in league. You've sold your immortal soul."

"Sweetcharity, I think you are being a little bit hysterical. I'm not in league with anyone."

"The bee did your bidding!"

"No it didn't."

"Oh, dear Lord. You're lying, Mathewmark. You are the familiar of the liar bees. You speak to them in their own lying tongue!"

"He does, too," said a voice about a meter above our heads.

Sweetcharity gasped and looked up. Then she fainted into a crumpled heap on the ground.

"Good grief," said the bee, "She's as loopy as that halfwit with the whip."

"She's his grand-daughter," I said.

"Poor kid," said the bee. "I thought my olds were assholes, but that fruitcake..."

"Who are you?" I said.

"I'm a cyborg bee, you know that,"

"Where are you from?"

"The metro. You know, outside your Valley of Goddess or whatever you call it. Let me introduce myself. I'm the voice of Amanda Kolby-McAllister. This is not the bee that is talking to you, this is me, Amanda. I'm shut up in my room, controlling the bee. It's only a machine."

"What do you want?" I said, shaking a bit.

But before the bee could reply we were interrupted by a piercing shriek from Sweetcharity, who had obviously regained consciousness.

"See, see," she cried. "You are the liar bee's familiar. Oh get thee behind me, Satan!"

And then Sweetcharity was away and running, tearing through the woods in the direction of her grandfather's cabin.

"Another nutter," said the bee. "The bloody place is rife with them."

"She's my beloved," I said, "and in the fullness of time I hope to make her my betrothed."

"Not any more, buster," said the bee. "You owe me, Mathewmark. You owe me for saving your ass from the mad guy with the whip." The bee cleared its throat. "And you owe me for saving you from the clutches of that crazy little bint."

"Do you mind!"

"No, I don't mind at all," said the bee pleasantly. "Uh-oh, that's my Mom at the door, time to log off. See you around, Mathewmark."

6: AMANDA

By the time Mom was in the door, I was perched innocently with Strad the Lad under my chin, sawing away at the Tchaikovsky concerto like my life depended on it. Mom looked at me suspiciously, but my room is well sound-proofed, for obvious reasons—during the first few years my violin and I had made noises like a tormented cat, although these days I maintain that I should be allowed to charge admission to my practice sessions, so delightful are the musical strains I coax from the Stradivarius. Well, maybe not the Tchaik. I admit it, the Tchaik is dreadfully difficult, and I'd been working on my doublestop triplets for weeks.

You have to play two notes at the same time, three times in a single beat. There's a passage of blindingly fast doublestop triplets at the end of the last movement. My music implant helped, but I'd been practicing for hours a day to get even near it. To sound those notes simultaneously, you need to bring the heel of the bow, near your hand, hard down on both strings at once. That makes it difficult to control because the bow wants to move like a hammer. Literally—imagine holding the heavy head of a hammer between your fingers, thumb tip underneath, and trying to direct the end of the handle with great delicacy and speed, changing angle in split seconds. Strike two strings at once, precisely, then instantly switch to another pair, off-set from the ones you just played, each of the strings with a distinct resistance. Do it again, and again. Your left hand is crazily pressing the doublestops, then dancing to the next pair. Most of the time the sound goes crunchy and vile. I was determined to master it.

Strad the Lad isn't a true Stradivarius. Those lovely ancient violins are hundreds of years old, and rare as hens' teeth, not to mention expensive as real estate on the Sunway Coast or Utopia Valley. My Strad is an exact knock-off, a computer designed replica built by a molecular shaper machine on the basis of extensive mag res scans, CAT scans, PET scans, and probably DOG scans for all I know. He spoke with the voice of an angel, when I stroked his whispers with my bow. I think that's a mixed metaphor or something, but who cares?

"Your father and I will be dining with the commissioner this evening," Mom told me, looking at me with calm tiger's eyes. She obviously didn't know I'd been toying with the tender and vulnerable mind of a

Valley of God kid, even though they'd installed a NannyWatch surveillance program on my computer link to record and trace the URLs of every call I made out. What they didn't know was that Vikram and I are the school's ace hackers, which isn't something you go about advertising, let alone boasting of. Under a dozen handles, we were known and feared and majorly respected by the cryptonauts and other buzzboyz and grrlz in seven continents and a few islands, but none of those streetwise d00Ds knew we were upscale prisoners of refinement and taste. Naturally we yearned to be down&durtee, but instead we were trapped in Durance Vile by the likes of Dad and Mom and the terrifying Dr. Singh and his seldom seen wife, not to mention our community Magistrate, the hissing Mr. Abdel-Malek.

"I'll be okay, Mom," I told her airily. "*Spine-chiller* will be on the vee, Mrs. Ng will prepare her usual excellent dinner, and I'll catch some early zees before the geography test tomorrow."

I realized even as I spoke that I'd taken the wrong tack entirely. Mom's eyes narrowed. She'd been expecting me to whine and bitch and moan about how incredibly *bored* I was, and how *small* the house was (all twenty rooms of it, including the arboretum), and why couldn't *Vikram* come around or even Bessie or Steve, Mr. Abdel-Malek hadn't said *anything* about Steve and Bessie not being allowed to visit, and—

If I'd had the brains to carry on like that, Mom would have raised her voice the tiniest bit and invited me to grow up a little, young lady, you are nearly Mature and this is scarcely the behavior of an adult. Too bad, but if I started to grizzle now it would look rather odd and even more suspicious, so I just turned away from her dubious glance, tucked the S Man under my chin, and drew out a perfect middle C. The hairs on my arms were standing up, but I didn't even hear the door seal behind her when she left the room.

Once I was sure Mom and Dad were out of the house for good (I wouldn't put it past them to double back and try to catch me red-handed), and the lower half of the house was filled with the delicious scents of Mrs. Ng's preparations for our scratch meal, I re-opened my system, still using Dad's crappy old discarded computer.

There was no way I could reach Vikram direct, not legally, but that didn't stop me for a moment. I popped up a couple of fairly impregnable layers of counter-measures, then opened a window to an e-pal in Austria, Rupert Hochschauble. He was a 45 year old glass-blower with an interest in medieval illuminated manuscripts. Well, that's the bio on his home page, but for all I knew "he" could be a seamstress in Honan Province or a retired rocket engineer in Kurdistan. Rupert was my "beard', patching my encrypted messages through a series of email lists to a place where

Vik would see them when he went on-line himself. He'd reply through his own "beard', someone I didn't know and didn't want to know, and his answer would be forwarded almost instantly through another list, maybe devoted to waterskiing or face stencils.

How come we felt so secure? It wasn't the number of links we sent these messages through—that helped, of course, but could be traced. No, we chatted behind the security door of an excellent Steganography program we'd both installed.

Steganography? Never heard of it? Shame on you! Here's how it worked, in a nut-shell: I spoke my end of the conversation into my machine's acoustic hood (or typed it if I was feeling really paranoid and thought they might be listening to my room through a micro-bug). My words were digitized in the usual way into a stream of ones and zeroes. These binary digits were used to modify a standard "one-use pad" of other zeroes and ones, which cost nothing to prepare. Vikram and I had made up a hundred pads and stored them for whenever we wished to communicate in absolute secrecy.

Anyway, the new blend of message bits and pad bits were woven artfully as colored pixels into the background of a painting or photo, and the whole thing was transmitted as a graphic attachment. The picture might be a bland little portrait of me playing Strad at the Prom last season, or a heart-warming pic of a doggie doing tricks with a food bowl, or a shot of ring-a-ding Saturn from high over its north pole. Some dull and ordinary, some beautiful and memorable—anything, really. In this case, since I was going through Hochschauble's site, it was a gold-leaf encrusted page from some ancient German Bible (the book of Deuteronomy, as I recall).

The manuscript was being shown backwards. We didn't touch the words of the sacred text, which would have been a relief to my weird new buddy Mathewmark if he ever heard of this hitech game of ours, not that he would have understood the first word of it. No, what our Steg program did was find bits of grey parchment in the background and ever so slightly tweak the bits and bytes. You couldn't see the difference in shades of grey with the naked eye, trust me. You could see speckle if you boosted the magnification, but so what? Who's to say what shade of dull grey or brown a random pixel is meant to be? Without the key—the shared and prepared one-time pad—nobody in all the world could decrypt our messages.

Okay, enough with the science and art of skullduggery. The point is, me and Vik could natter away to our heart's contents and no one was going to intercept our forbidden conversation. Not even the dreaded Mr. Abdel-Malek.

<Hey, Vik.>

<Hey, grrl. I'm bored shitless.>

<Tell me 'bout it. Luckily, I Have a Plan.>

<Oh, no. Look, Amanda, you know I am devoted to your genius and beauty, but I don't think my parents could take another of your plans. I don't think I could, for that matter. The last one almost got me sent home to The Punjab.>

<'Home'? I thought you were a naturalized citizen.>

<True, but you know the olds. They claim I've been corrupted by your alien ways.>

<Funny, that's exactly what I'm planning to do next, but not to you, bopper. Ever heard of the Valley of God and its weird old hippies?>

There was a pause. I watched my main screen. A series of lovely illuminated pages was being displayed, each held on the screen for fifteen or twenty seconds. At Vikram's end, the display might well be showing a cricket match in progress, or a map of the points of the horse. The pause had nothing to do with the mechanics of Steganography. Vikram was being indecisive. The kid was easily flummoxed by raw fear. I've never understood it.

While he was mulling over his trepidation, I patched in a map of the deep maglev route, with a small blipping red rectangular box laid over the spot where the tunnel curved through the Valley. A green dot marked the vent. We'd never paid much attention to the route itself, since our plan—well, *my* plan—had involved hopping the rails at the metro hangar, webbing onto one of the shiny freighter tubes, hanging on for grim life with the wind screaming in our hair and around our carbon fiber composite goggles, and then jumping off at the coast when it came to rest. One part of a thousand kilometer tunnel hundreds of meters deep under the rock is like any other, or so we'd assumed. Just blackness pierced every 100 meters by blue maintenance lamps no human ever clapped eyes on. I mean, it wasn't as if anyone was meant to go down there once the system was up and running.

<The mad bastards have put a kink in the track,> Vikram remarked. <That will slow the bullet train down a bit. Why would they do that, Amanda?>

<Well, it's not quite a kink,> I said pedantically. <More a slow and gentle curve. But you do see that it's right under the Valley I just mentioned?>

<Of course. Something to do with the rock, you think? Or maybe they had to divert around an underground river?>

<Around an above-ground sacred site, Grasshopper,> I told him. <The faithful felt that having the transport route of Satan's Minions

drilled under their landscape was a shocking affront to the God of Their Choice.>

<Which god is that?>

<Well, it's not just the one, is it? They all get to worship whichever god they fancy. Mainly the menfolk like an old bearded chap who spits fire and brimstone, and the ladies go for Mother Gaia or one of the blessed Virgins. You dig it? "Of their choice'?>

<All right, no need to be narky. How does this have anything to do with anything?>

I smirked to myself. It pays to do your research.

<Turns out Mom did this secret deal. With one of the elders, don't know which one. For the right to take the tunnel through the Valley— well, deep *under* the Valley, but they owned some kind of legal mining rights that stopped the corp from just ripping ahead without permission.>

<In exchange for—?> I could imagine Vikram's big laugh. He was probably imagining bribes, civic corruption in high places, dirty deals and guilty secrets. It was what his own father specialized in, according to rumor.

<Mom's arranged to send them all directly to heaven.>

There was another pause. The display flipped back another page. Adam and Eve, and a snake with conspicuous teeth and a rather cheesy smirk, were twined around a tree. One of them was about to chow down on an apple, while the gaudy snake looked on, rather pleased with itself. How appropriate, I thought, sniggering.

<Excuse me?>

<It's true. Mom agreed to have a diamond disk engraved with the names and histories of every member of the Church of the God of Their Choice, and send it up into space on the next convenient deep space probe. Cost millions, probably, but cheap at the price. Oh yes, and this is the bit that makes it all worthwhile. In exchange for a vent in some grotty old disused field, the corp agreed to slow the freighters down to the speed of a running horse. Fifty kays max, I reckon."

<Good grief,> Vikram said. <Bless my soul.>

A red stockpot appeared in the upper right corner of my screen, steaming over a crackling fire. Dinner was served.

<Gotta go,> I told my bad if reluctant buddy. <Mrs. Ng calls. But you do get the big picture now, I hope?>

<I do indeed,> Vikram agreed. The manuscript showed God brooding over the unformed earth, which was empty and void. He was about to make something really, really dread. So was I.

<We'll go down the vent,> I said. <Now all we have to do is get in there.>

<But Amanda,> Vikram started to say, <I've heard that those bastards are completely mad and armed with pitch—"

I cut him off, closed my cyber defenses, and scampered downstairs to dinner with Mrs. Ng. Chicken and steamed Vietnamese vegetables! Yum.

7: MATHEWMARK

I always look forward eagerly to Beanfeast Night. Each village in the Valley has a Beanfeast Night once a month. It's pretty well compulsory to go to the Beanfeast at your nearest village hall, but you can go further afield if you wish. Our village has its Beanfeast every New Moon. That's a mixed blessing. It makes it harder for outliers to drive their carts home after the feast, so we get more people staying over afterwards than the Sickle Moon and the Full Moon villages. We have to provide more food and candles and hot water, it's a bit of a strain on the local community, but we get the kudos.

And there's some splendid cooks in our community. My Mom makes the best pickled pork rolls in the Valley. My dad's cheeses are legendary. Auntie McWeezle bakes wheat bread and corn bread with herbs only she knows about. Try winkling the recipes out of her—try to get water from the moon.

So all that day, as I went on my rounds, each house and farm and cabin and mud hut I visited smelled better than the last. And at most places I was given a taste or a bite or a sip.

"What do you think, Mathewmark? A little more chopped chives?"

"Don't overdo it, Auntie. Remember what happened to old man Old-wood and his Fragrant Sausage."

"Fragrant! You could smell the pong of it the moment you entered the hall!"

"It's a lesson to us, Auntie."

"I'm talking about chopped chives, Mathewmark, not essence of liverwort."

"Moderation in all things, Auntie. Could I have some more?"

"Begone, Mathewmark, or I'll have nothing to bring to the feast."

Beanfeast days are great days. I always make sure I visit as many people as possible on a feast day. But this particular day, for all the tasting and sipping, had an uneasy feel to it. Beanfeasts are jolly affairs, but they can also be the occasion for airing grievances and circulating rumors. And there were going to be some grievances aired—the Valley was alive with rancorous debate over the granting of permission for the ventilation shaft. And old man Legrand and his grand-daughter, Sweetcharity, would be there.

By the appointed hour I was scrubbed and ready. As were Mom and Dad and my brother Lukenjon. We loaded the basket of feast food, I put a daisy chain around Ebeeneezer's neck, we all piled onto the cart and we were away. We arrived at the village hall at sunset. It was a warm evening and those who had arrived already were still standing around outside, under the peppercorn trees, watching the sunset and discussing the ventilation shaft. I looked for old man Legrand's great lumbering wagon, but it had yet to arrive. I was going to need all my diplomatic skills, all my cunning, to keep out of his way while still managing to speak to Sweetcharity.

Ah, Sweetcharity. What did Sweetcharity think of me? She'd accused me of being the liar bee's familiar and gone running off through the woods. But I was no fool. I knew what that sort of behavior was called: a lovers' tiff. The thing about lovers' tiffs is that when, after a bit of argy bargy and tears and hot words, the two lovers fall into each other's arms again, their love is strengthened tenfold. Lovers' tiffs are like summer showers. Rain one minute, brilliant sunshine the next. At least this is what I was telling myself as I unhitched Ebeeneezer from the cart and led him to the village green, there to graze peacefully with the other mules until home time.

"Psst!"

I looked round quickly. The village hall with its little group of nattering locals and visitors was about a hundred meters away, but no one was watching me. I was alone on the village green with a dozen mules for company. I ignored the bee and bent to put the hobbles on Ebeeneezer's front legs.

"Look, all I'm asking for is a bit of advice."

"The devil and his winged messengers need no words of advice from a mortal," I whispered.

"Oh, give me a break. What's wrong with all you fruitcakes? I'm a girl, not a bee. Wake up to yourself, or I'll give you a nasty sting." The bee sniggered in my ear, a terrible buzzing sound for a mortal to have to listen to. I swatted furtively. Was that Jed Cawthorne peering in my direction from the shadows of the nearest stand of peppercorn trees? That's all I needed—another witness to my damnable persecution.

"A girl, eh," I grunted. "Did the Magistrates of Hades turn thee into a creature of the hive as punishment for thy infractions?"

"The magist—" The bee fell silent, as if astonished. "Out of the mouths of babes. But look, you idiot, what's with all this thees and thous and smites and begorrahs? You sound like a hick out of some 20th century hillbilly teev spoof."

I clung to Ebeeneezer's neck, hearing his patient chewing.

"It's just the way we talk. What's wrong with it?"

"What's wrong with it is that it's fake as a rubber dog turd. It's phony as a novelty puke toy. Your great-grandparents all had higher degrees from agricultural colleges, those that weren't running illegal chemical factories and software companies. The isolation's softened your brains! Is it something in the water, or what?"

"We have cast off the cool flippancies of the city slickers," I told the bee proudly, repeating something I'd once heard old man Teusner tell his stout wife. "The ways of the world are the worldly ways of the worldly wise, which isn't for the likes of the saved."

The bee sighed sadly in my ear. "Uh huh. Just another fashionable dialect, eh. Like, whatever. Listen, I need a favor, Mathewmark. I'll do you one in return. I can bring you a vee unit, or a self seating implant phone, or some really wicked porn, anything I can tuck into my pouch."

"I would accept no such thing," I blurted aloud, wondering what these wicked things might be, and again the shape lurking in the nearest trees shifted, as if someone were spying on my dreadful conversation. I lowered my voice to a hoarse whisper: "What would you desire in return?"

"A safe way to get in to your Valley," the liar bee said. "For me and my mate Vikram. Some way to sneak past the guards and into the new vent shaft. You know about the vent, I assume? Everyone here seems to be whining about it."

The ventilation shaft? Huh? The bee wanted to fly down that devilish tube to the bowels of Hades?

"I don't understand anything you're saying," I said in confusion. Ebeeneezer turned his head and looked at me. He didn't understand either. What was I doing here in the gloom still hanging about with a mule when all my human friends seemed so cozy over near the hall? I looked away. "Here you are already, liar bee, yet now you tell me you still wish to learn how to visit the Valley."

"You're just not listening, you dolt!" the bee rasped angrily. "I'm a girl, my name is Amanda, I live about forty kays from you as the crow flies, and I need to get in to your god-forsaken Valley while the moon's still dark and our chances of not getting caught are fair to good. Capiche?"

I caught the sound of a heavy wagon lumbering towards us. You get good at recognizing the sounds, this was a four wheeled, six mule job. Old man Legrand.

"Oh shit, here comes that mad old swine," said the bee. "The fruit-cake with the whip. Him and little miss prissykins. Her with the dopey face."

"Shut up," I snapped. The last thing I wanted was to be found by old man Legrand alone on the village green talking to a bee. And as soon as he'd dropped Sweetcharity at the hall, he'd be bringing his mules to the green. That might be the only chance I got all night of snatching a few moments alone with Sweetcharity. Once the pair of them were inside the hall, the old man's eyes would never be off her. I needed to get rid of the bee and sneak back to the hall at the highest of possible speeds.

"It's no good telling me to shut up," the bee said. "We're mates, you and I. You asked my cyborg bee into the Valley, after all. Now you've got to tell me how to get there in the flesh."

"Well, you just can't get in," I told the girl-bee. "Not unless you can fly over the mountains," I added sarcastically. "Shouldn't be too hard for the minion of Satan."

"Fly in!" The bee developed an excited rasp to its buzz. "Good grief, you're right. Vik and I could just unfurl our wings—"

"I thought you just told me you're an ordinary human girl when you're not pretending to be a liar bee. For god's sake!"

"Blasphemy now, Mathewmark...?"

"Yeah, it's blasphemy," I said making the sign o'god in the air, "But you drive me to it."

The sun was below the horizon, but there was still enough light to see that old man Legrand had unhitched his mules and was leading the team towards the green.

"Okay, friend Mathewmark," said the bee, "I owe you one. Run off and have a little chat with sourguts, though why you want to is a mystery to me. I'll keep the old fart amused for a while. You owe me. Catch you later."

The bee disappeared. And so did I, running low to the ground, keeping as many of the dark shapes of the mules between me and Legrand as I could, hopping over a fence and circling back to the hall. Under the peppercorn trees, Sweetcharity was standing in a group of young people. She was smiling sweetly at Jed Cawthorne, laughing at something Jed was saying. And you should have seen Jed's face: it was all scrubbed up for Beanfeast night, of course, but already there was a trickle of saliva running out of one corner, glistening in the last light of the day. And he was leering at Sweetcharity, staring at the embroidery on her best bodice, and saying something about work for idle hands. I knew just what work he wanted to put his idle hands to. Everybody fell silent as I approached. Abner O'Took and Gracie Sandinski looked at me and then looked away.

So did Zeb Teusner. Blessed-Bride-of-Christ Dwyer examined her fingernails in the twilight, fingernails cracked and chapped by hard work in the fields but probably trimmed for the occasion. Sweetcharity made the sign o'god. What did she think I was, the Prince of Darkness himself?

"Evening all," I said, sounding even louder than I'd meant to. "I trust I find you all in the pink of condition."

"Those'n who walk in the ways of righteousness be always in a condition of grace," said Jed. "Though whether'n it be pink or not, I cannot tell."

"Sure ain't scarlet," Will Orpington said.

"No, nor black as sin, neither," Krishna Dyson chipped in.

"Amen to that," said Sweetcharity and once again made the sign o'god.

"Amen," said the whole group.

"Got a bit religious, have we?" I said. "Got a bit holier than thou?"

"It wouldn't take much to be holier than a bee's soulmate," Jed said.

"An adder or viper that crawls in the grass is holier than the bee lover," Krishna said. "Yea verily," he added after a couple of seconds of silence.

"They do say that you are never alone on that cart of yours, Mathewmark," said little Light-on-the-hill. "Even on the lonesome road the very insects keep you company."

"Oh, really," I said. "Who's 'they'?"

Light-on-the-hill looked down at her feet. It was a bit hard to tell in the dusk, but I thought I could detect the hot blush that was creeping over her face. She's a shy little creature, Light-on-the-hill, it must have taken quite a bit of effort to come out with that remark in company. But I wasn't feeling very protective, I pushed on.

"Tell me, Light-on-the-hill, who is it that says I keep the company of liar bees? Is it my dear friend, Sweetcharity, here?"

"Don't call me friend," Sweetcharity said. "I have no friends who are the friends of the bees from Hades."

"Correct me if I am wrong," I said. "But I think I remember that the bee we met yesterday spent most of its time talking to your grandfather. Methinks it knew him well, addressed him in familiar terms: Old goat, Shit for Brains, Motheaten Old Fart. It was the merry blathering of old friends that I heard in the forest."

Half a dozen people giggled and snorted, trying to suppress their laughter. The mood of the group was changing, I could sense it. I pressed on.

"Hark!" I said cupping one hand to my ear. "Old Man Legrand is at it again, yarning with his mates, the bees."

And indeed he was. From the village green came the sound of swearing and cursing. The sudden crack of the stock whip. "Accursed of god! Foul fiend mired in slime. Filth of the air."

"The banter of familiars," I said, "if ever I heard it."

The violent crack of the stock whip sounded loud in the dusk. But not as loud as the hand that slammed across my face.

"Never speak to me again!"

Sweetcharity turned and flounced into the hall, the light from the hanging oil lamps suddenly catching the silver threads in the embroidery of her dress. There was more laughter from the group, but this time directed squarely at me. The mood was changing again. Despite the stinging in my face I managed a careless shrug.

"Ah," I said, "the lovers' tiff! A hint of pent-up emotion, a promise of passions to come."

I turned and walk as jauntily as I could into the hall. I wished to hell I could believe what I had just said.

I didn't get another chance to talk to Sweetcharity all night. She ate at the same trestle as old man Legrand and when trestles were pushed back and the fiddles started up, she danced with Jed and Krishna and half a dozen others. I didn't even try for a dance. And I didn't feel like dancing with anybody else. I just skulked around the side of the hall and listened to the oldsters. The oldsters were splitting into two camps, you could see that from the way they talked quickly and quietly to each other, falling silent when somebody they didn't trust ventured near. As Beanfeasts go, this one wasn't the greatest, but it was one of the most interesting. Trouble was, as the evening wore on, people started looking at me with suspicious, shifty glances. There was a certain amount of muttering. The rumor was getting around: Mathewmark talks to the bees.

Mind you, some people were starting to look at old man Legrand in the same way. I wasn't the only one subject to that particular rumor. I looked from under downcast eyes to where Legrand was sitting. But he seemed oblivious to the tensions within the hall, he was in a huddle with old man O'Grady and old biddy Witherspoon. They were muttering intently and planning something. You could be sure of that. By the time the feast ground to a halt and everybody stood up and sang Old Lang Jack, I was more than ready to leave.

8: AMANDA

<You on-line, Mr. Bones?>

<Indeed I am, Mistress Interlocutor,> Vikram replied via our Steganography link.

<I know how we can get in,>I told him.

I was halfway through a strawberry sundae Mrs. Ng had whipped up for me, and my mouth was all gooey. Somehow I had to get out of this house and into a real soda-joint in the Mall where Vik and I could engage in eye contact and I could tell that he knew I was on the verge of a stroke of brilliance and was appropriately impressed. Well, I'd settle for just getting out of the front door after sundown and taking a slow walk along the river. It had only been three days, but I was getting cabin fever. Watching through my bee-spy as Mathewmark mooched off for a feast of beans with his loony pals in the fading twilight had made me resentful and devious. Unlike my usual relaxed and sunny state of mind, you understand. (As if. I know.)

<We can't go in through the pass,> he said. <They have that blocked off with their damned Gatehouse.>

<Correct. And we can't get in at the other end, because that opens into the National Park and you need three kinds of official passes to go there, which we might be able to fake up, but it also requires the presence of at least one bona fide adult to take charge, as they so light-heartedly term it.>

<Well, duh. And we can't drive a fresh tunnel through the rock of the mountains, either, not without our own portable nuclear powered mole, and I've carelessly lent mine to Lata for the week.> Vikram made a smiley, and a canned bray of hyena laughter came out of my machine.

<Right again. But hey, this isn't just hot air I'm floating here.> I paused, added, <That was a Hint, Dodo-boy.>

<Oh my gosh.> I could imagine him sitting bolt upright as the Idea started to enter his brain. <You've got bats in your belfry.>

<Well, I ain't just flying a kite.> The idea was growing on me, but it still filled me with anxiety. I gnawed my lip, which was starting to look like the edge of a lace doily, I expect.

<We don't have enough pocket money to hire a plane, Mand, and traffic control wouldn't allow us to fly in anyway. Neither of us has a license for an ultra-lite. I suppose you're suggesting we hang-glide into the Valley, but you're forgetting something: we need to do this under cover of darkness, and there are no thermal updrafts at night. So what am I forgetting?

I'd been scouring the local news channel archives for something to help us out. This was my big find. I dumped it on his screen with an applet showing a flourish of triumphant trumpets:

<The Muon Power Station has been in trial operation for a bit over a month. It's quite a hike, but they're located right snug up against this side of Bell's Ridge. And from there it's only five or six klicks easy glide into the Valley, Vik. If we don't kill ourselves in the dark.>

Warm nuclear fusion. I laughed out loud, with delight. Vik would be seeing the possibilities now: we could use our suits' built-in carbon composite wings, no need to haul hang gliders. We could jump down off the Ridge and into the fusion plant's updraft and up and over and down in easy spirals into the Valley.

<Of course>, I added, <chances are we'll miss and be smashed into pulp on top of the plant's radiator vanes.>

Vikram was silent for a long moment, thinking it through. Not one for jumping into things, the old Vik—although he'd have to jump long and hard to make this one fly. Then he said, <Or be detected by the plant's safety automatics and gunned down by its protective lasers.>

<No, they're not allowed to use those, I saw a news report. Might harm the local rare species and we can't have that. They use nets. We won't be layered into ash and steam, we'll just be trapped by the nets and hauled off for the vets to check our beaks and wings.>

<Or our claws and tails,> Vik sent, getting into the spirit of the game. <There must be a dozen possums and feral cats trapped every night. We'll have a whole zoo for company. Then Mr. Abdel-Malek will lock us in and throw away the key.>

<Only if we crash and burn. Only if he learns that we were there. Don't worry, Vikram, it's a stroke of brilliance.>

<My heroine!> he keyed sardonically. <So smart! And so humble! Mad, of course. Utterly mad.>

I wasn't going to be put off. <We'll hit that bloody updraft and loft over into the Valley like autumn leaves in a gentle breeze.>

<Like two blind lunatics jumping into the river, more likely. Don't forget, there'll be no moon even if the weather is good for flying.>

<Nag, nag. The Global Positioning System satellites will see us safe and sound.>

Vikram fell silent. Then he said: <GPS's still only accurate to within a square meter of altitude, I think. We need more precise guidance from someone on the ground. You'll have to get your pal Mathew Mark Peter and Paul to light us a fire or two next to the maglev vent.>

<A landing strip. Hmm, I don't think so. They don't seem to use artificial lighting in their crackpot little utopia, Vik. Well, oil lamps and candles, I suppose that's artificial. Still, a string of small fires would have all the yokels for kilometers about rushing in with barrels of water and blankets to beat out the flames.>

<Two or three radar corners, that's what we need,> he sent. <Hey, why not? Do you think Believer Boy could hacksaw us a couple of reflectors? They have steel containers, don't they? Rusty old tins? Buzz him with your cyborg fly and put the idea into his head.>

<Ingenious, Watson. I'll give it a burl right away, before he gets home to bed. Nothing ventured.>

<What do you mean, "Watson'? I'm Holmes, you ignorant child.>

<Way cool, Homes. You da bomb.>

<Sometimes you alarm me, Amanda. I don't know where you pick up these outdated and jaded turns of phrase.>

<Funny, I was just making exactly that comment to somebody else. Anyway. Gotta go, babe. Have bat wings to scrub and pack.>

<Sure, Mand. Watch the skies! Over and out.>

His machine sent me a rude blatting, as of forty hogs a-farting, and he was gone. I grinned, then sighed and pulled up a GPS survey of the region, looking for exact co-ordinates of the Muon Warm Fusion Test Facility or whatever the engineers and politicians and publicity flacks were calling it this month.

* * * *

I woke my bee just after eleven that night and looked around the bit of the Valley in sensor range. The feasting was done, looked like, dishes and fiddles packed away. Were they allowed to sing and dance? In a modest, god-fearing way, naturally. Probably not. They were a dour-looking crew. A few couples stood about chatting by the soft glow of oil lamps, occasionally swatting mosquitoes. These people didn't seem to use insect repellent. Probably they didn't wash either. Did they even know about running water? I shuddered. With any luck, Vikram and I would be in and out without any of the smelly creatures even noticing us. Tomorrow night would be ideal, if I could get the love-lorn one to snap out of it and guide us in to a convenient landing right next to the vent.

When I tracked him down, he was clopping along the dirt road, with his Mom, dad and brother. Without moonlight, I needed to boost the bee's artificial eyes to get a good picture of his downcast mouth and wounded eyes. No one was saying anything, the other three looked sleepy and well fed. It was only Mathewmark who was full of gloom. The mule turned up a side track and, a few minutes later came to a grinding halt outside a small, dark hovel. Mathewmark muttered something about putting Ebeneezer in the lower forty. The other three made their way into the hovel, while Mathewmark unhitched the mule and began leading it along a narrow path.

"Psst! Mathewmark. Know anything about radar corners?"

He hardly twitched a muscle this time. Maybe he was getting used to me. All to the good. "Go away."

"I'm off just as soon as we've finished our little talk."

"I'll swat you like a bug."

"Ha ha."

"Don't think I won't! I'm still half convinced you're a limb of Satan."

"Six limbs, you'll find. And two pairs of wings. Quite pointless squashing me, though. There's more where I came from. You can't swat the lot."

"Look you, if I'm seen talking to you again, I'm dead. No one will want their goods carted by a familiar of the liar bees."

"Better talk to me out here, then. In this boring old field. You'll give me credit for not coming into the hall of fun and beans with you? Not alarming your olds on the cart."

"Go away. You make me tired."

"Sure, I'll nip back to your place and wait for you there. Hope we don't keep your old chedders up with our nattering."

"For the love of Shiva, what do you want? I've already said I can't tell you a way to cross the range into the Valley. At any rate, it can't be done from this side, and I've never heard of one of your heathen kind making his way in here."

Yeah, right, like we'd want to.

But that was an interesting throw-away remark, sounded as if he wasn't the first one with a sneaking, barely acknowledged interest in leaving this hell-hole and exploring the fleshpots. If that was true, and if I'd really managed to arouse his interest, I was home and hosed. Well, I was certainly home, damn it, grounded for weeks according to the Magistrate, and I don't know what that "hosed" bizzo means but I suspect the worst. Nah, I told myself, Vik and me are meant to do it. Down the vent, then web on to that freighter as it slows in its curved path deep under the Valley. Thrill of a lifetime, yeah. Worth being grounded until we were 64. By hook or by crook.

"Radar corners," I said patiently through my bee.

"I don't know anything about—"

"I know you don't. You're as ignorant as pig-shit, you poor boy. Relax, I'll explain. Do you have any sheet metal in this place? You know, for the roofs of your hovels. What's it called, they used it last century, gal iron?"

"Roofs is thatch."

"That grass stuff?"

"Reeds, dried sedge, straw..."

"Not what I'd call hygienic. What about oil drums? Do you people use oil drums?"

"Eucalyptus oil we store in bottles. With corks."

"Hicksville, this place is unreal..."

"Yeah," Mathewmark said sourly. Boy, the kid was really pissed off. I should have kept the bee's recording mode running while I was talking over my plan with Vikram. Something messy had obviously gone down with Sweetcharity at the bean feast. I really couldn't see what he found in the girl. Okay, there were the boobs, but it wasn't as if she had a decent bra or showed off her cleavage or anything. Her teeth were okay, apart from the missing one right in front. And that prim thing was never going to put out, not until they were married in the Temple of the God of Their Choice. I'd watched enough 20th century vids to know that for sure. But the boy didn't know what was in his best interests. He was still trying to give me the brush-off. "If you don't mind," he was saying, "I've got a lot on my mind. Please go away."

"Tell me your troubles. You help me with the radar corners, I'll help you straighten out your personal life."

"No you don't!" His bleat of alarm was so sharp that Ebeeneezer tossed his head, jerking the rope thing, the leash or whatever it was. Mathewmark patted the mule, muttering to it, ignoring the bee.

He wasn't going to get rid of me that easily. "What do you have in this place that's made of ferrous metal? Iron, steel, that sort of stuff?"

His eyes shifted shiftily. "Nothing."

I gave a beeish laugh. "And I thought I was meant to be the liar! Okay, come clean. What do you people use that's made out of metal?"

"Ploughshares, harrows, spades, crowbars, cross-cut saws..."

"What's a harrow?"

"A thing with spikes."

"Spikes are no good. A spade is a thing you dig with, right?"

"Don't you know anything?" he said.

Defensively, I made a guess. "Sort of flat device on the end of a stick? You shove it in the ground to make a hole, right?"

He widened his eyes comically and raised them to heaven and nodded, as if to a baby. In the darkness, only my bee eyes enabled me to see this. But see it I did. Patronize me, will you, farmboyo? I thought savagely. We'll see about that. You'll get your comeuppance. But meanwhile, one of these spades might just do the trick with our suit radar. Two or three would be even better. Drive them into the soil at the points of a triangle, and—

"Okay, Mathewmark, here's my plan," I told him. "You'll be at the vent tomorrow night at a quarter before midnight. Bring three of those shovels. Now listen carefully, unless you want me to buzz back to the hovel and tell the whole family about your dirty little wrestle under the trees with Miss Muffett the other day—"

9: MATHEWMARK

The morning after the beanfeast, I didn't cart anything. Ebeeneezer had the day off and Lukenjon and I weeded the cucumber patch—hacking away with the hoes, trying not to sever the cucumbers. Every now and then we did. The little cucumber would lie there on the ground, split clean in half. The best thing to do was to eat the evidence. We'd bought lunch with us, wrapped up in a cloth. A wedge of cheese and some pickles in a jar, a half round of corn bread. Lukenjon and I lay in the shade. We just picked at the food, we'd eaten too many cucumbers to be really hungry.

"Is it true?" Lukenjon said.

"Is what true?"

"You know," Lukenjon said. "What folks are saying."

"What are folks saying?"

"Come on," Lukenjon said, "I'm your brother. Folks say that you and old man Legrand talk to the bees. Or talk to the trees. Some daft, mad thing."

"Legrand sure does," I said.

"And you?"

I looked out over our patch of dirt. In the distance was the river. Weeping willows and old biddy Gonzales' cows grazing on the opposite bank. Beyond the Gonzales' place you could see the patchwork of fields and woods and villages. And against the bright blue skyline the rocks and cliffs of the Valley walls. They are our strength, the Valley walls, they keep us safe and unpolluted by the Outside. But sometimes they can look like the walls of a grim fortress, a jail maybe, seen from the inside. Off to our right, just over the boundary fence, the green tower of the ventilation shaft stuck up out of old man Grout's deserted sorghum patch, leading straight down to the tunnel, the tunnel to the Outside.

"Cat got your tongue?" Lukenjon said.

"The bee I've been talking to," I said to my brother, "is a girl called Amanda. She's shut up in her room and sick of it. So she's coming to visit us tonight."

What's a brother for, if you can't confide in him. I felt a huge wave of relief: just saying those simple words out loud was like coming up for air in the swimming hole when you've been down too long.

"If them bees exist," Lukenjon said, "them bees lie. They lie like the devil himself, if they exist. If the devil exists."

"Most people tell lies now and then," I said. "I don't reckon Amanda would be much different."

"It's a strange name for a bee," Lukenjon said, "Amanda."

"The bee isn't called Amanda," I said. "The bee is just a messenger. Ain't even alive. It's a sort of... sort of a machine... like a cuckoo clock. Amanda sends it her voice."

Lukenjon made the sign o'god, but he made it in a fooling around sort of way. "Sounds like the devil," he said.

"She's coming tonight," I said. "Her and a friend. I've got to guide her in—with spades."

Lukenjon laughed, rolling around on the ground. "I reckon you're touched," he said. "Taken total leave of your senses. Signaling to the devil's handmaiden with spades."

"Want to help?" I said.

There was another long silence. Eventually Lukenjon broke it: he burped mightily. The air was heavy with the smell of half-digested cucumber. "I'm not letting you out at night by yourself," he said, "you being a loony who talks to bees and waves spades at night-running chicks called Amanda."

* * * *

Mom and Dad were well asleep when Lukenjon and I slipped out of our bedroom window. Silent as mice we padded barefoot to the barn, collected the spades and made our way to the lower forty. It was only when we were sitting on the grass with Ebeeneezer's dozy form standing like a black rock half a dozen meters away that we pulled on our boots. The night was very clear and very still. There was no moon. The stars burned like glow worms.

"What you said this afternoon..." I said.

"What did I say this afternoon?"

"You said, "If the devil exists", like maybe you thought he didn't."

"Maybe he don't," Lukenjon said.

"And the God of Your Choice?" I said.

"Maybe I've chose a god that don't exist neither."

"Everybody in the Valley believes in the God of their Choice."

"God help them."

"Do you really think I'm touched?" I said. "Do you think I'm gone in the head? Do you think I'm imagining the bee when I talk to it?"

"Remains to be seen," said Lukenjon.

I was about offer Lukenjon a small wager, but we were both suddenly still, suddenly alert, listening.

"Wagon," Lukenjon said.

"Four wheels, six mules," I said.

"Your friend, old man Legrand," Lukenjon said. "Out and about at midnight. Now what would he be up to?"

"I can't think," I said. "And he's not my friend."

I was totally confused. The only reason I could think of for old man Legrand's midnight wandering was the same one that had brought me and Lukenjon to the Lower Forty: Amanda. But, as far as I knew, all Amanda had done to old man Legrand was to taunt him, tease, him, insult him. Surely she couldn't have asked him to help with the radar corner business.

"Sit tight," Lukenjon said.

We sat on the grass of the lower forty and listened. The stars were intense, but the starlight still wasn't bright enough to illuminate distant things at ground level. Our ears were our eyes. The wagon creaked nearer and then turned when it got to old man Grout's.

"The ventilation shaft," Lukenjon whispered. "He's going to the shaft."

We listened some more. We heard muffled voices: Legrand, maybe O'Grady and a woman—old biddy Witherspoon unless I was totally mistaken. A girl's voice said quite clearly, "There's nothing survives a good roasting."

"Quiet!" said Legrand speaking three times louder than the girl. "You'll wake the whole Valley."

Beside me Lukenjon laughed quietly. "He wouldn't leave that little bundle of purity at home alone, would he now."

"She's my beloved," I whispered, fierce.

"Was," chuckled Lukenjon. "Was."

"But what are they doing?" I whispered. This was the last thing I wanted: the whole place swarming with folks up to no good. Amanda and her friend would be landing in the middle of a jamboree. And they'd be coming in any time now.

"Don't worry about them," Lukenjon whispered. "Let's get these spades in position."

Silently, hardly whispering a word to each other, we set up the long-handled spades in the lower forty in the way Amanda had demanded. We made a small hole with the crowbar and then jammed the end of the handle in. Two sets of two. Little right angles of steel a meter above the ground. And all the time we worked, we listened to the sounds from across the boundary fence. It was pretty obvious what was going on. Legrand and his companions were heaping firewood around the ventilation shaft. They were going to burn it down.

"Reckon it will catch?" I whispered.

"Ain't steel, nor iron," Lukenjon said.

"I don't reckon the tunnelers would have used something that would burn," I said.

"Either way, old man Legrand's firewood is going to burn," Lukenjon said. "It'll light up the place like the fires of hell themselves."

"Might be useful to Amanda and her friend, they'll be able to see what they're doing."

"And Legrand will see them arrive."

There was nothing we could do. We retired to the far end of the lower forty, putting as much distance as possible between us and the boundary fence. We lay on the grass and watched the first little flickers of flame. Within a minute the fire was well alight. The crackling and spitting of the dry timber was loud in the still night air. A bright column of sparks rose up, enclosing the dark mass of the shaft.

"All they need is a saint," Lukenjon said.

"Saint?" I said.

"Yeah. Tied to the stake, ready for a bit of martyrdom."

I shivered in the warm night air. There was a drumming of hooves as Ebeneezer came galloping up to our end of the field. He's not fond of fire, our mule. I put my arms round his neck, whispered calming words into his great floppy ears. By the increasing light of the fire I could see old man Legrand's team of mules kicking and tossing in their traces. The mad fool had left his team standing far too close to the blaze. The mules brayed, and human figures could be seen trying to turn the team and the wagon away from the fire. There were shouts from the other side of the Valley. An oil lantern was swinging in somebody's hand on the track that ran down from the McWeezle place. I thought I could hear Mom and dad shouting something from our house. They were calling our names.

"It's all right," Lukenjon said. "We'll just say we thought we heard sounds and came to investigate."

"What about Amanda and her friend?" I said.

"If the buggers have got any sense they'll fly back where they came from."

"I don't think it's that simple," I said. "All they can do is glide. They can't fly upwards."

"Oh yeah," Lukenjon said. "What do you reckon those are doing?" and he pointed to the great tower of flame that was now totally engulfing the ventilation shaft.

"What are you talking about?" I said.

"Look. Up above. Right up there where the sparks stop."

I saw two huge bats. Great black-winged vampires swooping and wheeling, riding the new column of hot air, blotting out the stars, turning and twisting. Visible one minute, invisible the next.

"Daft gits," Lukenjon said. "Their wings will catch. Moths to the flame. You watch."

I watched. They were beautiful, free. They were riding the great tower of hot air for the pure joy of it. They circled, rose up almost to the stars, diminishing in size. They quit the hot air for the cooler blackness, disappearing. Reappeared lower down, swooping in over the heads of the groundlings and mules, twisting and spinning upwards again around and around the shaft and back into the airy reaches of the night.

Crack! Even the roar of the fire couldn't drown out old man Legrand's stock whip. The crazed figure was dancing around, leaping onto the back of his wagon, giving himself extra height, flailing with his whip at the night. But the black creatures were up and away, far out of reach. Oh how I wanted to join them, to be one with the night and the air and the stars.

A small crowd was gathering. In the firelight you could see their clothes. Britches pulled on overnight attire. Hair that was normally tight as a fist in buns, flowing and flaring in the firelight. People holding rakes and spades. A bucket. A figure that looked like old biddy Smeeth—down on her knees, praying.

"It's hot," Lukenjon said. "But it's not going to last. Most of them logs is ash. They'll not be flapping around up there much longer."

He was right. The fire was dying. The sparks now barely reached above the top of the shaft. The circling human bats weren't much higher than two or three times the height of the shaft themselves. It was only a matter of time before they'd be in reach of Legrand's stock whip.

They quit the dying tower of hot air. They were away into the night, lost from sight.

"Now where've they gone?" Lukenjon said. But the bats answered him themselves, wheeling round out of the blackness and rushing straight towards us, flying abreast, straight between the two radar corners, leaning back in their flight, bringing their feet down like landing herons. Almost colliding with Ebeeneezer who bucked, jerking my arms from around his neck.

"Yeeeeha!" said the girl. "What a ride! Sorry about the donkey. You should paint him with iridescent stripes."

The boy had fallen with a yelp when he landed. "Bloody ankle," he said.

"Upaday, Vik," said the girl. "We've gotta shift." She turned to me, "You Mathewmark?"

"Of course," I said.

"Sorry, can't see much in this darkness. You look a bit different. Damn bee—we get all this false color from its sensors. You ought to see yourself on the screen. Freakenstein!" Something especially unnatural was happening to her dark silhouette. It looked as if her great bat wings were shriveling away. In a moment, she was just a tall shadowy girl in the moonless night.

The sounds of people clambering over the boundary wall brought the conversation to a halt.

"They're coming to get us," Vik said, getting to his feet. His wings got in the way, and one buckled as he groaned and almost fell over. He pressed something on his chest, and the stiff fabric of his wings folded neatly away, its struts clicking together and sliding into a flat pack on his back.

"Let's skootle," the girl said. "Where do we hide?"

"You'd better follow me," Lukenjon said. "Mathewmark, go and head off the posse."

The two former bat figures, one hobbling, both jet black and nearly invisible except for their faces under hair tight hoods, followed Lukenjon into the night. I walked down the field towards the sounds of the pursuit party. The first person I bumped into was old biddy Smeeth.

"They went that way, Auntie," I said, pointing in the wrong direction.

"Fiends o'filth!" yelled old biddy Smeeth. "We'll boil ye alive in t-tree oil!" and set off, the others of her band following, laughing and brandishing their tools of trade. They sounded, I thought sourly, just like the very fiends of hell themselves.

10: AMANDA

Skulking like rats in a dusty barn, just our dimmed shoulder-patch nav lights to hold the gloom at bay—we didn't dare light an oil lamp, with those squawking loonies running loose outside—no, this wasn't my idea of fun. Not at all my neat in-and-out plan.

Poor Vikram had stopped speaking to me an hour ago, and I couldn't really blame him. Vik's grippo sneaker had been removed as soon as we reached the barn, and he had unzipped the black carbon fiber legging of his blackgear jumpsuit. His sprained ankle seemed to be half again its normal size, and as far as we could tell in the murky glow of our navigation patches it was also a rather ugly shade of purple. At least it didn't seem to be broken. It was going to slow us up, though. As for me—

"Ah-CHOO!"

"Keep the noise down, mistress bat," the kid brother said, jumping. "Do you want the whole village on top of us?"

I wiped my running nose on the back of my sleeve. My eyes were streaming. That unpleasant tickle started up again almost at once, and I could feel another big sneeze pushing at my swollen forehead and cheeks There are instant pharmaceuticals for this kind of thing. Of course we didn't have any in our packs.

"Ah— Ah— Arch—"

The rest of the explosion was muffled by something enormous and rough being crushed against my nose and mouth. I swung around in the dark with my fists, but it was only Mathewmark with his handwoven handkerchief. Last time I'd seen that coarse woven piece of cloth, I'd been watching through the eyes of a bee, and the boy had been trying to swat me with it.

"Keep your hands to yourself," I said, but took his snotrag and blew heartily. I took a deep wheezy breath, and felt my nasal tissues swelling again. The barn's air was choked with mule dander and a dozen kinds of grain pollen or whatever it is that sets off allergic reactions. I wondered if I were going to die, gasping on my own fluids.

"Auntie Maisie has a decoction for this blight," Mathewmark muttered to his brother. "Think you can locate her bag of simples in the pantry?"

"I know where she keeps her herbs, but not which among them is effective against the sniffles and snots."

"Fetch the lot like a good chap. We can't leave mistress bee to wheeze herself to death."

I lowered myself weakly into the embrace of a bale of hay that the boys had covered with a patched old sheet. Vikram was lying on his side gazing gloomily into the gloom, his damaged leg raised up on a bag of oats. A stout tomcat wandered across the straw covering the dirt floor of the barn, glancing at us with only slight curiosity, and positioned itself facing a crack in the timber of a stall.

"He smells a mouse," Mathewmark told me. "Perhaps a family of the sly beasts." He called in a soft, encouraging voice, "Good work, Kevin. Stand at your station like a god-fearing mouser."

"Bite they tiny nose and toes," added Lukenjon, slipping in with a bundle of twigs, a battered metal pot, and a ceramic bowl. He began to crush the dried leaves between the palms of his hands, watching the debris sift down into his bowl.

"Your cat might smell a mouse," I said thickly, swallowing gunk, "but I smell a rat. What was that fire doing all around the vent? The spades did the trick, homed us in perfectly. If I'd wanted a bloody great visible beacon, I'd have asked for one. All it did was rouse the mob."

"You don't think Lukenjon and I lit the bonfire, do you?" Mathewmark snorted indignantly. "That was the work of old man Legrand, the elder you've taken such a dislike to, and his gang of pestish cronies. Egged on by Jed Cawthorne, I shouldn't wonder, who's taken a wicked fancy to my beloved and would sway her from my wooing."

"Ah-ha!" I sat forward. My head swam, I really was feeling appalling. "I thought I heard the shrewish tones of your lady-love among the rabid horde. Where the mad old grandfather is found, they say, the dreary young grand-daughter is sure to follow."

Mathewmark started up an angry but whispered defense of the dull creature but I was too asthmatic by that point to pay any attention. He was crouched over a small portable stove of some kind, lighting its wick with a match. A match! Mind bogglingly primitive. He dipped water into the pot, pressed down its ill-fitting lid, placed it on the pale flame. Despite the blocked nose, I could smell its fumes—some kind of oil from a tree or bush, I suppose. I doubted that the Valley folk received weekly supplies of petroleum or kerosene from the awful Polluters they seemed so afraid of.

By the time Lukenjon had finished crushing and mixing his dried herbs in the bowl, the pot was boiling. No electricity, but not altogether hopelessly primitive after all. Lukenjon poured in steaming water and brought the stinking result across to me in the gloom. I took the bowl in both hands, and nearly dropped it. Hot!

"What am I supposed to do with this?" I asked irritably. My nose was running like a tap. "Drink the foul stuff?"

"Hold it up under your nose, madam bat," the boy told me, "or better still, put your face down just above the water. Take in the steam. Here, let me show you." He topped up the bowl with more boiling water from the stove, and gently pressed down on the back on my head until my sore nose was only a few centimeters from the surface. Steam rose in the cool of the night, rich with odors, making my skin flush and sweat slightly. "That's right," he told me encouragingly, "breathe of its healing vapors. Soon you'll recover your health, if such blessed medicaments have any power over those who fly in the night."

I let the strange smells rise from the bowl into my lungs and the blocked spaces behind my nose. Oddly enough, I found my mood improving almost at once. My nostrils stopped their seeping, my eyes felt less like a sore someone had rubbed grit into, and slowly the throb in my swollen head eased. I started to breathe normally. Vikram frowned at me from the darkness, and rubbed his foot meaningfully, but held his tongue. Clearly he didn't wish to ask these yokels for any help. Not him, son and heir of Dr. Singh.

"Thanks, boyo." I snorted loosened gunk back into my throat and swallowed it. Yetch. Salty. "This is doing the trick. Can you think of anything for my poor friend's sprain?"

Mathewmark had been fussing in the shadows. He came forward with a rolled and rather grubby bandage, and a vile smelling pot of something that looked as if it might have been used to treat the mule or perhaps to poison any mice that escaped Kevin the cat. Vik grudgingly permitted Mathewmark to rub the oily muck into his bare ankle. He winced but otherwise refused to show the pain he must have been suffering.

"You two are studying medicine?" Vikram asked skeptically.

"My brother and I treat the livestock hereabouts when they sicken," Mathewmark told him. "Now grit your teeth, this might cause some pain but it will help bring down the swelling over the next few days." He started to wrap the damaged ankle tightly with his bandage, cinching it with a knot. He rolled down Vik's unzipped trouser leg but left off the sneaker. I doubt it would have fitted back anyway.

"Days!" Vikram was horrified. He eased himself up into seated position. "Thanks for the help, pal. But look, we can't stay here. Our parents are going to find out we're missing in the morning, and there'll be hell to pay if they learn we're holed up inside the Valley."

Mathewmark looked at him suspiciously. " "Hell to pay"? Are you changing your story, now that we have given you sanctuary and—"

"Oh, lighten up," I said. I really was feeling a thousand percent better. If we could get the recipe for this stuff, we could make a fortune. "It's just an expression. Vik, we're just going to have to go ahead with the freighter burn, hurt or not. If we had phones, we could face the music. You know, get them to pick us up at the Gatehouse. As it is, nobody knows where we are." I shivered as the reality of our situation settled into my bones. "Our families are really going to go nutso. There'll be a five bell alarm, cops roughing people up, choppers scouring metro from one end to the other for our murdered bods." I shuddered. "We'll end up so grounded we'll die of old age before they let us out."

I glanced at my watch. It was after one a.m., and the farm boys looked completely done in. No wonder—they probably got up with the sun to feed their chickens or tote their barge or whatever farm boys do when the rest of the sane 21st century world is snoozing after a hard night of vee. I was starting to nod off myself. Damn good stuff, whatever it was in that herbal infusion. I yawned rudely.

Mathewmark looked flustered and embarrassed in the pale blue light of the stove, which was still flickering even though the pot had been taken off it. We'd be awake until morning if I didn't force him to spit it out.

"What's on your mind, M-man? Are you scared we'll run off with the family silver?"

He frowned. "You are frivolous." He cleared his throat. "There isn't any other place for you both. I fear you will have to stay here together for the rest of the night, even though it will compromise you, Mistress Amanda."

What? Do *what*? Vikram gave a sarcastic laugh from the darkness.

"No fear of that, pal. Amanda and I are already so deep in shit that spending the night together in a barn won't raise any extra eyebrows." Over Mathewmark's splutterings, he added, "Look, guys, we're very grateful for your help, but it's time to bed down. See you in the morning, okay?"

Lukenjon stood up at once, gathered his medicinals and bowl, turned out the stove's flame. He nodded shyly to me, extended his hand to Vik, left like a shadow. His older brother bumbled about for another minute, clearly distressed at leaving Vikram and me alone together. I thought this was rank hypocrisy. If he'd had a chance for some snuggling and snuffling with Miss Sourcharity, he'd have been in it quick as flash, if you ask me. I shocked him even more by grabbing his arm, pulling him down so his face was next to mine, and giving him a hearty and only slightly snotty smooch.

"You're a veritable saint, Emster," I told him. "We owe you. Oh, that reminds me." As he gaped guiltily, glancing sideways at Vikram who was more concerned about his bung ankle than anything else, I reached around into my backpack and pulled out a small flat cardboard box . It was wrapped in metallic foil decorated with prancing high stepping horses and carriages rather more upmarket the local carts and wagons. "For you and your brother. Don't eat them all at once."

"Eat—?"

"Open it, it's a present."

He tore clumsily at the foil as if he'd never seen such stuff before in his life. I suppose he hadn't. After a moment I took it back from him and slid my thumbnail down the seam, opened the box of assorted chocolates, held it out in the dimness. My newly salvaged sense of smell went bonzo at the happy odor of brandy-centered almond-crusted dark chocolates, and my mouth started watering involuntarily. A girl's got to eat, after all, and I'd missed Mrs. Ng's supper treat I snatched a choc and popped it into my mouth.

"Go on, Mathewmark, be tempted. But don't eat them all at once, you'll make yourself sick. And save some for Lukenjon."

Suspiciously, he took a choc and sniffed it. He put in between his teeth and bit down. Liqueur spurted. Startled, he coughed, dropping half the chocolate into the straw. Then his taste buds kicked in, and I saw the endorphin rush start. Golly, just imagine what it must be like—to go all your life without one of the basic nutritional food groups. He closed his eyes and sucked, then swallowed with a gulp. His hand reached out of its own accord and found another chocolate. In fact his hand found two chocolates and crammed them both into his gob. He chewed blissfully, making little moans. I slapped his hand as it darted out for more, and put the top back on the pack.

"That's enough, you pig. Now go and clean your teeth and get to bed. Don't you have work to do tomorrow?"

Mathewmark looked at me as if waking from a naughty dream. He stood up, shoved the chocolates under one arm, clomped to the barn door. Vikram gave him a languid wave and lay back in the darkness.

"Sweet dreams, farm boy," I called softly. "If you see any witch burners, tell them we've flown back to Hades."

But he was already gone. A moment later, it all caught up with me, and I was gone too. Not out like a light, we didn't have any to switch off. Just gone, down into exhausted dreams of running and someone shouting and a cat peering into my face with huge fangs and falling through blackness into sparks and pitchforks.

* * * *

An instant later, it seemed, I jolted awake. Morning sunlight streamed in through the open barn door.

Mathewmark had closed the door when he left.

Vikram was still lying like a log, wrapped in an old horse-blanket.

So who was—?

"Shh," a vaguely familiar voice hissed in my ear. I twisted convulsively, blinking sleep out of my sore eyes, and looked up at the really quite pretty face of bloody Sweetcharity. She smiled nervously at me, showing the gap in her front teeth.

"Oh shit," I said, "the witch-burners are here after all."

The girl looked frightened but determined. Can't say I blamed her, really. After all, last time she'd seen us we had been zooming down out of the sky like a pair of bats, riding the bonfire thermals on our foldaway carbon wings.

"You and the other one must get out of here," she told me, her eyes wide with fright. "At sun up my grandfather and some of the others started a house to house search. They've started at the bottom of the Valley and are working their way up. They'll leave no stone unturned. They'll be here soon. I don't want Mathewmark and his family to get into trouble just because they did an act of charity to strangers."

Vikram rolled over and opened one eye.

"Heavens," he drawled. "An angel! Good morning, beautiful. I'm Vik, I don't believe we've been introduced."

Sweetcharity blushed. I gave that bad boy a stern look.

"I have to go," she said. "Tell Mathewmark—" She stood in the doorway, framed by light.

"Yeah, yeah," I said. "I'll give him your regards." She hesitated for a moment, glancing over her shoulder into the open field at her back. I could see good old Ebeeneezer ambling up toward us. "Hey, Sweetcharity," I called, relenting, "listen—thanks, sis."

She ducked her head and was gone into the crisp, cool morning.

11: MATHEWMARK

There was no point arousing suspicion. So Lukenjon and I got up at our normal time, although we'd had next to no sleep all night. We did what we normally do before breakfast: got the fire going, let out the chooks, milked the cow. Dad was up and about and Mom was soon banging pots and pans and preparing breakfast. You can see the old barn from the farmyard, it stands in the lee of a row of trees half way up the hill behind our place, but there was no reason for me or Lukenjon to go there. So we didn't, just shot the occasional glance in its direction. But we needn't have worried. The two Outsiders were laying low.

At breakfast all the talk was about the fire and the strange creatures that had swarmed in the updraft. Mom had only seen the two of them, but Dad—who has a bit of imagination—had seen a whole host.

"How many's a host, Dad?" I said.

"They are legion, the fiends from the infernal regions."

"How many did you actually see?" I said.

"Maybe two dozen, maybe a thousand," Dad said. "They was ascending into the night sky, getting smaller and smaller as they spread their contagion across the heavens."

"Oh, rubbish," Mom said. "I was there too, Fred Fisher. I saw two children with those hang glider things. That's all I saw."

"If they were children with hang gliders," Dad said, "how come they came flying out of the shaft. It ain't wide enough for their wings."

"I reckon they just come over the ridge," Mom said. "Like that poor git the year before last. The one Elder Robinson had to cart off to the Gatehouse. He just got blown off course. Them children were the same."

"I saw them as we were running across the field," Dad said. "Pouring out of the shaft, dozens of black winged fiends."

"That was sparks," Mom said.

"Either way, it is all Elder Legrand's fault," Dad said. "He never should have done it—building fires in the middle of the night. Stirring up the devil with no thought for his neighbors."

We spent the rest of breakfast discussing old man Legrand. Mom and Dad both reckoned he was a lunatic.

"That poor girl," Mom said. "Being brought up by a madman. It's a wonder she's as sane as she is."

Mom and Dad don't know about Sweetcharity being my beloved. You don't want to tell your parents everything.

* * * *

After breakfast Lukenjon and Dad took the fencing equipment and went down to the river paddock. I hitched Ebeeneezer to the cart and trundled up the hill to the old barn. I'd said I was going to cart some hay to Auntie McWeezle. She didn't actually need the hay for a fortnight, but I'd said there was no point in putting off that which one can do today. I pulled the doors to the barn wide open. There was no one inside. Then Amanda put her head over the top of the old feed bin. Her hair, now I could see it in the morning light, was bright purple and spiky like a weed.

"You alone?" she said.

"Yeah," I said. "I'm alone." I kept staring at her. On her forehead was a bright picture of a mythical beast—a tiger, I decided. Shameless!

Vikram's head appeared. "We must leave at once," he said.

"Not with your ankle," I said. His hair was very black and strangely knotted in strands. These people might not be fiends from hell but they were clearly heathens.

"The searchers will be here soon. We must leave."

"No one will come searching," I said.

"Get real, farmboy," Amanda said. "That nutter who lit the fire, the one with the stock whip. Him and his mates are going around doing a house to house search."

"I don't think so," I said.

"Listen, Mathewmark. Sweetwhatshername was here just after dawn. She ought to know. She's his grand-daughter."

"Sweetcharity?"

"Poor girl. What a name!" Amanda said. "How could anybody call their kid something as yucky as Sweetcharity? You might as well start calling kids Sugarbun or Toasted Marshmallow."

I ignored her. I was a bit vexed that Sweetcharity had been roaming around on her own, talking to the bat people, while I'd been tucked up in bed.

"Did Sweetcharity say where they were searching?"

"She reckoned they were going to start at the bottom end of the Valley and work their way up. Methodically, she said. Leaving no stone unturned. Quite frankly I'm not too keen to get caught. I suppose it would be the gibbet for us..."

"The what?"

"Gibbet. Isn't that the sort of mad mediaeval thing you people use: gibbets, ducking stools, stocks, pillories, priories, thumb screws... Don't you lot go in for that sort of thing?"

"No," I said. "Now do you want me to help you or not?"

"Sure do."

"Right," I said. "I'm going to put a load of hay on the cart. You can hide in it. Then I'll set off towards the bottom of the Valley. With luck we'll slip through the net."

* * * *

We met old man Legrand and old man O'Grady on the track up to the McWeezle place. They were on foot and both were carrying long pointed sticks.

"Morning, Uncles," I said.

Legrand just narrowed his flinty little eyes. O'Grady was pleasant enough.

"Been traveling around a bit, young Mathewmark?" he said.

"I'm taking hay to Auntie McWeezle," I said.

"Seen anything on the road?" O'Grady said. "Anything that might indicate the whereabouts of the fiends?"

"Those hang-glider people?" I said.

"They were no hang-gliders, no ordinary folk. They had the wings o'Beelzebub."

"So my Dad reckons," I said. "My Mom, now, she's of the contrary opinion. My Mom reckons they was just Outsider teenagers, joy riders, blown off course by the winds."

"And you, Mathewmark?" Legrand said, speaking at last. "What thoughts on this matter bubble in your cesspit of a mind?"

"Easy on, Elder Legrand," I said. "My mind is not—"

"As I hear it," Legrand said, "Your mind is as filthy as your paws. Those paws that fain would despoil the virgin purity of—"

This time it was O'Grady who muttered, "Easy on."

"I'll not be easy on any young scoundrel who gets his filthy paws on the snow white purity of my grand-daughter's—"

"We'll be bidding you good day, young Mathewmark," said O'Grady, speaking quick and loud. "Come on Theophanous Legrand, we have work to do."

O'Grady more or less dragged old man Legrand out of my way by the sleeve. I gave Ebeeneezer a good flick with the reins and the mule started forward. As we passed the two men, Legrand poked his stick into the load of hay, but before he could do it again, O'Grady had him out of harm's way. When I was no more than fifty meters down the track I heard

Amanda say from inside the load, "That swine missed me by an inch. He ought to be chained up."

"Hush," I said.

Ten minutes later we were at Auntie McWeezle's place. My plan was to keep Amanda and Vikram on the cart all day, hoping that by the time I arrived home, the barn would have been searched, and the searchers would have disappeared further up the Valley, or given up and gone home. I climbed down off the cart and knocked on Auntie McWeezle's door.

"Begone," came a muffled shout from inside. "I'll put up with no more harassment from the likes of you, Legrand."

"It's only me, Auntie," I shouted. "Mathewmark. I've brought the hay."

The door opened. Auntie McWeezle said, "Well, it's a relief to see a friendly face. And a sane one. Come in, Mathewmark. You wouldn't know what sort of rubbish I've had to put up with. A witch hunt. That's what it is."

I entered Auntie McWeezle's cabin. It only had two rooms and normally it was a neat, cheery place. Now it looked a mess.

"Drat that Legrand," Auntie McWeezle said. "The man is a walking offence to the Lady herself. You should have heard him: "It's for your own protection, Myrtle McWeezle, the fiends could be under your own bed and you'd not know it." Him and that O'Grady, poking their sticks under the bed. Rootling through the camphor chest like pigs after acorns. As if the fiends of hell would worry with a poor cottage like mine..."

"Take it easy, Auntie," I said. "I reckon they were just hang-gliders. Outsiders blown in by the wind."

"One way or the other," Auntie McWeezle said. "They certainly aren't here."

From where I was sitting at Auntie's table, the plate of corn bread and the mug of buttermilk already in front of me, I could see out the window to the cart. The hay moved, bulged. Auntie turned and followed my gaze, but the hay was still.

"You've brought it early," she said.

"No time like the present, Auntie."

"You've not bought rats with you?" Auntie said, still looking at the load of hay.

"Rats?"

"They do like to nest in the hay. You can easily carry rats as well as hay."

There are some people I can lie to all day with a straight face. If I needed to lead Jed Cawthorne up the garden path, I'd spin him a yarn, tell him a tale with never a word of truth in it. But not Auntie McWeezle, the task was beyond me.

"The truth is, Auntie. I've got the hang-glider people on board."

"And do they look like the familiars of the devil to you, Mathewmark?" Auntie said, showing no surprise at all.

"They're just Outsiders." I said. "A boy and a girl. The boy has twisted his ankle."

"Well, they can't be too comfortable with all that hay sticking into their soft Outsider skins," Auntie said. "And I'll warrant they're a mite peckish."

Five minutes later, Amanda and Vikram were tucking into a plate of beans and barley bread, mugs of butter milk beside their plates.

"This diet milk is really good," Amanda said. "Better than Slimmer's Delight."

"And what'll that be, Slimmer's Delight?" Auntie McWeezle asked. It was clear she didn't approve of Amanda's appearance, purple hair and all, but she kept her own counsel on that matter.

"It's the lo-fat, high calcium, cholesterol reduced, energy-enhanced, soy milko-lite drink my mother insists on. It's not half as good as this buttermilk stuff. I reckon if you drank buttermilk all day, you'd lose five kilos a week. It can't have any nutritional value at all."

"And you'd see that as a good thing, young lady. No nutritional value at all?"

"Well, you know, you wouldn't get a spare tire, would you?"

"I don't know about no tires," Auntie McWeezle said. "But it don't do to throw good food away, and she as makes butter, makes buttermilk."

"I've heard about butter," Amanda said. "They say it's poisonous."

"Rubbish," said Auntie McWeezle. "And now, young man," she said turning to Vikram, "I'd better have a look at your ankle. Mathewmark and Lukenjon are reasonable hands when it comes to fixing a poultice for a mule or sheep, but humans need a lighter touch."

We spent most of the morning with Auntie McWeezle. She mixed and mashed and steamed some herbs and changed the dressing on Vikram's ankle. She chided Amanda for her Outsider ignorance of everything useful, she let it be known that she thought the actions of some of her neighbors were a disgrace.

"It happens," said Auntie McWeezle. "Folks get scared and they start seeing the polluter behind every bush. And then other folks won't be outdone, they see the devil behind every flower, every blade of grass. Folks get carried away. I reckon you two want to lie low for a day or two and then get young Mathewmark to take you up to the Gatehouse. Your own people can collect you there."

THE VALLEY OF THE GOD OF YOUR CHOICE, INC. | 73

"Well, the thing is, Auntie," I said, stretching, "I've got to be getting on. And without all your hay on the cart, hiding Amanda and Vik might be a bit difficult."

"Sure, they can stay here," Auntie McWeezle said. "Stay the night, if they like."

I left Amanda and Vik at Auntie McWeezle's and drove off on my rounds. Auntie hadn't been wrong about people trying to outdo each other with hysterical talk. The story of the vampire bats dancing in the updraft had reached the furthest corner of the Valley. The funny thing was that the greater the distance from the ventilation shaft that people lived, the more numerous were the fiends they swore had come out of it. My last load for the day was a pile of dried cow dung to be carted from the Old Nirvana Commune to the Apple Orchard. Old Communard Williams knew all about the fiends. They had wingspans as wide as windmill sails, and there had been ten dozen of them, screeching and cackling like parrots as they flashed their talons.

"I don't think so, Communard," I said to Williams. "I was there. There was only two of them and they looked like hang-gliding teenagers. Outsiders."

"They've addled your mind," said Williams. "There were dozens of them." He made the sign o'god.

After I left the Apple Orchard, I took the river track back to our place. Ebeeneezer knew we were going home and needed no guidance from me. The cart still stank slightly of manure, I would have to wash and scrub it before I could call it quits. And Ebeeneezer was in need of new shoes—there'd be a bit of blacksmith work to be done in the morning. After a normal day's carting, I trundle home with my mind a blank, or just wandering from thought to thought in a random, sleepy sort of way. But this evening things were different. All I could think about were Amanda and Vik.

There was a lot wrong with those two—they seemed to have no appreciation of the simple pleasures of life. They were driven by some crazy desire to experience more and more. I got the feeling they'd never be satisfied. But I knew this: they weren't fiends from hell. They were just adolescents, with all the desires and problems of adolescents anywhere. We're no different in the Valley—often kids don't get on with their parents, get thrown out of home. Often they fall in love with someone who doesn't love them and start thinking about ending it all. Girls get pregnant when they shouldn't. Some young buck gets hold of a jar of cider and before you know it, him and a few mates have rolled his old man's cart. Snapped the shafts, broken the mule's leg. It happens. So, on a deep level, I didn't reckon there was very much about Amanda and

Vik that I didn't know about. But they came from the Outside, they controlled liar bees, they could spread their strange black wings and soar in the updrafts. And they could thumb their noses at authority. They weren't meant to be here—there were laws and regulations and treaties that said they shouldn't enter our Valley. All manner of edicts from the Council of Elders also said that Valley people like me couldn't leave—or if we did, we couldn't come back. That's what Elders do: tell other folk what they can't do. And from what Amanda and Vik had said, it's the same on the Outside as it is in the Valley.

But Amanda and Vik hadn't been frightened by all the prohibitions, all the thou-shalt-nots of their society. They'd grasped the freedom given them by their wings, they'd paid us a visit. Dropped in. Oh, when I'd seen them playing in the updraft from the fire, twisting and turning against the stars, the familiars of that tower of sparks, I'd wanted to be like them, to be *with* them. I was about the same size as Vik. I started to wonder if he'd lend me his black jump suit, show me how to unfurl the wings and float in the heavens. I could lend him my Sunday Best outfit. Maybe he'd like to experience real handmade clothes for a little while: homespun jerkin, goats' wool socks, cowhide boots. But maybe he wouldn't. I didn't want Amanda and Vik to leave the Valley, but I knew that in a day or two, they'd be gone. Back to the Outside, back to a world I'd never know.

Unless I went with them.

What a sin! What a terrible, wicked thought. In our Valley just about the worst thing you can think is that you might leave, might pass through the Gate into the hell of the Outside. We're taught that as soon as we can talk. In the schoolhouse there is no lesson more serious. The God of Your Choice takes many forms, but he, she or it is always a Valley god, never an Outside god. Sitting on the cart, rumbling along the river track with Ebeneezer clip-clopping like a tune that has got stuck in your head, I told myself I mustn't think the thoughts I was thinking, told myself that the wisdom of the Elders was the true wisdom. But what you tell yourself to think, and what you do think, are often at terrible odds with each other.

I arrived home with my mind in a spin. Mom gave me a dipper of spring water and an apple and then sent me and the cart downwind.

"Get it scrubbed, Mathewmark, or the smell will sink into the boards. Decent folk won't ride in it."

I scrubbed the remains of the manure from the cart with a yard brush and many buckets of water. From where I was standing on the cart, I could see the ventilation shaft. It was slightly blackened around the base, but otherwise unharmed. If old man Legrand had thought the tunnelers were so stupid they'd make the thing out of flammable material, he was off his head. What a place to live—a Valley where the likes of Legrand were considered solid citizens. I looked some more at the ventilation shaft. The daylight was dying, our place was already in shadow, but the sun still slanted down to the shaft. It glowed. And it led, through its infernal passageways, to the Outside. I couldn't stop looking at it. I was like a mouse looking at a snake.

12: AMANDA

"I like Myrtle McWeezle," Vikram said. "It doesn't seem right to repay her kindness by nicking her ladder."

"I like her too, Mr. Bones." It was still dark, with just the slightest sliver of moon in the starry sky. You don't see stars like that in the metro, not with all the glow from the street lights and the neon and lasers. Quite restful, actually, or I suppose it would be if you didn't have a posse of paranoid witch-hunters on your tail. "But we're not really stealing it. She'll get it back."

"How's she going to lug it back through the fields from the vent? Heavy damned wooden clunky thing." He was having trouble getting his end of the ladder up on his shoulder, hampered by the pain of his stoutly wrapped foot no doubt. I had my end hoisted, backing out of the low shed into the yard. Luckily old Myrtle didn't have a large barking guard dog or she'd have been awake and out of her bed ten minutes ago. Actually I had a sneaking suspicion that she was lying inside her little cottage with one eye cocked, knowing full well that we were making a break for it. She didn't know our plans, but she wasn't going to be a nuisance and get in the way.

"I wish we could have left her a gift of some sort," I muttered, narrowly missing a sleeping chook. It squawked and flapped, then settled. Vikram banged his end of the heavy ladder against the shed's simple brush gate. I gritted my teeth, jumpy although I didn't want to show it.

"We did," Vik said, to my surprise. "I left her my solar powered watch."

"Useful. She'll be able to time how long it takes when they burn her as a witch."

"Come on, Mand," he said a bit crabbily, "you know they don't actually do that stuff in the Valley. The worst we'd face if they catch us is a night or two in the stocks. More likely they'd march us up to the Gatehouse and send a message to the metro cops."

"How's your foot?" We were in the clear now. My own watch showed it was a little after midnight. Everyone else in the Valley was well asleep by now, even bloody old man Legrand and his soppy grand-daughter. According to my calculations, it should take us twenty minutes to hoof it to the vent, even with Vik's bad ankle and the ladder. Then a couple of minutes to ace the fairly mindless computer chip that controlled the vent access, down to the deep root of the ventilation shaft using its own elevator, and wait another twenty minutes max until the next freighter came ripping through. Well, not ripping, with any luck, because of the ridiculous deal my Mom had secured with the local sell-outs. Because of their sacred prohibitions, the bullet train turned into a slow-coach for the length of its trip under the sacred Valley before it accelerated again to supersonic speeds for the remaining stretch. Ride of a lifetime, eh.

"My foot's not too bad," Vikram said in a tone that showed how much it must be hurting him, this dreary ladder lugging. Well, if it weren't for his injury we wouldn't need to lug the ladder, because we could use our blackgear's fiber grapples to climb the vent. As it was, I didn't want to take the chance that he'd get stuck halfway up. The ladder it had to be.

It's surprising how well you can see when your eyes have become adapted to a skyful of stars and a scrap of moonlight. I don't suppose we banged into fences and dropped the ladder on our toes more than twenty or thirty times in the whole trip. I was feeling a bit bruised, and Vikram must have been in agony, by the time we reached the field where the ventilation shaft rose in its dark green glory, now rather smudged by the ash from the dead bonfire. Scraps of hardly burned timber leaned against its base. I kicked a path through for us, and we hoisted the ladder up against the side.

"Piece of cake," I said. My breath smoked a bit in the cool night air. Even in summer, it seemed, the world outside of snug buildings could get quite crisp well after sundown. For a moment I wanted nothing more than to curl up in my own bedroom, my vee system running some de-lightful fantasy quest, music roaring from the surround speakers, Mrs. Ng building me a yummy treat downstairs. I was missing Strad the Lad and my violin practice. I caught myself having these cowardly thoughts and suppressed them at once. We were adventurers. We would boldly go where no teeners had gone before.

"You'll have to give me a hand up," Vikram said dubiously. It must have hurt him to admit that, but the trouble he was having with his sprained ankle made me realize that embarrassment was the least of the poor boy's problems. Okay, let's do this thing and get home. We'll be legends. We'll be Mall gods at last. We'll be able to have a decent shower and sleep all day in our own soft and comfortable beds.

The ladder, for all its weight and hand-made clumsiness, was only about two meters tall. Less, with it leaning against the vent column. So the top of the vent was another two meters higher, maybe more. I scam-pered up the ladder, shot out a fiber webbing strand that settled over the top of the vent and tightened into place. I climbed the web hand over hand, grippo sneakers holding firmly to the slick, stealthed surface of the vent's thick column. I certainly needed all four limbs to manage it, though. I looked down at Vikram who had dragged himself up the ladder and was perched on the top rung, arms outstretched to the curving wall of the vent. I didn't trust him to climb up the rest of the way with his bad ankle, but at least he was already halfway to the top so I should be able to help haul him up.

Something caught my eye. Something moving in the field. Oh shit, not the witch hunters! We were in deep doo-doo if they caught us now. Here we were, the two devil-spawn, poised to fly away on bat wings into Satan's grim land of polluters and real estate dealers. It'd be even worse if they realized we weren't going to fly off but instead had every intention of plunging downward into the hellish bowels of the earth.

Vik saw me peering about.

"What?"

"Dunno. Thought I saw some kind of— Nah, just a farm animal. Probably Ebeeneezer having a squint at us."

I left Vik on his perch for a moment and stared around for the control panel cover. The top of the vent was absolutely solid, to look at it. The thing did its ventilation trick using invisible micro-pores in the vertical stack. Although the top wasn't open, it would give access to an elevator designed for use by maintenance crews during their planned once-a-decade visits. I fiddled with my hand-held notepad, searching for a hand-shaking protocol. Voila! A rectangle of light shone up from the middle of the circular platform at the top of the cylinder. I left the two machines to chat with each other using their infrared beams and went back to the edge.

"Okay, Mr. Bones, ready to scale Mt Everest."

"Get on with it, Amanda," he said. He sounded fed up. The poultice Myrtle McWeezle had put on his ankle must have well and truly worn off by now. I could almost feel the painful throbbing in my own foot.

"Okay, here goes." I made sure the webbing was secure at the top, then shot down a length of triple weave fiber net. Vik looped it around himself as we'd been taught in abseiling sessions in gym, grabbed the remainder firmly with both hands. He leaned back, letting the web take some of his weight, and lifted his good foot against the side of the vent. Instantly, his injured leg sagged, and he cried out in pain. He dropped back to the top of the ladder. Without any ado, the ladder gently teetered and slipped slowly away from the wall. It crashed noisily into the bonfire remnants.

"Shit!"

Vikram was left dangling, held by the web but not in any good position to recover. I yelped in fright, and again seemed to see something or someone move suddenly in the field to my left. Mathewmark? Could the silly boy be spying on us? Could he have followed us to see what devilish prank we were up to? I didn't have time to think further about such distractions. I leaned over the edge and grabbed the webbing with both gloved hands.

"Come on, you slacker," I yelled in a silly, jolly voice, "put your back into it."

Vikram gave a throttled gasp, then started laughing. He hung in his harness of webbing, swaying slightly, and laughed like a lunatic. It was enough to wake the dead. Worse still, it was enough to wake the living.

"Stop laughing," I told him, my own shoulders shaking, "this is serious."

Five minute later we'd calmed down enough to get sorted out. I hauled and hitched and Vik clawed his way up the webbing, kicking with his good foot and finally throwing his crook leg over the edge with a terrible groan. We lay there panting, gazing up at the stars. My handheld beeped. I sat up, set my blackgear jumpsuit to gather the webbing and tuck it away neatly in its designer pack ready for its next use, and crawled over to the vent's control site.

Bright patches of green and red showed in the night. The cryptic abbreviated words on the display would have revealed interesting information to engineers if there had been any with us. Numbers flickered steadily, showing changes in the transport system. I had a feeling at least one of those glaring numbers told a tale of a freighter rushing at this very moment toward the Valley, maybe even slowing as it entered the sacred site.

"Now all we have to do—" I peered at the display doubtfully.

"It's this one, I reckon," Vikram said, and poked his finger at a symbol like a door. Silently, part of the floor near our feet lifted a few centimeters, slid across another portion of the cylinder's roof, revealing a surface a meter square edged in comforting green light. A slender panel surface slid up, showing one arrow pointing down, one pointing up, and one with a square white dot. Maybe the white dot meant standing still.

"Dread," Vik said with satisfaction. "Going down."

He limped to the panel and looked at me. I shrugged, pretending to be relaxed and pleased that our interrupted plans were about to come off. Actually I felt as if my gut were squeezed tight into my chest. I wanted really badly to go to the toilet, but didn't think this was the moment to mention it. My mouth was dry and the palms of my hands were wet. I shivered, although it wasn't that cold, and went to stand beside him. He raised one eyebrow (a trick he'd been practicing in front of the mirror, I bet). I nodded. Vikram stuck his thumb on the down arrow.

With only the slightest tremor, we sank into the heart of the ventilation shaft.

13: MATHEWMARK

I didn't sleep well that night. I woke up sometime past midnight and lay listening to the sounds of the night: little scurryings, the hoot of a night bird, the wind in the trees. That and Lukenjon's snoring. You could tell *he* was having no trouble sleeping. I kept wondering how Amanda and Vik were doing at Auntie McWeezle's. There was no room for them inside Auntie's little cabin, but she had a snug stone barn, almost as big as the house itself. And there was hay in the barn. I'd put it there only that morning.

Then, just faintly, I heard something different, something that didn't belong with all the usual sounds of the night. I wasn't sure what it was, but I knew I'd heard it. I listened intently. But it was no good, Lukenjon's snoring seemed to grow louder the more I strained to hear what was happening in the fields. I suspected that old man Legrand was coming back for another attack on the shaft. I swung my legs out of bed and reached as quietly as I could for my clothes. A couple of minutes later I was standing in the dark beside the cart shed, straining my eyes in the starlight. Actually there was now the thinnest of sickle moons hanging low on the horizon, it gave me just a little bit more light—I couldn't tell what I was seeing, but I knew there was some sort of activity at the shaft.

I began to creep closer, using my knowledge of the terrain more than any of my senses to guide me. Then I heard something quite clearly, a yelled curse. I knew immediately who was at the shaft: Amanda and Vik. I quickened my pace. A burst of mad laughter, Vik's. Some sharp commands from Amanda, but she sounded as if she were trying not to laugh too. Finally I was close enough to see them, very faintly, silhouetted against some sort of glow coming from the top of the shaft. They appeared to be standing on the top, on what must be a lid or grille.

I stopped just inside the boundary fence, and strained my eyes. Some more conversation I couldn't quite catch, then the two figures disappeared from view, sinking downwards into the shaft. I ran forward, stumbling over the stalks and roots of old man Grout's wrecked sorghum crop. When I reached the shaft I stubbed my toe and fell over. A ladder was lying on the ground. As I picked it up and leaned it against the shaft I recognized it from its feel. The miserable pair had stolen Auntie McWeezle's ladder.

I was up it in a shot. I stood on the highest rung, but the top of the shaft was still just out of reach. I didn't stop to think. I bent my knees and then jumped upwards. If I missed I'd tumble to the ground, maybe break something. But I didn't miss, I gripped the slightly rough edge of the top of the shaft and with a superhuman heave got myself up so that I was resting on my elbows. There was indeed a lid, but it had an oblong hole in it. I reached over, grabbed the edge of the opening and pulled myself onto the top. I looked down. The shaft was softly lit, although the source of the light was not immediately apparent. Below me I could easily make out the forms of Vik and Amanda. They were descending. Whatever they were standing on was going steadily down. They were leaving me. A staggered series of foot- and hand-holds was cut into the side of the shaft, descending into the depths like a kind of ladder. I knew that if I stopped to think I'd be overcome with fear, I'd never move, never leave the Valley. So I didn't stop to think. I swung myself through the opening and began to descend, spread-eagled on the wall of the shaft like a spider.

14: AMANDA

I heard something scrambling above us, looked up in fright. Something large, something that looked like an ape or maybe a clumsy human, was peering over the edge of the shaft's entrance. I wondered why the sliding panel hadn't zipped shut behind us as we started our descent. Fail-safe, I supposed—the proximity of someone standing there. A human voice called down to us, echoing strangely. I couldn't make out the words, but it sounded awfully familiar.

"Oh great," Vikram said. "Your new boyfriend has decided to join us."

"He's not my—" I started hotly, craning my neck backwards. Mathewmark had his legs dangling into the shaft now. We were already a hundred meters below him, and dropping steadily. If he let go, he'd fall and break his back. Strips of yellow light shone in the tube as we descended. I could hear a clang as his heavy leather work boots struck the sides of the shaft.

"What's the idiot up to," Vikram yelped in alarm. "He's going to set off the fail-safes. The whole bloody thing is going to shut down. We'll be stuck here like flies inside a bottle until the Maglev cops come and nab us. Damn it, Amanda!" He looked as if he was about to break into tears. "First I bugger my ankle, now this. We'll look like fools. Everyone in the Mall is going to laugh at us."

"Calm down," I said, wishing I could follow my own advice. "He can't come down, he's going to have to climb back up and out and then—"

But as we fell deeper and deeper into the solid rock at the elevator platform's steady pace, I finally noticed the hand-holds that some machine had cut at regular intervals, every 15 centimeters it looked like, into the side of the shaft. It was like a ladder reaching down toward the centre of the earth. Hell's teeth! And Farmboy, far above us, was climbing down that grim ladder. We could hear his yells, the clatter of his boots as he made his vertical descent in pursuit of us.

"He doesn't realize this shaft is 200 meters deep," I said faintly. "He'll get tired before he's halfway down. He'll slip and fall and land on us and we'll all get squashed like bugs. We've got to stop the elevator and go back up for him."

Without a word, Vik shot out his right hand and slammed the white dot on the control panel. We slowed almost instantly, and I felt my guts rise again in my throat. Then we were motionless. High above us, monkey boy was clawing his way down an endless set of vertical hand- and footholds. He was still calling hoarsely.

"Well," I said in a thin voice, "push the up arrow, Mr. Bones."

"Don't call me that," Vikram said angrily. "This is stupid. Damn him. I'm not going back there, they'll tie us up and make complete jackasses out of us. No way." He slapped the down arrow again, and once more we dropped gracefully toward the freighter tunnel.

I couldn't believe it. Didn't he care if Mathewmark was hurt, maybe killed? My own arm jerked out, but Vik grabbed my wrist and held it.

"No."

"Don't be bloody stupid, Vikram Singh!"

We stood face to face, both furious and tired and confused. It took a moment to realize that we were motionless without either of us touching the controls. High, high above us, the faint sounds of Mathewmark's fearful hand over hand descent continued.

"We're here," Vikram said. Behind him, a vertical panel showed a rim of blue light. He touched it with his right hand, and it slid open: a door. A gust of odd smelling air entered the shaft, somehow dead but electric, faintly oily. I could feel the hair stir on the back of my cropped neck. Somewhere, almost at the edge of hearing, came a rushing. Air was moving, pushed by a projectile approaching at terrible speed.

Vikram was still holding my wrist. He lifted my arm and checked my watch.

"Good timing, kiddo. Here comes our ride to the coast." He stepped through the opening. Before I followed him, I tapped the up arrow. The door closed with a faint hiss. In a minute or so, Mathewmark would find firm footing had risen to meet him. With any luck, he'd have the sense to continue back up to the surface. If he followed us down, he'd arrive too late. The freighter was due in about eighty seconds, if my time-table was still on the money.

This was the scary bit. All the rest of our adventure had been easy. Sneaking out of our homes, thumbing a ride to the bus station, getting to the outskirts of the Valley, climbing the cliff above the Muon power station, unfurling our bat wings and throwing ourselves headlong into its updraft, lifting across the mountain and down into the goddam Valley of the Nutters... all that was just the prelude. I could already hear the story of our heroic journey set to music, violins wailing. No, that wasn't violins, it was the on-rushing wind of a freighter drawing closer, slowing, but not to a stop, not a chance, not even slowing to walking pace. This monstrous thing that we planned to jump down on and ride like one of the sand worms of *Dune* would be skimming along on its magnetic fields at 30 kilometers an hour. Miss the connection, and we'd go head first into the tunnel under its hundreds of tons of thundering metal and plastic.

I really wanted to go to the toilet now. Why do you always leave these things to the last minute?

"Over here," Vikram called. He was peering down from a catwalk that jutted into the top of the tunnel. It was guarded by heavy-duty glass or plastic. We would need to crawl out past the safety barrier. The sound was rising, like a storm wind. I fancied I could feel the freighter's forward wind blowing up, cool and sparky. I put one leg over the edge of the barrier and crept up to Vikram.

"Time to get our webs ready," I said. It was almost instinctive by now. My fingers danced over the buttons on my belt. I hung over the superconducting rail far below. When the freighter came through, we had to be poised to jump. No second thoughts.

Like a deep organ note, the air moved about us. And then the freighter was there, in a rush, humming at thirty klicks an hour, the speed of a galloping horse. It did not cast a beam of light ahead of it, like old-time locomotives. There was no driver in the train. The whole process was entirely automatic. Vikram reached out his hand, and I took it. Light flared suddenly at our backs. *What?* I twisted my head around, horrified. A dark shape loomed out of the illuminated square of the doorway. The train was running under us. Mathewmark leaped forward, clutching with his long arms. Our carbon webbing shot out, spraying and solidifying as it fell. We leaped, and the farm boy came behind us, yelling my name. My web latched on to the roof of the rushing freighter, snagged, locked, tightened. I rolled forward on top of the freighter, taking the shock in all the muscles of my legs, arms, abdomen. There were two awful banging noises. Vikram's hand was torn out of mine. He rolled ahead of me, his web tearing free. Mathewmark flashed past, bouncing, his mouth open and screaming in terror. His clod-hopper farm boot struck Vikram in the face, with a bright spurt of blood from a torn lip. Vikram slid, slipped, ripped free. He bounced over the curved edge of the roaring freighter. I clung on to my web for dear life, screaming so hard I hurt my throat. Somehow Mathewmark had caught the edge of my web and clung to it. The web started to curl up, break free. Vikram was gone, smashed under the freighter. Already we were speeding up. The Valley tore past, two hundred meters overhead. We accelerated, and my poor friend was battered under the freighter while the stupid, ignorant farmboy clung to my web and lived. Vik stayed alive despite everything, long enough for the crashing harmonies of the freighter to pick him up and smash him down, head first, into its unyielding metal skin. Pick him up, smash him down. Again and again. He bled in a river of red that I could see only as blackness in the blipping, blurring maintenance lights edging the maglev tunnel. He smashed against the side of the freighter until he was unconscious, his fingers and one leg trapped in my carbon web. By then I was crying too hard to see anything.

15: MATHEWMARK

Click click clickety-click CRASH boooom hiissssss is that a Mooooo Cow I think I see her big brown eyes ROARING bang bang cockadoodle-oo says the fat old rooster and Mommy is rocking me in the lovely warm sun CLICK CLICK oh that was a bad bad thing I've gone and wet my bed No he did it Daddy that Lukenjon baby did it CRUNCH CRUMP the light is so bright all Red and Purple and Golden oh so pretty but SHOCK tinkly tinkle.

Rosy that's her name, that brown dear cow of ours, old biddy Grand McWeezle is leaning over the wooden bucket and I can hear the SHOOSH HUSH SHOOSH of the warm milk squirting into the bucket and splashing All the nice stinky smell of those cows doing a poo in the straw and Daddy grunting as he puts his back into the shovel, cleaning out the stable, and Bossie our old mule hee-hawing and clop-clop, the rain coming down, SPLAT SPLAT cold running down my back CLANG BANG I wish I could stop this noise in my ears.

So bright and then pale, stripes of colored bars, ping ping ping.

Oh. What can that man be? Is it a devil? Is it a fiend risen up from Hell's Teeth to carry me off? His face is blurry and green. No, he is wearing some sort of cloth over his mouth and the top of his head. He says to the other person it's a garble garble garble NOISE darkness now he's back Superior auditory cortex damage extensive temporal lobe damage I think his auditory cortex is compromised doctor NOISE garble babble.

Yes I am watching the moving light. What's wrong are you all deaf? I can hear you but I can't speak. I am so tired. What—

Ten nine eight um five? CRASH tinkle Sorry what was that? Um eight, the next one is um is it six? Ow! That hurt! Who? Who? Mathewmark. I'm Mathewmark. I can't hear you, there's all this noise and light in my head.

Ahhhh... That's a bit better.

They tell me I had a freighter accident. I tell them no, there are no freighters in the Valley. They tell me the accident was under the Valley. In a tunnel. Sure, I tell them, I know about the tunnel. There was a shaft that appeared one night in old man Grout's field. Maybe there were freighters down below. But I never went there, I say, I'm a good boy. No, they say, you did. You followed Vikram and Amanda down the shaft. There's nobody in the Valley called Vikram, I say. And the only person called Amanda is old biddy O'Conner who lives in the deserted windmill and she's ninety if she's a day. No, they say, the rescue team found you in the tunnel with Vikram and Amanda. I don't know any Vikram, I say. Vikram was dead, one of them says and the others shoosh him. Whoever he was, I say, may his soul rest in peace. It's normal, they say, memory loss. There are two different causes, they say. The freighter banged your head rather badly, and that will cause the memory loss. And maybe post-traumatic stress syndrome is also to blame—you're blanking out things you don't want to think about, don't want to acknowledge. No, I say, I want to remember everything, there is nothing I do not want to know. The scans are encouraging, they say, there is significant brain damage but nothing we can't emulate on a chip. I don't understand, I say. This is the best neurological unit in the country, they say, we will make a new man of you. Auntie McWeezle says that, I say. She says, glug down this potion, Mathewmark and it'll make a new man of you. Auntie McWeezle knows every herb, every mineral deposit, every property of bark in the Valley. We respect the traditional wisdom of other cultures, they say, but this is a neurological unit, we can map your brain here. And we can reproduce and repair the map in silicon. I don't understand, I say. I'm tired. Sleep, they say, sleep, Mathewmark. Sleep cures all. This will help you....

The walls change color. Sometimes when I'm feeling sad the nurse will look at the little windows with the wavy lines and say, this will enhance your mood, Mathewmark. And then the white wall becomes a warm rosy color—like firelight, like the candlelight at a bean feast. And then I feel both content and melancholy. It seems a long time since I danced at a bean feast. I remember the bee talking to me on the Village Green and our mule Eben, Eban, Eb.... Hey, nurse, I say, I can't remember his name—our mule. The nurse says, hang on we've retrieved that. He plays with the little buttons below one of the little boxes with a window. Ebeeneezer, he says reading from the window, your mule was called Ebeeneezer. That's right, I say. And then I say the name—Ebeeneezer. I say it a few times, there's comfort, there's solace in the name.

16: AMANDA

Our metro Magistrate, Mr. Abdel-Malek, didn't give a hoot about tradition and formalities. He had his own ways of dispensing law and order. I'm sure he kept within the strict letter of the law, but he preferred to cut through the ceremony and strike straight for the heart of the case. Anyway, that's what Dad and Mom's lawyer told them before the hearing. I had horrible nightmares every night, mixing up poor Vikram's dead body and Mathewmark's smashed head and me strapped to a table in court while Mr. Abdel-Malek ripped through the skin and bone of my chest with a scalpel, looking for my heart...

Dreams are stupid, especially bad dreams that turn a figure of speech into a scene out of a horror movie. I knew that, but it didn't stop me jerking up in bed in the darkness, clutching my sheets, yelling out loud in terror, sweating like a pig. Mrs. Ng ran in the first time, frightened out of her wits, and comforted me for an hour until I went back to sleep. To sleep, to dream— To re-run the stupid, awful accident over and over. The third time this happened, Mom came into the room and spoke sharply to me.

"Amanda, pull yourself together, for heaven's sake."

I was sobbing and shivering. After a moment she crossed the room and sat gingerly beside me on the bed. I clutched at her.

"I know you feel awful, darling," she said. "Don't worry, we have an excellent lawyer representing us at the hearing, one of the best young advocates at my firm, Cecil Jones. We have every reason to hope for a suspended sentence."

How could I tell her what was in my heart, the sorrow and guilt? I wasn't worried for myself—well, I suppose I was, in fact I was sick with anxiety, but really the pictures I kept seeing when I closed my eyes were Vik being torn from the webbing in the rushing blue darkness and sliding, falling, crashing under the humming freighter. He had been buried in a closed casket, but one of the shock jocks in vee did this gruesome sim of the whole accident. I didn't mean to catch it, but once I was plugged in I couldn't leave, and I went through the whole horrible thing again, in slow-mo, moving around in space as the three bodies fell to the top of the accelerating freighter, one of them snagging tight, one tearing loose and falling, rolling into darkness. The vee followed him down, showed him in sick close-up detail as he twisted and his arms and legs were broken and his skin tore and the blood—

It was just a computerized simulation, of course, I knew that. They didn't have much to go on, as the automatic vid feed from the security system on the freighter was grainy and limited. So they made it up, based on the coroner's report of the injuries. It was probably fairly accurate. There are laws against misleading the public, after all.

I'd sat there in vee, linked to the virtual reality reconstruction, trapped like a bug under the paw of hungry cat. I couldn't get out, switch off, pull the plug. Action replay. Mathewmark slipping, tumbling, smashing Vik as he fell, catching in the carbon webs, his head banging and banging in the rapid turbulence of the air rushing past the accelerating transport. It had taken nearly a minute before the on-board sensors of the freighter knew something was badly amiss and slowed the transport down, sending out emergency shrieks for a human to come and see what had gone wrong. Most of it after that I can't remember, except the coldness in my body, the shaking, the stink of my own sweat. Yellow lights darting up ahead as an emergency crew ran a small trolley back to us from the next vent shaft access point. Someone peeling Mathewmark's bloody head free of the carbon mesh, someone else's strong hands getting me out of my webbing and lowering me into the blue and yellow dark to the trolley, someone zipping up my sleeve and injecting—

Mr. Abdel-Malek bent the rules, as usual, instructing us to gather in the chapel of Memorial Neurological Hospital where Mathewmark was still struggling for life in the intensive care unit. They said his badly damaged brain was being supported by a computer, which sounded scary as hell to me. The chapel was carefully non-denominational, without crosses or stars of David or any other sacred symbols of a particular faith. But there was a hushed and special feeling about the place. Maybe it was something left over from all the people who must have come down here crying while their loved ones lay upstairs surrounded by bleeping sterile machines, hoping and praying that they wouldn't die. It seemed wrong to raise your voice.

That didn't bother Mr. Abdel-Malek. He never had to raise his voice.

We were all there, and none of us could bear to look at each other. Except for Auntie McWeezle, who had bustled up the moment she caught sight of me huddled between Mom and Dad and put her arms around me and pulled me tight against her chest.

"You poor child," she said. Mom and Dad were exchanging appalled glances, I could tell. Mrs. McWeezle was dressed in her Sunday best, a modest bonnet that covered her hair and a long quilted jacket over a rough-spun grey skirt that fell to her leather-booted feet. She even wore gloves. I don't think I've ever seen dress-up gloves before, outside a vee sim. It made me think for a moment of the carbon fiber gloves Vikram and I had worn during our prank. When she let me go, I clung to her gloved hands, squeezing tight.

"I'm so sorry about..." I started.

"The boy was always head-strong," Auntie McWeezle said. "He's in the custody of the Goddess now."

My father was trying to introduce himself and my mother, but I kept clinging to Auntie McWeezle's hands.

"How come you're here?" I blurted. "I thought you Valley people weren't allowed..."

"Somebody has to come and fetch the boy," she told me, scowling a little as her eyes studied the others in the chapel. Two sturdy young men in conservative black suits were setting up a table in front of the altar, placing audiovisual equipment here and there for a full recording of testimony and judgment. This might be an informal hearing, but everything else was going to be done by the book. Dr. and Mrs. Singh stood across the room, distant and grieving and stiff with anger. I cringed. It was my fault. It was all my stupid, stupid fault.

"They'll let Mathewmark go back?" I managed to stumble out. "I thought once you'd crossed the mountains you'd done your dash." We were guided to our seating near the front of the chapel, and I made sure Mrs. McWeezle stayed with us. Mr. Abdel-Malek entered the room, walked placidly to his chair behind the desk, nodded to my parents, to the Singhs, to the advocates. A flunky stepped forward.

"All rise. This hearing is now in session, Magistrate Abdel-Malek presiding. Step forward as you are called, and speak only when the Magistrate asks you to."

Mr. Abdel-Malek settled himself comfortably. He glanced at his screen.

"Dr. Singh, Mrs. Singh, good morning."

They rose, went forward. Mrs. Singh looked unsteady on her feet.

"Sir, may my wife have a chair?"

"Of course. You may both be seated. Tipstaff."

One of the black-suited flunkies moved two of the chairs forward, held out his arm helpfully as Mrs. Singh sat. She hunched forward for a moment, openly weeping, then sat straight, pushing her hankie back into her sleeve.

"While this is primarily a hearing into the circumstances of the death of your son Vikram, you have petitioned this court for the privilege of cloning the deceased. As you know, this is a forbidden procedure except in the very rare cases when a court grants authorization. Please tell me why I should rule in your case against overwhelming precedent."

One of the advocates stepped forward, holding a notepad, primed to deliver an oration. I've seen this scene in a thousand vids and vees. Mr. Abdel-Malek waved him back irritably.

"I shall hear from the petitioners, thank you. I am conversant with the law. Madam?" Mrs. Singh made to stand, swayed. "Please remain seated, ma'am. Why should I allow this cloning to take place?"

"Why— Vikram is a fine, brilliant..." She stumbled to a halt. "Was. Vikram was a wonderful boy, everything we could have asked for in a son, except that he was led astray in a moment of foolishness. We would not allow that to befall his twin brother, if you allow us to bring him into the world in place of our wonderful lost child." She could not go on. Tears were streaming down her face.

"Dr. Singh?"

"I cannot improve on my wife's words, sir. Our son was the light of our lives. We gave him everything, and he flowered into exceptional young manhood. It is not right that a single accident—no, I admit it, a single error of judgment—should deprive the world of his unique endowments."

"You could parent another child," Mr. Abdel-Malek said, unimpressed. "That boy or girl would also be yours, blessed with all that you can provide. Why a cloned twin of the deceased?"

Dr. Singh shook his head, as if he could not understand the question. "You met the boy, Magistrate. You have seen his school records, his sporting attainments, his genome scan. This was an exceptional human being. He was destined for great things. Yes, another child would be just as much ours to love with the same devotion, but what are the chances that he would match our lost boy's potential?"

He stood up, stepped forward slightly. The Magistrate said nothing, watching impassively. "Each new child's genetic endowment, as you know, is a kind of lottery," Dr. Singh said. "Vikram was a jackpot, if I may put it so crudely. He was our winning entry. His cloned twin would share that same wonderful promise. Mr. Abdel-Malek, do not mistake me. We do not expect to get our son back. We would not impose unrealistic demands on our new child. He would not be forced to retrace the footsteps of his illustrious predecessor. But he would bring us special joy, and offer the world those rare gifts which an... accident... has taken from us." He sat down again, and I noticed that he did not take his wife's hand.

The Magistrate steepled his own hands. "Thank you, Mrs. and Dr. Singh. I shall take your arguments under advisement and deliver my judgment at the end of these proceedings. Please accept my commiserations in your loss. You may return to your own seats now." He looked straight at me for a moment. He knew exactly where everyone was in the room. "Mrs. Myrtle McWeezle, please step forward."

Auntie McWeezle stood up and made her way to the front.

"You are Mrs. Myrtle McWeezle of the Valley of the God or Goddess of your own Choice?"

"I am."

"Do you wish to be seated, Mrs. McWeezle?"

"The Goddess has given me legs. I know how to use them."

"As you wish," Mr. Abdul-Malek said. If Auntie's reply surprised him, he did not show it. "May I say," he said evenly, "that the court fully appreciates the sacrifice you have made in leaving your Valley."

"Someone has to take young Mathewmark home."

"Well, perhaps. In the fullness of time... Now, Mrs. McWeezle I believe you are the last person, apart from Amanda Kolby-McAllister and Mathewmark Fisher, to see Vikram Singh alive."

"He was a polite, well-spoken boy. A bit soft, if you ask me."

"A bit soft, Mrs. McWeezle?"

"That young lad would have been no use in the fields."

"I should think not," Mrs. Singh said quite loudly.

Mr. Abdel-Malek raised his eyes and looked at Vik's mother for a couple of seconds but didn't say anything. He returned his attention to Auntie McWeezle.

"Ah, I see', he said. "You mean his hands were soft, not his brain."

"Well, I don't know," Auntie McWeezle said. "Plunging down that stink pipe into the depths of the infernal regions wasn't the brightest thing."

"He was led astray," Mrs. Singh said and she spun around in her seat to look straight at me. "She made him—"

"Mrs. Singh!" Mr. Abdel-Malek said. He spoke sharply but without raising his voice. "I know this is a trying time for you, but I must insist that you do not interrupt these proceedings again." Slowly the Magistrate took his eyes away from Vik's mother and then said to Auntie McWeezle, "Now, Mrs. McWeezle, I understand that Ms. Kolby-McAllister and Mr. Singh stayed the night at your house? Is that correct?"

"It's correct until about one o'clock, then they borrowed my ladder."

"In order to climb up the MagLev Authority's ventilation shaft?"

"The devil's ass."

There was a slight intake of breath in the room, some people suppressed giggles. Mr. Abdel-Malek let nothing show on his face. He said smoothly, "Let us just refer to the structure in question as the shaft. We all know what it is."

"And we know what comes out of it."

"Quite, Mrs. McWeezle. Now could you tell us, please, what impression you formed of the two young people while they were your guests."

"Amanda has a way with words. She's a headstrong young lady. Willful maybe. But I can't abide a dishrag. Some young ladies have got no backbone to speak of, but Amanda, for all her Outside ways, is what I'd call a girl with a bit of spirit."

"And Vikram Singh? What impression did you form of him?"

"Like I say, a bit soft, but a polite, helpful young man."

"Your honor, with respect," began the young lawyer from Mom's firm.

"Yes, Legal Jones?"

"With respect, these questions are doing nothing to further the course of this hearing. The witness's hastily gathered impressions of the two young people have no bearing on what eventuated later that night in the MagLev Authority's tunnel. The witness was not in the tunnel. The witness was at home in bed."

The young man appeared quite pleased with the point he had just made. Mr. Abdel-Malek looked at him sadly. He might have been looking at a foolish young puppy who had knocked over a vase of flowers. "Legal Jones," he said, "are you of the opinion that what happened on the night in question was the result of an exploit entered into by your client, Ms. Kolby-McAllister, and young Mr. Singh?"

"Yes, of course, your honor,"

"And are you of the opinion that when exploits are entered into, a certain relationship develops between those whom we might call the exploitees?" I had the strong impression he was taking the mickey out of Legal Jones, but his face was bland, utterly expressionless.

"Er... I dare say, your honor."

"Well, if you don't mind, Legal Jones, I think the court might spend some time examining this relationship. Do sit down."

"Umm... if the court pleases," mumbled the young man, sitting down.

"What a dork," I whispered to Mom.

"Jones is your lawyer," Mom hissed. "If you want to stay out of prison, you'd better take him seriously."

"Now, Mrs. McWeezle," Mr. Abdel-Malek said, "did you form an opinion about who was in charge? Whom would you say was the dominant member of the couple, Ms. Kolby-McAllister or Mr. Singh?"

"They was a couple of teenagers. They meant no harm."

"But who was in command?"

"Command? They wasn't an army."

"Did you form the opinion that one of the young people was making the decisions? That perhaps the other young person was being led?"

"Young people have got to take responsibility," Mrs. McWeezle said. "It's no good blaming things on others."

"My boy was bewitched," Mrs. Singh said. "Hush," Dr. Singh said quietly, putting a hand on his wife's arm. Mrs. Singh shook him off but didn't speak again.

"About Mathewmark," Mrs. McWeezle said. "I've come to take him home."

"We shall consider what is in the best interests of Mathewmark Fisher in due course," the Magistrate said.

17: MATHEWMARK

I'm feeling much, much better. I can remember all sorts of stuff. I can remember Amanda. She was a bat. A huge bat playing in the sparks from a fire. She had a friend, they twisted and swooped in the air above the fire, they blanked out the stars with their wings.

"Hey nurse," I tell the pretty girl nurse who is sitting by my bed, "Amanda was a bat."

" Amanda Kolby-McAllister is staring a Reckless Endangerment charge in the face," says the pretty nurse. "Custodial sentence, unless her rich olds can hire the right lawyers."

"I can remember the shaft," I say, "I climbed down it. Down the handholds. Like a spider on a wall. I remember as clear as day—only it was night. There was this weird light in the shaft. I remember everything."

"Of course you do. They've hooked you up."

"Hooked me up?"

"To a dedicated computer," the nurse says. "You've got computer enhancement by the ton. Terabytes of supplementary network."

I try to sit up. Someone gives my hair a good hard pull. I don't think it's the big fat man in the blue clothes who is washing the floor with a mop. He's too far away. I yelp and shake my head.

The nurse jumps up and she's fussing with my scalp. "Hey, be careful with the jack."

"Jack?"

"The optical cable coming out of your head. There's more two-way data transmission going through that little baby than you could count in a million years."

"I don't understand," I say.

"You're connected to a neural net, a machine, Mathewmark," says the nurse. "It is doing a lot of your thinking for you."

"We don't believe in machines in the Valley," I say. "Machines are the devil's handiwork."

"Could have fooled me," says the pretty nurse. "It was machines that saved your bacon."

The orderly over on the other side of the room laughs in a nasty way. "Right. Turn that thing off and he's a drooling vegetable again."

"Watch what you say, Carl," the nurse says sharply. I can tell she's upset at what the man said. "The boy is regaining his memory and there's nothing wrong with his ears."

"Sorry, nurse," the fellow mumbles, and pushes his mop and bucket out into the hallway. The nurse leans over me again and gives me a big smile. My eyes go out of focus, and there are two smiles and four eyes. I'm very sleepy. At least nothing hurts. I'll just nod off—

18: AMANDA

The hearing dragged on, despite Mr. Abdel-Malek's irritable insistence that the lawyers present speed matters up. One of the legals even brought in a bearded guy called Superintendent Holesworthy. At first I thought he had been part of the MagLev rescue crew, but he turned out to be the chap who'd been in charge of the warm fusion plant. He said that on the night we'd ridden the updraft all his sensors had gone crazy.

"It was as if we were being attacked by pterodactyls, sir."

Quiet laughter in the chapel.

"Thank you, Mr. Holesworthy. That will be all."

I sat there in the chapel-courtroom, a mess of mixed emotions. I was pissed off with the proceedings. They seemed to have less and less to do with what really happened, the reasons we did what we did. This flash young lawyer who was meant to keep me out of jail, Legal Jones, was a nerd, no two ways about it. Each interjection, each question he asked a witness, was more irrelevant than the last. The Singhs' lawyer was no better, although she was nerdy in a different way. She was too clever by half, endlessly trying to blind Mr. Abdel-Malek with obscure bits of law. Luckily, Mr. Abdel-Malek knew even more law than she did and put her sharply in her place. So I fumed. But, of course, I was miserable as well. I was just full of guilt for what I'd done. All I really wanted was to get up and tell the court what had happened and why it was all my fault. But Mom said that she'd no more allow me to give testimony than she'd allow me anywhere near a MagLev tunnel. And Legal Jones agreed. Legal Jones was so full of himself he didn't need any help from me. And it was *my* case, *my* trial!

By the end of the day, nothing had been decided. Mr. Abdel-Malek wearily instructed us all to come back the next day.

"Sir," Auntie McWeezle started to explain, plainly put out by this decision, "I need to take Mathewmark home immediately. It's not right for the boy to be separated from his—"

"I understand your concern, madam," Mr. Abdel-Malek said, "but I fear that matter will have to wait as well." He glanced at the screen on his table. "My understanding is that Mathewmark's recovery is still far from complete. I shall hear from his doctors tomorrow, and then we'll see how soon he can be released into your care."

Outside the chapel I breathed deeply, telling myself that everything would pass. That time heals all. But I didn't believe it. I just felt depressed and angry at the same time. Mom and Dad were already in the family Autoglide, waiting for me to get in. I wondered if they'd let me walk home by myself. I couldn't face the intimacy of the Autoglide's cabin. I noticed Auntie McWeezle still standing there on the far side of the parking area, just outside the chapel doors. The huge edifice of the Memorial Neurological Hospital rose up behind her, like a cliff. She looked little and old and lonely in her handmade clothes.

"For heaven's sake, child," Mom told me, "stop dithering and get in."

I bent down to the Autoglide's open side.

"You go home," I said with all the firmness I could muster. "See you later." Then I ran across the forecourt to Auntie McWeezle. The car lifted into the air behind me, and its headlights came on. I ignored my parents. "Come on, Auntie," I said, taking the old lady's hand. "Let's go back in and see if we can find Mathewmark."

19: MATHEWMARK

I'm sitting up in bed. The cable coming out of my head feels as thick as my thumb, and when I crane my head back I can just see the curve of it rising over me. It's supported by a sort of lever jutting down from the ceiling. Then it disappears into the wall behind my head. Today the walls are blue and white like sky in summer. The nurse is new, he's called Tony and he has green hair and a rose tattooed on his cheek.

"Sorry, wrong room," Tony suddenly says quite loudly. "No visitor access here."

"We've come to see Mathewmark," a girl says and walks straight into the room. It's the bat. It's Amanda. Only she is dressed in ordinary Outsider clothes. An old woman comes into the room, in decent Valley clothes.

"Auntie!" I say. "Auntie McWeezle."

"Sit down!" yells Tony. "The jack, mind the jack!" He grabs me by the shoulders and forces me back against the pillows. "You two, get out," he says to Amanda and Auntie McWeezle.

"They're my friends," I say.

"We're his friends," says Amanda.

"Well, everybody stay calm," Tony says. "No sudden movements. Mathewmark isn't supposed to have visitors until his chip has been installed."

"Oh Auntie," I say, "What are you doing here? This is the Outside."

"Someone has to take you back," Auntie says.

"I'm all hooked up to machines," I say.

"No good will come of it," Auntie McWeezle says.

"They reckon I couldn't speak properly without the machines."

"Machines are the devil's handmaidens."

"Look, I really must ask you two to leave," Tony says with authority. "Mathewmark is in a very precarious state."

"Let them stay," I say. "They're my friends. I haven't seen any friends since I woke up."

Tony looks quickly at the two women, makes up his mind and presses the button that closes the door. "Just don't excite him," he says. "And you can't stay long."

Auntie McWeezle sits on the side of my bed and holds my hand.

"How are Mom and Dad?" I say. "How is Lukenjon?"

"Your parents will come round," Auntie says. "Don't you worry, Mathewmark."

"Come round?"

"They'll want you back, you're their flesh and blood."

"But," I say, "but at the moment?"

"At the moment," Auntie McWeezle says, "they are being a bit literal about those who venture Outside without permission."

"They've cast me out?" I say. My voice sounds funny, but then everything sounds a bit odd right now. I'm near to tears. My own Mom and Dad. "Have they scrubbed my name out of the Holy Book of Our Choice?" I whisper.

"Yes, yes," says Auntie McWeezle, waving one hand as if this was of no consequence. "Anything that has been scrubbed out can be rewritten, Mathewmark. It's just ink on paper. Don't you worry. Lukenjon is working on them. As soon as I get you back they'll see the error of their ways."

"Look," says Tony, starting to sound worried. "Can you just make your conversation more general, please. Just talk about the weather. If you upset Mathewmark the brain-state monitors will activate every alarm channel in the network."

"I don't know what you are saying, young man," Auntie McWeezle tells him, "but Mathewmark needs to talk about his parents and his foolishness in the tunnel, there's no point running away from things."

"If the monitors pick up unusual brain activity they'll automatically feed a powerful sedative into Mathewmark's system, they'll shut down his higher faculties."

Auntie McWeezle makes the sign o'god. She turns to Amanda, "What's he saying?"

"He's saying that the machine that's running Mathewmark will put him to sleep if..."

"Put him to sleep!"

"No, no, Auntie," Amanda says quickly. "Not that sort of sleep. Just, you know sleep-type sleep."

Auntie makes the sign o'god again. "The sooner we get him away from these polluter machines the better."

"I think he'll have to be connected to a brain simulator for the rest of his life," Amanda says, looking unhappy.

"He'll be connected to no such thing," Auntie says sharply.

"No, don't worry, he won't have this cable and all these monitors," Amanda says. "They'll just put a chip in his head."

"Not if I have anything to do with it," Auntie McWeezle says.

"Don't fret, Auntie," I say. "Maybe some machines are good..."

"Good! Oh, Mathewmark, what have they done to you?"

"It's just that... I want to be able to talk properly... to think properly."

"Of course you can talk and think properly. What do you think you're doing now?"

"It's the machine, Auntie."

"Machine! There's nothing that faith in the God of your Choice and lots of rest and the proper use of herbs and potions won't put right. I'll not hear about good machines! You'll be talking of good devils, righteous princes of darkness, wise hobgoblins..."

Auntie was getting quite upset. So was I. And I was feeling tired, and sort of hungry without actually wanting to eat anything. My mouth had gone numb. I was almost asleep. Some lights were flashing and a soft beeping noise came from somewhere. I heard Tony talking, but he was a long way away, at the end of a long dark tunnel.

He was saying, "Now you've done it! The system is closing him down. The neurosurgeons will be here in a minute. You've got to go. Both of you, now..."

I tried to speak, but through my tiredness all I could do was burble, the words wouldn't come. I was collapsing sideways. Tony caught me. He said something about balance feedback circuits. More people were in the room. Auntie McWeezle was saying, "What are you doing to him, what are you doing..."

Amanda said something about the machines cutting me out for my own good. I'd be all right, I'd be....

20: AMANDA

I wanted to take Auntie McWeezle back to our place, and Mom reluctantly said it would be very nice to have her with us until this whole ordeal was done, but it turned out that a room had been set aside for her in the hospital. I came out from the public call booth and found an anxious orderly searching for Auntie. That shouldn't have been a major difficulty, you'd think, given the strange clothes she was wearing. He located us just as I was explaining my arrangements to Myrtle McW, so then I had to go back into the booth and phone home again, and Dad said he was already on the road so he would pick me up out the front of the hospital instead of sending a cab for me.

It was infuriating having my implant phone disconnected and needing to go out looking for a hard phone like some peasant. I started to say this is Auntie McWeezle and she frowned at me in a way that made me feel instantly ashamed of myself.

"I don't mean a *real* peasant, Auntie," I said, covered in confusion. "I mean, that is, not a farmer, like you, I mean a layabout—"

"I know perfectly well what you mean, Amanda." She looked at me sorrowingly, and I felt even worse without quite understanding why. "You're a child of heedless privilege, a daughter of the bad machines. That's why you harbor ill feelings for the poor. You should come back with us and learn what it's like to do an honest day's toil with your own hands." She went on like that for a while, explaining my character defects, and the orderly stood there looking embarrassed.

I'd started out feeling ashamed, which is something I'm not used to, but this ticking-off put my back up. What would she know? Yes, she might be a nice old biddy, but what gave her the right to swan around offering sarcastic and holier-than-thou opinions about *my* life? She didn't know the first thing about modern life. I could feel my face getting red, and I was about to blurt out something rude when Dad came through the double doors into the hospital lobby.

He pushed his hands into his pockets, giving us a rather stern look. The orderly took Mrs. McWeezle's arm and said, "All right, now, dearie, I'll just take you up to your room now." I swallowed hard, looking from one to another, and bit my lip, and gave Myrtle a peck on the cheek. She gave me a big hug before shaking hands with Dad and then trotted after the orderly, following the scuffed green line to the lift. She still looked little and old but not quite so lost. Not lost at all, maybe.

* * * *

In the morning we gathered again in the chapel. Mr. Abdel-Malek was behind his desk at exactly 10 a.m., and we were all in our previous seats except for Superintendent Holesworthy, whose testimony had been quoted on the previous evening's news along with a satirical animation of a flapping troop of giant prehistoric pterodactyls menacing his muon warm fusion plant. I suspect he took the day off work as well.

Myrtle McWeezle looked rested and resolute. The Singhs were fierce, and all the lawyers seemed ready to drone on endlessly with rare and unusual cases of precedent and points of order. Mom and Dad sat on either side of me, beautifully dressed, of course, and pretending to be utterly relaxed. I could tell that Mom was actually about to leap out of her skin, which always made Dad extra jumpy as well. I was starting to feel sick, and a bit of my breakfast jumped up into my throat, sharp and sour. I couldn't help thinking about poor Mathewmark with the optical fiber cable stuck into his head, piping hundreds of millions of bytes of data in and out of his computerized brain back-up. Vikram was dead and buried, which left a horrible hole inside my chest, a hole plugged up with guilt and shame. Mathewmark was still alive but he'd never be the same again.

Because of my stupid prank, the dill had left the security of his own weird world and got himself trapped into something he never could have dealt with, even if he'd had a careful guide. And now a great big chunk of his brain was gone, and a team of technicians was preparing to replace the destroyed tissue with a specialized sim chip.

It wasn't the simple idea of plugging a sim in his head that threw me—I'd had my first neural implant years before, when they gave me a math chip, and then my phone module on my 12th birthday along with the immunities. It was just that this chip wasn't a kind of optional extra. It wasn't an improvement—it was a replacement. If Vik and I hadn't gone flapping around like giant pterodactyls and got the poor farmboy stirred up with the romance of the forbidden Outside, he'd still have all his brain. And he'd still have his home, and that dorky girl Sweetcharity to moon over and maybe marry and have a dozen Valley kids. Now he'd never be allowed back, unless Auntie McWeezle could pull off a miracle. I felt myself sob, and two hot tears ran down my cheeks. I really felt so awful.

"I call Amanda Kolby-McAllister," the flunkey was saying. "As she is a minor, she may be represented by counsel."

Legal Jones bounded to his feet, looking especially self-important, and opened his mouth. I tapped him on the arm, stepping past Mom's Italian-shod toes, and said as clearly as I could, "I'll speak for myself, if that's all right."

The Magistrate looked at me for a silent moment, and then nodded. "Step up to the front, Amanda. Take one of those chairs. We will not stand on ceremony this morning. I have a busy schedule, and this matter has already been unduly protracted." He cast a cold glance over my shoulder, presumably at Legal Jones, who probably shrank instantly by several centimeters. Or maybe not—the rebuke might have gone right over that dork's head.

"You've heard the accounts given by all the witnesses, Amanda. In the light of that evidence, it seems plain that you and Vikram Singh understood the risks you were taking, and just went ahead anyway. Is that correct?"

"But I never thought he'd—"

"I am not interested in self-serving excuses. You had been intercepted not one month previously attempting to enter the sealed loading bay of the metro MagLev deep rail Project. I'm sure you have not forgotten appearing before me on that occasion, together with the young man who is now tragically absent from our company."

I dropped my eyes, stung again by a stab of shame. "Yes, sir."

"Yet you devised a scheme to evade the precautions your parents had put in place to restrict your movements and access. You conspired with the deceased to enter a prohibited sacred locale, despite your certain knowledge that this would cause grave offence to the people whose sanctum you would be intruding upon. Once there, you invaded the private property of the MagLev consortium, interfering dangerously with the electronic safeguards to a ventilation access shaft. You allowed an innocent from the Valley to follow you into—"

"We didn't mean for Mathewmark to come after us," I said desperately, wishing I could curl up, shrink away, and vanish off the face of the world.

"Hold your tongue," Mr. Abdel-Malek told me in a cold, level voice. "You did nothing to prevent this unfortunate young man from entering with you into the direst peril, even after you knew that he was following you down the shaft. You could have turned back at that point. You could have returned to the surface with him, closed the access entrance, and left the Valley. You did not. While you plainly did not connive at his horrendous injury, you took no steps to avert it."

I started to sob, quite loudly. I couldn't help myself. My chest shook, and my hands shook as well, even though I locked them together against my waist. I said nothing. The sour taste in my mouth got worse, like vomit.

"As a result of this extraordinarily foolish escapade, your joint exploit with the deceased has led directly to a death and a most serious injury. If you were an adult, you would now be liable to sanctions under the criminal code. As it is, your youth allows you to escape the serious consequences that would befall an adult responsible for such violations. Do you have anything to say in mitigation?"

Behind me, I heard Legal Jones push back his chair and clear his throat. The Magistrate silenced him with a cold glance. I had a thousand things I wanted to say, explanations, excuses. I wanted to say how much I regretted my foolishness. I wanted to tell him how sorry I was. Poor Vikram! Poor Mathewmark! Poor Auntie McWeezle! I couldn't say a word, which was just as well. I shook my head.

"Perhaps you are belatedly learning a little discretion," Mr. Abdel-Malek told me. "Very well. Here is my summary judgment: you will not have a criminal conviction recorded against your name, but you will be restricted to the following places until you reach your 18th birthday: your parents' home, your school, and any other places supervised by educators where your school mandates your presence. A NannyWatch chip will be fitted to your net access to ensure that you are under surveillance 24 hours a day, seven days a week, during that penitential period. Any attempt to evade surveillance—" he looked at me with piercing eyes, his tone hard and implacable, "—will result in your immediate arrest. Believe me, Ms. Kolby-McAllister, you do not want to appear before this court a third time."

In a very small voice, I whispered, "No, sir."

"Very well. Return to your seat." As I blundered back to sit down between my white-faced parents, I heard him tap a gavel on his desk. "Now, as to the disposition of Mathewmark Fisher, currently still in intensive and remedial neurological care in this hospital. Mrs. McWeezle. No, please remain seated. I have conferred with the young man's medical specialists, and I understand that they have spoken to you as well. I realize that the technology of their procedures is rather alien to the practices familiar to residents in your sacred enclave—"

"The work of the devil," Myrtle McWeezle called clearly from her chair near the front of the room, across from where I sat. "A tube sucking at the poor lad's brain!"

"Just so. Now I'm afraid that any hopes of moving—"

"Not that I'm ungrateful," she said just as clearly. "Devil's work, but the devil has his tricks and uses. The boy would not have survived such a terrible fall in the Valley."

"Quite. We must be grateful for such small mercies. However, it is apparent that without a neural prosthesis to augment his severely damaged brain, Mathewmark will suffer a significant mental impairment during the rest of his life. Do you understand the choice you must make, Mrs. McWeezle?"

"The boy will go simple," she said in a gloomy voice. "Good for nothing but herding cows and mucking out their droppings."

"Worse than that, perhaps," the Magistrate told her, gazing over his steepled fingers. "Much of the left side of his brain has been destroyed. Many of his faculties are now lost, or would be except for the heroic medical treatment available in this hospital. Do you follow what I am saying now, madam? Your grandson—"

"No relation of mine, though I love the boy like a son, the young scamp."

"I misspoke. In any event, do you grasp what the doctors here propose to do to help young Mathewmark go on with a healthy life? I must be certain that you do, since your informed consent is required before the medical staff can take the final step and replace the temporary computer prosthesis with a specially grown chip."

"You're saying you'll put a machine inside the boy's head? An instrument of Satan?"

"Not of Satan, madam. A contrivance of human design, built by human hands, just as your own poultices and herbal remedies are the product of human wisdom and care. I do not believe you need fear for the lad's spiritual well-being."

I watched sideways, across the width of the chapel. Myrtle McWeezle was standing in her place, hands pressed together in silent prayer. Her eyes were closed. I could see anguish in her lined, old features. Her lips tightened. The moment stretched on and on. I glanced at the Magistrate. He sat stock-still, his own fingers steepled, as if he'd wait forever for the old lady to reach her decision. She nodded, then, once, sharply, and opened her eyes.

"Do what you must to aid him," she said, and sat down.

"Thank you, madam. You have chosen wisely. Now," the Magistrate said, clicking to a new display on his screen, and reading it for a moment, his eyes flicking back and forth like a snake's, "we come to the petition made at the outset by Dr. and Mrs. Singh. Would you please come forward?"

There was some shuffling and muttered words with their legal. They stood side by side before the desk.

"I have considered your request to be allowed a clone-twin of the deceased youth, Vikram Singh. I have drawn your attention to the psychological hazards of such a procedure, when it is conducted in such sad circumstances. The pressure upon such a child to match the perhaps unrealistic and increasingly rosy expectations of his grieving parents would be very great."

"Please, sir," Mrs. Singh burst out, "we would definitely not place any such—"

"Allow me to finish." Mr. Abdel-Malek was crisp and chilly. Mrs. Singh recoiled, as if she'd been slapped. I guess not many people talk to the Singhs that way. "I am also obliged to take into account the fact that this lad was not, in fact, an angel. He contributed to his own death by his reckless decision to partake in this absurd and dangerous escapade. Do we wish to bring into the world a carbon-copy of such a foolhardy if talented person?"

His question was obviously posed only for effect, but again Mrs. Singh started to speak angrily. Her husband silenced her with a hard jab. I felt a bit sick, watching this. Vik had always gone on and on about how his parents were so great, but I'd always had a sneaking suspicion that things weren't everything they were cracked up to be. If he'd been having such a wonderful time at home with his terrific olds, what was he doing out crawling into the bowels of the earth with me in the middle of the night? But after all, my folks were okay, sort of, weren't they? And it had been my idea.

"Taking all these matters into balanced consideration, and placing them against your notable and well-deserved reputation in the community, I find that your petition, while unusual, is justified in these tragic circumstances. You have the permission of this court to begin a cloned twin of the deceased, which I understand will be carried by a surrogate mother."

Mrs. Singh began to blubber tears, murmuring, "Oh thank you, thank you."

"I do caution you once more not to place impossible hopes upon the shoulders of this new infant—and to remember that by the time he is born he will have parents who are nearly two decades older than they were when Vikram was born. You will be raising a child young enough to be your grandson, which will be a drain upon your reserves even with today's life-extension technologies. I wish the three of you well. Please take your seats now."

The Magistrate cast his cool gaze across the whole room. No doubt he foresaw the media uproar this decision would set off. I suppose he also knew that nasty rumors would be flying at once—rumors about the Singhs' links to organized crime, their wealth, suspicions of corruption and special deals. None of that was obvious in his disdainful attitude. He snapped his notepad shut with the flick of a finger.

"This has been a distressing hearing. I trust I never need listen to such a sorry tale again. Thank you, ladies and gentlemen. Court is adjourned." He stood, and flowed from the chapel surrounded by his black-suited flunkies.

I stood up myself, after a moment, and my legs were weak. Mom and Dad were exchanging a sour glance. I looked across the room at Mrs. McWeezle. She had nobody to help her and a shockingly sick boy upstairs to look after in a strange, a terribly strange city. I wanted to go over and talk to her, but I couldn't think of anything to say that would help.

21: MATHEWMARK

"Hey, Tony," I said. "Do you know when Amanda is going to visit me again?"

"She can't," Tony said. "Court orders."

"What do you mean, court orders?"

"She's only allowed to go to school. Otherwise she has to stay at home."

"Why?"

"Because of the list of crimes as long as her arm, that's why."

"She's not that bad," I said.

"Vikram Singh's dead. You've only got half your natural brain..."

"That's not her fault," I said. "Both me and Vikram chose to go down that shaft—she didn't make us."

"She's lucky she was up before Abdel-Malek," Tony said. "Any other Magistrate would have sent her off to Juvey Hall."

"Well, anyway," I said. "I want to see her. The only visitor I get is Auntie McWeezle."

"When you get moving, maybe. Then you can visit her at home."

"When I get moving," I said, "I'm going back to the Valley."

Tony didn't say anything. He had heard all about my troubles with the Valley Elders. He'd been there when Auntie McWeezle showed me the Elders' letter. Auntie McWeezle had been writing letters to them every day. They'd sent one back. A special messenger had to bring the pieces of paper from the Gatehouse to the Neurological Hospital. Tony and some of the other nurses had thought it was the funniest thing they'd ever heard of: sending messages on bits of paper. Real olden days stuff, they said. I didn't tell them that was one of the things I often did when I was carting loads with Ebeeneezer: carry notes from one farm to another. But even if Tony and his friends thought letter-carrying was a funny occupation, the contents of the letter weren't funny for me.

The Elders said that even though I'd left the Valley without permission, I'd be allowed back in, but not if I had an infernal machine in my head. That they weren't having. "If Mathewmark is to become a foolish simpleton, he will be God's foolish simpleton," the Elders wrote. "But if he carries the machinery of a cunning wisdom in his head, he will be the devil's mechanic and he will know the devil's wisdom." The letter went on like that for five more pages. There was lots of stuff about casting out evil and serpents in paradise and speaking with forked tongues. And I recognized the handwriting, I'd carried notes for its author on a number of occasions. Officially the letter was from the Assembly of Elders, but it had been written by old man Legrand.

"But Auntie," I said, when Auntie McWeezle showed me the letter, "look at me now—you know I'm not in league with the devil. You know the mainframe thing is just letting me be my old self."

"They'll be putting the... the... chip thing in your head next week," Auntie said.

"It'll be just the same," I said. "It's like the mainframe only smaller, Tony's explained it all to me."

"Explained what?" said Tony coming into the room.

"About the chip," I said. "The Elders reckon I'll be the devil's mechanic."

Tony stifled a giggle. "Sounds like a band," he said. "Tony and the Devil's Mechanics. I might just start it up."

"They want me to be one of God's foolish simpletons," I said.

"Even better," Tony said. "God and the Foolish Simpletons. What a winner, with a name like that the band would be number one by Exmas."

"This is not a laughing matter," said Auntie McWeezle making the sign o'god.

"Then why are you laughing, Auntie?" said Tony.

"I am not," Auntie said with a snort.

"Could have fooled me," said Tony. So, a couple of days later, when Tony told me Amanda was only allowed to leave her home to go to school, I said, "Could you take a letter to her?"

"A letter?" Tony said. "Like one of those crazy collections of paper. All about God and the Devil and the casting of stones?"

"It won't be crazy," I said. "It will be written by me, not old man Legrand."

"So what are you going to say?" Tony said. " 'I am the devil's mechanic and it is my fiendish desire to perform a grease and oil change on your soul'?"

"I want a piece of paper and a pen," I said.

"I'm not sure about the ethics of being an old fashioned postman for patients."

"Go on, Tony," I said.

22: AMANDA

Life was a dull, dreary, boring, mind-numbing series of oscillations. Home to school. School to home. Home to school. At school everything had changed. Everybody knew what I had done. Everybody knew what Mr. Abdel-Malek had said. Some of the kids who'd been my friends muttered in my presence that Mr. Abdel-Malek ought to be thrown out of the judicial system. They said it was a disgrace to hold a court hearing in a chapel. They said he should have sent me to Juvey Hall. My parents had bribed Mr. Abdel-Malek. They knew this because it was what their parents said had happened.

One day when I arrived at school, the janitor was very slowly cleaning some graffiti off the wall outside the science block. ....DA SHOULD HAVE DIED WITH VIK.

"You should of, too," said the janitor under her breath as I walked past.

Some kids went out of their way to be my friend.

"Come and hang with us," Juliet Burkenstock said at lunch time.

"We still regard you as a fellow human being, Amanda," Tomasina Gainotti said, keeping a straight face, "even if you did kill Vikram."

"We can help in your rehabilitation process," Itzhak Posner said, staring earnestly through his glasses. He was the only kid in class whose parents didn't hold with remedial surgery, and he couldn't tolerate contacts. His eyes were watery. Mine were, too, by that stage.

"I didn't kill Vik," I said.

"It's all right, Amanda," Juliet said, "we learned about denial in Domestic Psychology, it's natural."

"It's the first stage of your rehabilitation process," Elizabeth Wing told me, "we can help you to the second stage: acceptance."

"Fuck off," I said.

"It's all right, Amanda," they said, "we learned about anger as well. But you've got to learn to use your anger, Amanda, it's natural but you must learn to use its energy for your own good."

Every lunchtime after that I ate by myself, glowering at anybody who came near me. At home I told myself I deserved everything that happened to me. I deserved the cold shoulders of my friends, of Vikram's old friends. I deserved the attentions of the do-gooders. It was true—what had been hinted at during the hearing—I *had* been the dominant partner. Vik would still be alive if he'd never met me. It gave me a creepy feeling to know that somewhere on the other side of the metro, in Right To Life Maternity, repro technicians were already growing Vikram's tiny clone twin. So I paced my room, flicked the vee on. Flicked the vee off. Flicked it and flicked it. And turned to my only real friend. Who saved my sanity as nobody else could. There's no doubt about it, I'd have gone round the twist without Strad the Lad. I played my violin for hours, the second movement of the Mendelssohn concerto, the third movement of Max Bruch's concerto in G minor. There were grooves in my fingers from the strings, my arm ached from the bow. But I only played melancholy stuff; if it wasn't in a minor key, I didn't want to know it. I lost myself in the music for half an hour, an hour, two hours, I *was* the music. And if I was the music, then I wasn't Amanda Kolby-McAllister bringer of death and destruction. I ripped into Peter Sculthorpe's *Irkanda 4*, with its harsh outback loneliness mimicking just how I felt in the desert of my guilty heart. Someone tugged my elbow. My music stopped abruptly. It was Mrs. Ng. She always knocks before she comes into my room, but I hadn't heard her, I hadn't heard anything but the mournful and angry notes of the violin. My eyes had been closed.

"Tony said to give you this," Mr. Ng said.

"Eh?" I said. "Who's Tony?"

"You don't know him?"

"I can't think of anyone called Tony," I said. "What did he look like?"

"Green hair," Mrs. Ng said. "A rose tattooed on his cheek."

Good grief, that Tony. The muscle-man nurse from the hospital. Downstairs? This sounded like trouble. "Could be anyone," I said. "Did he have any distinguishing features?"

"Nice smile."

"I don't know anyone with a nice smile," I said.

"Cheer up," Mrs. Ng said. "Read what's written on the paper. They might be wise sayings."

Yeah, right, like the wise sayings of the do-gooders at school. Smart-ass wise words to help with my rehabilitation, or more likely warning me and Mrs. McWeezle to keep our distance. I had half a mind to throw the handwriting away unread. But it's hard to throw handwritten messages away unread. Curiosity is a powerful force. I unfolded the sheet. Tony had weird handwriting—it was like nothing that was taught in any of the schools around our neck of the woods. I flipped the single page over to see if he signed himself with his full name. But the name was Mathewmark.

* * * *

Dear Amanda,

My friend Tony the nurse says he will bring you this letter. I am writing to you because you are the only person who has ever visited me in hospital apart from Auntie McWeezle. I am alone. I don't think I can go back to the Valley—they want me to be stupid, half dead. But I'm from the Valley and I don't think I can live in the Outside. I have not seen the Outside, but this hospital place is so strange. It is like nothing in the Valley. The Outside must be worse. I'm frightened, Amanda. I'm frightened and you are the only person I know in the whole Outside. Please Amanda, come and see me. I know that your Elders have said that you can't come to see me. Just like my Elders have said that I can't go back to the Valley unless I'm a simpleton of god. But please Amanda. You are so clever, you can fly through the air and blank out the stars with your wings. Please fly to me.

Your friend Mathewmark.

* * * *

Yeah, yeah, Mathewmark, I thought. But there's no muon warm fusion plant right next to the Neurological Hospital. And anyway, they've taken my wings away. That was the first thing they did.

I went to my net link and stared at the screen saver for a while, trying to think of something I could dictate and print out for poor Mathewmark. But what was the point of that anyway? How was I supposed to get a snailmail letter to him? I wasn't even sure they *had* snailmail any longer. I couldn't order a courier, because Mom and Dad had frozen my credit card. And I didn't know how to reach this Tony the nurse dude.

I had another look at the rather pathetic letter and saw that there was some pale printed code running along the top right-hand corner. Well, if this was hospital stationery, the code might be for the neuro ward where they had Mathewmark hooked up to the optical fiber cable. On the other hand, Tony might have grabbed it from some buzz-joint he was having a drink in after work, or it could be part of a pharmaceutical company order form... or anything, actually. So let's assume it's from the intensive care unit or wherever he is now and do a quick search through the hospital's organizational chart. I'd cracked my way into the place the day after we got home from the last hearing in the chapel, but I hadn't found anything useful. And I didn't want to bring the wrath of Mr. Abdel-Malek down on my neck, so I just put in some bookmarks and picked up Strad the Lad instead. I played for fifteen minutes, but my mind wasn't on the notes. I kept seeing Mathewmark, tethered to the wall by the fiber optic cable.

Enough sulking and remorse. Time for action, Amanda.

"Open the hospital link," I told my computer. I was sick of feeling as if everyone in the world was staring over my shoulder and waiting to pounce on the least little misdeed. If some chip snitched on me, damn it and too bad.

My system played me some Philip Glass, and opened up a series of embedded objects. I raced through them, and inside thirty seconds I found the code from the slip of paper. Yep, the postoperative convalescence unit. intensive care unit. There was a table of staff on and off duty, and another with doctors and yet another with patients. Mathewmark was in stable condition and awaiting a dedicated neural prosthesis. I couldn't make head or tail of all the medical notes and charts. It didn't look as if he was in any immediate danger of dying. Now what about this Tony character?

Anthony James Doyle, charge nurse, rostered to evening duties this week. He must have dropped off the note on his way to work. There was a phone number to his work station, but I didn't want to talk to him just yet. Anyway, maybe someone else in the unit would answer the phone and then they'd see where the incoming call was coming from and I'd be in trouble if-

No, this was sheer paranoia. Why would anyone be looking for my number? On the other hand, all the calls into the hospital were probably logged and recorded. Maybe it made no difference, but they might start asking questions about how come I happened to have their private unlisted phone number. Better find another route in.

I went back to search through Mathewmark's file. It was extensive, page after page of entries and charts and diagrams of his brain, functional magnetic resonance scans and other sly ways of peering inside someone's head. Not that it would have been all that hard to look inside Mathewmark's braincase. There were horribly graphic and highly colorful digital shots in 3D that seemed to have been taken without anyone needing to open up his skull. The poor dork's skull was already open, a large chunk of bone had broken free, pulsing brain tissue and blood vessels visible... Urk and barf. I really did feel dizzy and woozy for a few minutes, and had to flick the screen back to my favorite saver, a green and brown tree growing up from a tiny seed and spreading out its twigs and branches until its wide leaves filled the screen and blocked the sky.

Mathewmark's head wasn't like that anymore, of course. A team of top neurosurgeons had gone in and cleaned out the swollen and bruised and tattered brain tissue and tidied up the torn veins and linked the whole mess into something they called a temporary nano-scale neuro-integrated interface boundary, which in the photos looked to me like a kind of ceramic plug. Then they'd run a cable as thick as a couple of fingers up to the plug and fired digital information down it into the poor boy's brain.

Weird science. I shivered. Half-man, half-machine. This took implants to a new level. It made my chips look like a splinter under the skin. This was industrial strength techno-magic.

I sat straight up and made a noise that surprised even me.

"Oh my god," I mumbled to myself. "I can probably run a virt right into the boy's head."

Maybe. I spoke some commands, and the screen jumped around. While I talked to one level of the system, I pulled out the keyboard and started hammering. There are some programming jobs where speech just can't hack it. Sometimes I prefer to let my fingers do the talking. I dragged in objects, patched them together, pulled down a game interface I liked a lot—*Zone: The Wizard Rebellion*—and plugged myself into vee. Laser light speared into my retinas, acoustics focused on my eardrums.

And then shot the whole sub-program down the line into Mathewmark's neural prosthesis.

Cool mist everywhere, and the soft music of birds waking at dawn. I shivered, and tightened my long silk gown around me. I wasn't actually cold, of course, but it *looked* pretty damn chilly. Violet and pale green flushed one horizon, above a distant edge of sea visible through the leafy trees. My breath smoked a little. Beneath my sandals, old worn flagstones were uneven and probably icy. In places the path had subsided, but the ruined city was not entirely overwhelmed by nature, not yet. I walked quickly toward the east, and light came more brightly into the sky, cinnamon now and soft blue. I found the sandstone hut where I expected it, and pushed open the low creaking door. A small fire burned in a simple fireplace, and someone sat hunched over on a stool, hands extended.

"How are you feeling, Mathewmark," I said, a little timidly. He turned his head, and I saw that he was wearing a dully gleaming helmet of gold or brass. A sword blade had slashed it open on the left side, and dark red blood dripped slowly from the terrible wound. Baffled and confused, he lifted his hand and touched the helmet, shivered as his fingers felt the wetness. He drew his hand down and gazed at the blood. He looked up again at me, eyes wide in fear and astonishment, and blundered to his feet. The stool went over behind him, and the fire flared up as he kicked a piece of timber with his boot, sending embers flying.

"Amanda? Oh dear God of Our Choice, where am I now? Is this Hell's Mouth?"

I waved my hands anxiously, and the wound in his helmet was gone. The far wall of the hut now opened out into a courtyard where several large steeds stamped and snorted. A boy ran past with a heavy armful of jingling chainmail.

"Don't be frightened, Mathewmark. This is just a—" I paused. He'd never understand that we were in a shared simulation. "A dream," I told him. "I'm visiting you in a dream."

"I'm in the devil's hospice," he said, eyes wide, palms outstretched, warding me off. "This can be no dream. It is something put into my head along that wicked cable."

The boy was quick, no doubt about it. Not a dill or a dork at all.

"Don't worry about that for now, Mathewmark," I told him. "Here, come and sit down for a moment by the fire and tell me how you've been. See, this is the only way I can get in to visit you. In this... in this dream."

Heavy rain was falling into the courtyard, and the sky was dark with thunderheads. A brilliant slash of lightning snaked across the bit of the heavens I could see through the double glass doors now leading out to the court, and an instant later a terrifyingly loud bang of thunder cracked through our chamber. The mirror set into the timber wall shivered and broke. A piece of silvered glass fell from the frame, shattered into smaller pieces on the tiles. They melted and ran like spilled droplets of mercury. Mathewmark stared, frightened out of his wits.

"You have to calm down," I told him, slightly hysterical myself.

"This is the work of the polluters and their demons," he said through chattering teeth. The fracture in his helmet was back, and the helm itself was thick, cracked old leather. Blood dripped down his cheek.

"No, it's you," I shouted at him. I made the clouds go away, and out of the corner of my eye saw the puddles drain into the soil. A field of golden flowers reached upward to the sun. "We're both doing it, Mathewmark. Haven't you ever had a lucid dream?"

"A Lucy what?" He stared at the flowers, and they grew thorns.

"Dream, and for heaven's sake *stop* that." I grabbed his arm and gave him a shake. "It's when you know you're asleep and dreaming, and then you can sort of make it go the way you want. It's good. We learn it in Domestic Psychology, I like to dream I'm flying."

My stomach lurched as I saw the ground plunge away. Mathewmark clutched at me. We started to spin and tumble. I flung out one arm like a skater trying to slow down, and it worked a bit. Mathewmark had his eyes clamped tight shut. I made us lighter than air and let the breeze blow us across the midday fields of cotton, hectare upon hectare, tended and cropped by great red machines that moved along the rows of genetically engineered plants. I could just make out the muon warm fusion plant in the distance, and the bluff rising above it.

"All right," he said, opening his eyes and then quickly closing them again, gulping as if he was about to puke. I suppose he'd never been in a plane. "So this is what it's like to fly like a bat?"

"Not quite. You can be hurt when you're hang-gliding. Nothing can hurt you here in the sim unless you let it. So be careful what you wish for. Time to go down and have a chat, would do you reckon?"

"Yes, Amanda. Let's go down." We fell to earth like thistle fluff and walked through white sand while the long breakers came in and went out, making a hushing sound. I imagined that the air was salty. I brushed a fly off my face, and it came back and settled on my back. This wasn't possible. My vee system didn't have full sensory interface. I couldn't possibly be smelling the crisp sea air or feel a fly crawling on my neck. I slapped it. Mathewmark was doing this somehow, cross-wiring my senses. His own linkage to the game scenario must be amazingly powerful, and that was surprising, really, since it was now running inside the hospital's neural nets.

"What's that strange smell?"

Actually I *couldn't* smell it now that I'd doubted it, but I guessed what he must be sniffing. "Seaweed," I told him. "Lots of people call it ozone. If it really was ozone, they'd be dead, oxygen's a dangerous poison if you're not careful."

"This whole demon's world is dangerous, if you ask me," Mathewmark said glumly, rolling up his trousers and stepping cautiously into the water at the edge of the sea. A million tiny broken fragments of shell shifted back and forth, and tendrils of green and purple weed waved in the froth.

"It's a dream," I insisted.

"I'm not talking about the dream," he said. "I'm talking about the hospital."

He lay back in his bed, cable hanging down from its supporting lever to his wounded head. I was seated in an armchair beside the monitors flashing and beeping beside him. A young man with tufts of green hair and a rose tattooed on his cheek was half-turned away from us, poised on one foot, holding a gleaming metal bed-pan. He looked like someone frozen in position in a slo-mo movie.

"Tony, I saw him here that other time."

"Yeah." Mathewmark stared at the softly golden ceiling, face expressionless. "I got him to bring you a letter. Or was that just a dream?"

"No dream, boy-o." I hitched the chair forward on its glider, and took one of his hands between mine. There was no sensation in the vee, but I imagined that he felt a bit cold. "Now let's cut to the chase. We have some planning to do. The damned NannyWatch chip is going to catch on any minute now and shut me out. Next time you'll have to make the contact."

"How can I do that? This is all black magic to me."

"Hey, buster, you're the one with the chip in your head. Or you will be in a day or two. Here, I'll give you the links you'll need to memories. It's just like dialing a phone."

"What's a phone?" Mathewmark asked.

23 MATHEWMARK

It was night. Things are always worse at night. I didn't know what to think. The dream—whatever Amanda called it, the sim. Surely it was the devil's work. I wanted to rip the cable, the jack, out of my head. I'd been bewitched, possessed by the dark forces. Amanda was the familiar of the prince of darkness. There was no doubt about it. She'd lifted me up and flown me through strange skies, over the playgrounds of goblins and machines. Though it had been pleasant on the beach: the sun and the sand and all that water, even the funny smell of the seaweed, I'd liked that. But then the devil's blandishments are like a poisoned cup of honey-mead, sweet to the taste but deadly as sin. I wanted to rip the cable out, so that no dark force could ever take over my mind again.

But no I didn't. I was just telling myself I wanted to be rid of the jack. I was just pretending. What I really wanted was to meet Amanda again. I wanted to meet her in the real world, I wanted her to come and visit me. But maybe, if I was honest, I also wanted to meet her in worlds of our own dreaming. I didn't touch the cable. I lay and waited for dawn and Auntie McWeezle. When she arrived at breakfast time, I made no mention of the dream, the sim.

Auntie McWeezle was worried. In two days time I would have my implant. Then I wouldn't be tethered to the wall any longer by the jack. If all went well, I'd be let out of the hospital a week later. I could go home. Only I couldn't.

"I've written to the Elders again," Auntie McWeezle told me, looking away.

"And," I said.

"And they've told me to return to the Valley."

"With me?"

"Oh, Mathewmark..." Auntie McWeezle said. I thought she was going to cry.

"It's all right, Auntie."

"No, it's not," Auntie McWeezle said. "Oh, Mathewmark, what is going to happen to you?"

"I'll be all right, Auntie," I said.

"On the Outside? Away from everything you know. Surrounded by machines."

"It's all right, Auntie," I said again. "Amanda will show me around."

"Oh, don't be silly!" Auntie said, and now she sounded really cross. "That young slip of a thing can't run her own life without causing death and destruction."

"But you like her, Auntie."

"I've liked new-born puppies in my time, but that hasn't stopped them chewing good boots to shreds and knocking over the milking pail."

"She's the only person I know on the Outside, Auntie."

"That Magistrate man has confined her to her house and her school. And a good job too. She wouldn't be allowed to show you anything, Mathewmark."

"What if we talk to the Magistrate, Auntie. Maybe he'll make an exception for when she's with me."

"She'd lead you astray."

"I'll keep her under control, Auntie."

"Oh for goodness sake, Mathewmark. The machine has addled your mind. You! Keep a wild Outsider girl like Amanda 'under control'!"

"Well, let's try to talk to the Magistrate anyway, Auntie. You said he's the only Outsider you've come across with half an ounce of brain."

"I'll talk to the Goddess now, if you don't mind, Mathewmark." And Auntie started to pray. She prayed in silence, her eyes closed, every thought concentrated on what she was saying to the Goddess of her Choice, and what the Goddess was saying back to her. I envied Auntie her easy access to her Goddess. Sometimes I think that the God of my own Choice was actually a rather poor choice. I've never said this to anyone, but when I pray to my god, I'm none too sure that he listens, he certainly doesn't reply in good plain English.

I lay on my bed and watched the wall while Auntie and her Goddess discussed my case. The funny thing was, I realized, I'd just started talking about my new life on the Outside as if it was an inevitable fact. The Elders didn't want me back, well I wasn't going to argue. Maybe I actually wanted to be an Outsider. At least for a while. Tony came into the room. He was going to say something cheery, but he saw that Auntie was praying, so he started tiptoeing around not making a sound. He shouldn't have worried. The truth is, when Auntie and the Goddess of her Choice get into a discussion, you could jump up and down on the floor and it wouldn't make any difference.

"Hey, Tony," I said. "Come round the other side of the bed and talk to me." He drew up a chair and quietly sat down. "What do you think of my chances of getting permission for Amanda to be my guide in the outside world?"

"Nil," said Tony.

"Say I asked the Magistrate?"

Tony looked like he was going to say nil again, but then he shrugged. "That Abdel-Malek guy has a reputation for unconventional behavior. Anything might happen if you petitioned him."

"Good," I said. "How do I go about using a phone to contact Amanda?"

"There's an old fashioned hard phone just down the hall. You can use it when you get on your feet again."

"Will you show me how?"

"Mathewmark, I'll show you how to clean your teeth, if that's what you need."

"Just the phone, Tony," I said. "Just the phone."

24: AMANDA

The damn NannyWatch caught me, of course. Except the thing didn't bother to tell me, didn't bother to kick up a fuss on its own account. It had known I was playing sim games with Mathewmark from the word go. All it did was shop me to Mr. Abdel-Malek or one of his staff. You'd think the Magistrate would have sent the Juvey cops around pronto. But no. Mr. Abdel-Malek isn't that famous for asking for outside help. He decided to pay me a little call himself. Unannounced. Or, rather, he got Mrs. Ng to announce him. As usual I was playing Strad the Lad.

"Don't stop, Ms. Kolby-McAllister," said the Magistrate, following close on Mrs. Ng's slightly flustered heels, and flinging himself casually into my armchair. "Play on."

"Mr. Abdel-Malek," I said, agog. "What are you doing here?"

"I was rather hoping I might catch the end of the nocturne."

"I'm not very good."

"You are a lot better than I am, Ms. Amanda Kolby-McAllister. The family dog forced me to abandon the violin when I was twelve. It kept joining in. It thought it could do better. It could. Now please, play on."

I needed time to think and there was only one way to buy time. I tucked Strad the Lad under my chin, turned to face my music stand and began to play. Luckily I had an old-fashioned music stand, my grandmother's, the sort that displays the notes on a screen. If I'd used a holographic display to project the score into my retinas, it would have been harder to completely turn my back on the Magistrate. But I did, and while I sawed my way through the rest of the piece I looked at the screen and the dim reflection of Mr. Abdel-Malek that lurked behind the notation.

Out of his official court gear he was a stylish dresser. He was wearing a high necked body-hugger with an open black leather jerkin. The jerkin was trimmed with silver. While I played he appeared to close his eyes, as if listening with all his attention. Perhaps he was. Perhaps he had realized that I was studying his reflection. Perhaps, through half-closed lids, he was studying mine. I tried to think. What was he doing here? Doubtless the NannyWatch had told its sorry tale, doubtless he knew of my latest indiscretion. But surely he was being indiscreet himself, just being here.

I don't know much about the public ethics of the legal profession, but the impression I get from Mom is that judges and Magistrates have to be pretty damn careful about the company they keep. Visiting miscreant teenagers in their own homes at a time when their parents are absent can't be standard procedure. Say he tried to get heavy with me, couldn't I get heavy with him? It was a strange, fearful, forbidden thought: power over Mr. Abdel-Malek himself. My music came to an end. There was no score left on the screen, only the dull reflection of the Magistrate's face. I lowered the violin slowly and turned to face the music—so to speak.

"You play very fluently, Ms. Kolby-McAllister," the Magistrate said, opening his eyes. "The fluency of the distracted. Had you been concentrating on the music and not thinking about other things, would the notes have come so smoothly?"

"Perhaps not," I said.

"And yet, although less smooth, would the music then have had more feeling? If you had been concentrating on it, Ms. Kolby-McAllister?"

"It is hard to judge one's own playing," I said. "And in my own bedroom I am called Amanda."

"I'm sure you are, Ms. Kolby-McAllister. And it is from this very bedroom that you fly through the sky in the company of brain-damaged young men from the Valley of the God of their Choice. In computer-generated simulation, of course."

"If the NannyWatch program has told you about the sim," I said. "I'm sure it told you where I was at the time."

"Indeed it did."

"Can't you give it a better name?" I said. "NannyWatch! It sounds like something you'd employ to babysit a toddler."

"In a manner of speaking, it is babysitting."

"In a manner of speaking, it is my jailer. What about calling it Crim-Watch, or Ball-and-Chain, or... I don't know... StickyBeak. It's degrading, being spied on by something called NannyWatch."

"I didn't create the program, Ms. Kolby-McAllister. The naming of it is not in my gift."

"Must be about the only thing that isn't in your gift," I said. "Does it satisfy you, having all this power over other people's lives?"

"If I told you how little real power I have," the Magistrate said, "you wouldn't believe me."

"You seem to have complete power over me. You control where I go. Who I get to see. What I—"

"I cannot even stop you from hacking into the Neurological Hospital's mainframe, and from there into Mathewmark Fisher's head."

"So you've come round here to admonish me for it. Well, you'd better do it. Tell me the full extent of my wickedness."

"Do sit down, Amanda."

"I rather like pacing about. I'm like a caged animal in here. It's what caged animals do: pace about. Totally neurotic, of course, but then that's what confinement does to a spirited young animal..."

"Sit down. And stop waving that bow, you'll break something."

The man had total cheek. It was my room. If I broke anything, it was my thing to break. And there was nothing I couldn't replace with my money. But after a second or two's silence I twiddled the knob that released the tension in the bow. I put it and Strad the Lad into their velvet lined case and closed the lid. When I was good and ready, and not before, I went and sat on my bed, pulling my legs up and crossing them in a half lotus. "Okay, Mr. Abdel-Malek, about my latest crimes against civilization as we know it..."

"Ah, the egoism of the young," said Mr. Abdel-Malek sadly. "It simply hasn't occurred to you that I might not be remotely interested in discussing your latest misdemeanor. Given the scale on which you operate, Ms. Kolby-McAllister, the latest prank was pretty small beer. I can't even remember if the court order made specific reference to computer hacking or not. Besides, I believe you used an address that was freely available to the public, was printed on the Hospital's notepaper... Why should I bother with that?"

"So why are you here?"

"In the interests of civilization as we know it," the Magistrate said. "We have to introduce it to someone who doesn't know it, who knows a completely different civilization."

"Mathewmark?" I said. I felt a bit deflated. What the Magistrate had said was completely true—it hadn't occurred to me that he'd come to discuss anything but me.

"Mathewmark," Mr. Abdel-Malek agreed. "He has experienced a great shock. He may experience an even greater one when he leaves the hospital."

"Well, that's no problem," I said. "He can go home. That's what Auntie McWeezle is here for, to take him home."

"They will not have him back," Mr. Abdel-Malek said. "Not with a chip in his head. He is going to have to live with us, in what he would call the Outside."

"Pack of assholes!" I said.

Mr. Abdel-Malek looked pained. But he did not say anything.

"Well, they are, aren't they?" I said, "What sort of society would turn its back on one of its own people, just because he wants to have a proper mind, just because he doesn't want to be a gibbering idiot falling down in the street all the time? It's outrageous. They ought to be made to take Mathewmark back. Can't we send an armed guard or something?"

"You seem very concerned," Mr. Abdel-Malek said. "It does you credit, Amanda."

"Look, I'm not trying to curry favor, Mr. Abdel-Malek. But the Valley is Mathewmark's home. He doesn't know any better. He's happy plodding around with his donkey—"

"Mule."

"There's a difference?"

"The mule is the sterile offspring of a male donkey and a female horse."

"News to me. Have you ever seen one?"

"Alas, no, my knowledge of these matters comes from books and the net."

"I have," I said. "Vik and I were loaded onto a cart pulled by one. We were covered in straw."

"Hay, actually. I am familiar with the details of your case."

"And I suppose there is a difference between hay and straw?"

"Indeed there is," said Mr. Abdel-Malek. "Hay is dried grass, it is very nutritious. For mules and other ruminants. Straw, on the other hand, is the dead stalk of wheat, oats or other crops. Its value as food is dubious, but it makes good bedding."

"Fascinating," I said.

"I'm glad you think so," said the Magistrate, "because I'm sure there will be ample time for Mathewmark to instruct you in the rudiments of peasant life."

"Ample time?" I said.

"Ample time," said the Magistrate. "I think it would be a good idea if you were closely involved in Mathewmark's rehabilitation and his introduction into our society."

"Er... look," I said. "Mathewmark is a nice boy. I like him a lot, but..."

"But?"

"But he *is* a peasant, a Valley hayseed. He only knows about mules and things like that. We don't have much in common."

"I know you don't," Mr. Abdel-Malek said, "yet."

I sat cross-legged on my bed and looked at the Magistrate. He sat quite at ease in my armchair and looked at me. There was a long silence.

"All right," I sat at last. "What've you got in mind?"

"I believe," said Mr. Abdel-Malek, "that it would aid your own process of rehabilitation into society if, as both an act of penance and restitution as well as friendship—"

"He's not my *friend*, I barely know him."

"Friendship," the Magistrate repeated firmly. "You seemed quite friendly with Mathewmark in your sim game. The NannyWatch program was most impressed. It said so."

"Sneaky little..."

"Quite so. As I was saying, I think it would be a good idea if you took Mathewmark under your wing. Showed him around."

"Around where?" I said. "You seem to have forgotten I'm not allowed to go anywhere."

"You seem to have forgotten that I am the sentencing Magistrate. I can vary the court's orders at will."

"That's the deal? Freedom of movement in exchange for dragging Mathewmark around with me?"

"Dragging isn't quite what I had in mind."

"I don't think he'll go down a bundle in the Mall," I said.

"But you, yourself, would like to revisit the Mall," Mr. Abdel-Malek said. "Sometime between now and the distant day of your eighteenth birthday?"

"This is bribery," I said.

"That is not a charge you should bring lightly against your local Magistrate."

"I'll have to think about it," I said.

"A good idea," said the Magistrate. "You might also like to think about how you are going to persuade your parents that what they really need in this vast house of theirs is a boarder."

"A boarder. I really don't think we are that hard up."

"But Mathewmark will need somewhere to live, and what finer place than the household of his guide and mentor?"

"Bloody hell."

"You have a way with words, Amanda. And also the violin. So if we could just listen to that nocturne again, I'll be on my way."

25: MATHEWMARK

I was feeling ridiculously calm when they came to wheel me down the corridor. Some wicked juice in the tube in my arm, I expect. It wasn't much like that time Julian Witherspoon and Tom Haughton and me drank a whole jug of fermented apple cider, and got silly and danced under the autumn moon wishing some girls would come down and join us, and then Tom took offence at some passing remark of Julian's and smacked him a beauty right in the eye, and we all ended up laughing and then puking our bellies out in the hedges and nursing our poor heads for two days. It wasn't like that, not really, but that's as close as I could remember to anything this light and floaty. Tony handed me over to a couple of men even burlier than him, wearing green clothes and masks over their faces like bandits, and foolish clear caps over their hair. One of them pushed my enormous bed, which sort of floated along a rail down one side of the hallway, while the other followed pushing a bunch of devil's machines, including the one with the cable that ran into the top of my head.

"Best of luck, chum," Tony called down the corridor behind me. "See you back here in a flash."

Into a room as bright as the inside of a newly-opened honey dew melon More machines with lights that blinked on and off, and little windows with lines that pulsed. I watched this with innocent pleasure, as if it was a dream even stranger than the sim dreams Amanda and I had shared, flying and watching the landscape shift and the weather change whenever one of us chose to make it happen.

"Good morning, Mr. Fisher," a young woman said, smiling down at me. Her whole head was covered by a kind of clear bubble, and her voice seemed to come from somewhere on her shoulder. "How are we feeling this morning?"

"Mr. Fisher is my Daddy," I said, and then laughed because that was quite silly. "I'm Mathewmark, and I feel nice and cozy but to tell the truth I'm absolutely shit scared."

The woman in the bubble grinned, and glanced at another person beside her, a dark-skinned man with very short yellow hair. I blushed and started to apologize.

"We've given you a little tranquilizer, Mathewmark, and it's suppressed your inhibitions. Don't worry, I've heard a lot worse in my time."

"Couldn't have been that long," I said, "your time. You look as young as Amanda."

"Ah, we have a little crush on Ms. Kolby-McAllister, do we?" said the dark man teasingly in a deep dark voice. "I can assure you, it's been quite a long time since my colleague was at school."

"Not *that* long, Dr. Ganunji." The young woman was doing things to the cable plugged into the top of my scalp, and although it didn't hurt I could feel the tug. "Now Mathewmark, we are not going to put you to sleep during this procedure, because we need you to tell us what you experience as we insert the prosthesis and initialize its settings. But don't worry, you won't feel any pain. We have by-passed your pain gates, and the brain itself has no sensitivity to local pain in any case."

A big, very bright light was coming down toward my face from the ceiling. I felt perfectly relaxed and completely terrified at the same time.

"I didn't understand any of that," I told her. My lips felt rather numb.

"Sorry, we get in the habit of talking jargon. Don't worry, all that matters is that you won't have any pain while we fix up your injuries. I know the counselors have been explaining to you that parts of the inside of your head were extensively damaged during your adventure. We have built a replacement for you, and now we'll be putting it in and resetting your—" She twisted her mouth. "It's very hard explaining this stuff to somebody who's never watched a television set, let alone experienced a vee."

"Oh, I've done that," I said. "Amanda took me to a land where everything changes when you think about it. She called it a vee, and then she said it was a sim. I thought she said 'sin' at first." I gave a foolish giggle.

The woman doctor was looking alarmed. She said to her friend, "Someone's already interfaced with him at the virtual reality level? What, that girl he was in the tunnel with? Who on earth let her inside the—"

The dark man said testily, "It's in your in-mail, Janice. The girl hacked through the net for ten minutes two days ago. No harm done. We ran calibration checks, everything's nominal."

The woman doctor was furious. "Damn it, Toby, this is the kind of slackness I'm always complaining about! How can I be expected—"

"Janice, little pitchers have big ears. He's fully alert."

"Shit." The woman doctor's face came down again over me, shadowed in the brilliant glare of the light. I could make out a cheesy grin on her face, like Jed's when he's caught with his hand in the till at the store.

"Just let yourself drift off, Mathewmark. Nothing to worry about. In a moment we'll take out the cable, and start to link you up to your new chip." Her face withdrew, and I heard her mutter crossly, "In the bloody email. Good god!"

The lights went out.

No they didn't. It was like when you've been staring up at the sky with your eyes shut, on a summer's day, and you turn away from the red brightness on the inside of your eyelids. Patterns bloom and shift, swirl and change color. It's magical and beautiful. You can't hold any of it still. The shapes are incredibly complicated and keep changing, except for the spot in the centre which changes slowly from white to red to blue to green and back again. The shapes are like the paisley shirts old man Smeeth used to wear before they all wore out, like a garden of a hundred sorts of flowers if you could look down from the top of the hills. That was something like what I saw.

But that's not it either. There were cones of darkness spinning in crimson. I watched spirals of deep luminous blue twisting into gold. Something like a net opened out, and then closed over me. Meteors flung themselves across the thick green, and I heard a humming like bees. My mouth filled with saliva, and the taste of roast beef with Myrtle Mc-Weezle's best mustard. An itching started in my left foot and raced up my leg, and a muscle in my calf cramped until I cried out. Then the pain was gone, in an instant, and I felt long scratchy fingers run over my shoulders and down my back and reach inside my back, through the bones, and down into my guts like ice that was hot as melted butter. My nose filled with the scent of fuchsias, and I wanted to sneeze but something was gripping my head tight. I couldn't move. Birds sang out.

Everything drained away. I felt my soul rush from my body in a dizzying, sickening flight. And I didn't go with it. I was left behind, dull clay, numb and thick and stupid and without a soul. If I could have screamed I'd have raised a shout to break the light pouring down into my blind eyes. They were shoving something huge into my ear, forcing it past cracking bone, but I was dead so it didn't hurt and it didn't matter. No, not my ear, the whole side of my head. For a moment I was floating up over my body, looking down. The two doctors were prying into my skull with fingers covered in blood over some white skin-tight covering that looked like a pig's bladder. I looked at my face, and felt worse, if that was possible, because it was obvious that I was dead.

I looked awful. I was white and breathing with a raspy asthma sound. Another person in green and bubble-helmet came over and put a mask on my face, and some color came back into my cheeks. The thing they were pushing into my head was quite small, on the end of a kind of mechanical arm. They looked at a screen which was like a box you could see right into, and the thing inside it was raw meat close up, red and blue veins or arteries pulsing. It reminded me of the afterbirth of an animal. A curdling wave of shock went through me, cold rising up from my toes and making the hairs on my dead legs and arms stand up. My stomach clenched very slowly. The thing shown in the box was a picture of me, my brain, and the huge metal bar and glinting stubbly object fastened to its end was just the thin rod the doctors were pressing into my head. The box held a kind of magnified picture of the inside of my brain.

I'd never seen a human brain, well or ill, only animal brains prepared for the table, but this one looked completely messed up. There were nasty gaps and bits that looked like the crinkled skin all over poor Lucy McWeezle's leg the time the log fell out of the fire when she fell asleep after quaffing too much cider and crisped her flesh with a stink like roasting meat. In fact it looked exactly as if someone had reached inside my head with a hot poker and fried my brains. Maybe that's what it was, on a smaller scale. Maybe they'd seared the torn vessels with their dreadful devilish machines to save me from dying of blood loss.

"Holding up, Mathewmark?"

And I snapped back into my head again. I gave a yelp, and the woman doctor blinked. Her arm didn't move, though, as much of it as I could see from the corner of my eye.

"You killed me, you bastards," I heard my numb lips say.

"No, Mathewmark," dark doctor Toby Ganunji said in a complacent voice, "on the contrary. We've given you back your life."

"No need for melodrama," Dr. Janice told him. "All in a day's work. Okay, Bruce, you can close up." She stepped away, and again I saw her face looming over me. "We have the prosthesis in place, Mathewmark. The scans look good. In a few minutes, after we glue in some bone and patch you up, we'll sit you up and run you through some calibration questions."

"That's all?" I blurted. "You're done with me already?"

Dr. Toby stretched, and twisted his neck around like someone getting a kink out. "Eight hours on the table not enough for you?" He gave a tired laugh. "You're a better man than I am, Gunga-Din."

I moved my own shoulders, feeling them creak and crack. Eight hours? I'd been dead for eight hours? Auntie McWeezle was right. I shook my head in disbelief, and there was no pain and no drag from the cable. I reached up carefully and touched the top of my head. There was a bald patch, but no cable.

"Okay, big boy," one of the people in green said through the speaking device on his shoulder, "we're going to sit you up now. Ready?"

I nodded, unable to speak, unable to find words. I was awash in loss and sorrow. They had stolen my soul, I was sure of it. They'd cut it out and put in their goblin machine instead and I would never, ever be allowed back into the Valley. Even if Auntie McWeezle talked the Council of Elders around, I'd never permit myself to sully that place with my presence. I was doomed, and that was that.

"Now, I want you to tell me what you feel when I do this," the new doctor said cheerfully, and pressed a button. I seemed to be standing in the sorghum paddock with Ebeeneezer, looking west at the setting sun, and at the same time I knew that I was sitting propped up on a marvelous bed in a hospital in the Outside.

"What do I feel?" I said bitterly. Ebeeneezer turned his head and looked at me, munching slowly on some tasty weeds. "What do you think I feel? I feel damned to be gnawed by hell's teeth forever."

26: AMANDA

I didn't play the nocturne again. I played a short piece I'd composed myself. I know my own work by heart, so I stood facing the Magistrate, looking at him down the neck of the violin, a bit like a target shooter with a gun. Mr. Abdel-Malek closed his eyes again. When I'd finished, he opened his eyes and said, "You have real talent, Amanda. You played in a style that totally suited the composition. It must be a great joy to be able to invent music as well as interpret it. I'll let myself out." And he was gone.

Invent music! Compose is the word he was struggling for. But how had he known the piece was my own? I hadn't told him. With my room to myself, I really did take to pacing up and down. I was a caged animal, no doubt about it. And I needed to get out. And Mr. Abdel-goddamned-Malek was dangling the key in front of my face. To get the NannyWatch off my back, all I had to do was become a nanny myself—a baby sitter to a poltroon. Me, who used to hang round the Mall with Vikram Singh. We'd been Mall heroes, me and Vik. We'd been the dreadest item on the patch. We'd made that scene. We'd created it. Things came alive when we sauntered in. And now I'd been banned from my own scene for life. I'd been turfed off my own turf—unless I sauntered back in with a hayseed. G'day guys, this is Mathewmark, he's a mule driver. That's a sterile cross between a male donkey and a female horse—or maybe it's the other way round. Which way is it, Mathewmark? Please explain about mules to all the dudes here assembled. It wouldn't be fair! It wouldn't be fair to Mathewmark, let alone me. Poor kid, he didn't deserve the sniggers and the patronizing questions. What did Mr. Abdel-Malek think he was playing at? Oh, Vik, Oh Vik, I want you back. I want you back so much.

And then I wasn't pacing around like a caged animal. I was lying on my bed crying into the pillow. I cried for maybe five minutes and then turned over and looked at the ceiling for another five minutes. Then I got up and went into my bathroom and washed my face. I looked at myself in the mirror, I was a red eyed wreck. But I managed a bit of a grin. I knew I was going to accept the Magistrate's bribe, I was going to become a nanny, there was no way I could refuse. Well, kid, I said to my reflection, if you are going to do it, you might as well do it good. I was going to introduce Mathewmark to the delights of this sin-ridden, machine-driven world, and I was going to introduce him to them with a vengeance. I went back to my bedroom and yelled at the computer to play something thought-provoking. I needed to think.

"Thought-provoking is not a recognized sub-set of music," said the computer. "Please refine your categorization."

"Just play the *Ode to Joy*," I said. "And get on with it."

"Which recording? Please select from the following list..."

"Yukio Lee Smith conducting the St Petersburg Philharmonic and the Choir of Angels at Carnegie Hall circa 2010..."

But already the music was filling the room. I sat in my swivel chair and did an Abdel-Malek. I closed my eyes.

For a while I just let my mind go blank, let my senses have free rein, gave myself over to the music, and then, when the voices started piling on the freude, freudes, I turned my attention to the problem of our future boarder, lodger, paying guest. The smell of Mrs. Ng's cooking, wafting up the stairs, added its own inducement to thought. She's an ace cook, Mrs. Ng, but my parents don't fully appreciate her talents. They keep telling her to go easy on the sweet chili sauce. So, for all her culinary wizardry, Mrs. Ng's dishes are sometimes a bit bland, a bit less than ethnic. Not tonight, baby.

The music reached its crescendo and the room fell silent. I opened my eyes in the manner of Mr. Abdel-Malek and said to the hovering ghost of Yukio Lee Smith, "You have a fine control of the baton, Ms. Yukio, you are a joy to the ear." Then I padded downstairs.

Mrs. Ng was at the wok, crooning quietly to herself in Vietnamese. All her herbs and spices were within arm's reach. I looked at the dishes already prepared, the ingredients still awaiting cooking.

"Hell's teeth, Mrs. Ng," I said. "This is a veritable feast."

"Your parents have invited guests to dinner," Mrs. Ng said.

"Who?" I said.

"Dunno," Mrs. Ng said. "A man and his wife. Just the family meal, nothing formal, your mother said."

"Bully for them," I said. "Do you want a hand?"

"You could lay the table," Mrs. Ng said.

"Sure thing," I said and wandered through to the dining room. Three minutes later I'd dropped the vase of flowers I'd been moving onto the table for a centerpiece. It was in bits all over the floor, the flowers lay among the spilt water. "Yikes!" I said. Mrs. Ng came running.

While Mrs. Ng was at work with the mop, yelling for the scullion-bot to get its mechanism into gear and pick up the pieces, I lingered for a few seconds in the kitchen. I reached for the spice rack. I had the top off the *nuoc mam* sauce bottle in a flash. A few of Mrs. Ng's dishes rapidly became very ethnic indeed.

The dinner guests were a bit of a surprise: Legal Jones and his wife. Jonesy was looking as dork-like as he had in the court. His wife wasn't much better. Her name was Iolanthe. By the time we all sat down to eat, the adults had got a few snifters under their belts. The smell of Mrs. Ng's cooking wafted from the kitchen with considerable authority.

"Umm," said Legal Jones in appreciation. "That smells delicious."

"Ms. Ng is a treasure," Mom said.

"Are you sure you're up to it?" I said to Legal Jones.

"Sorry?"

"Are you man enough for Mrs. Ng's cooking?"

"Darling..." Mom said.

"Mrs. Ng's *muc rang muoi* packs a punch," I said to Legal Jones. "It's ripped better men than you to shreds."

"Really, Amanda," Mom said, shooting me a warning glance. "You know perfectly well that Mrs. Ng only goes in for the most subtle blends of traditional herbs and spices."

"Some of which can dissolve a human tooth overnight," I said. "Are you game?"

"Cecil has a fire-proof throat," Iolanthe said to me. "It's amazing what he can eat. When we were in India on our honeymoon he—"

But just what young Cecil did in India was never explained, because at that moment the doors to the kitchen sighed open and the food trolley wafted into the dining room, followed by Mrs. Ng. "Yumolla!" I said. "This is going to be great! Legal, you're going to love this, assuming you're up to it."

I gave Mrs. Ng a hand unloading the dishes onto the table. Her eyes were a bit red, as if she'd been cutting up too many onions. She gave me a suspicious look, but didn't say anything. Mrs. Ng withdrew. I sat down and everyone started to help themselves to rice and a selection of the other dishes. We gorged for a while on appetizers—crab in tempura, dipped in sweet *nuoc cham*, bean sprouts, lettuce, the whole deal, then some spring rolls made out of shrimp, pork and who knows what else, some egg rolls and lemony grilled mussels. I'd spiced up half a dozen of the dishes (the *cari ga* had a bit of a bite) but it was the *muc rang muoi* that was the real killer.

"Here," I said to Legal Jones, "let me help you. Have a go of this stuff."

I dolloped a few heaped spoonfuls of squid onto Jones's plate. Mom said something rather frosty about being sure Cecil could make his own choices, but I said, "Legal and I are real fans of *muc rang muoi* aren't we, Legal?"

"Call me Cecil."

"Sure thing. Thanks for keeping me out of jail, by the way, Cecil."

"My pleasure. Now let me help you..." And the guy went and dumped as large a serving of *muc rang muoi* on my plate as I'd dumped on his.

The strips of squid had been deep-fried, then lavished in my spiced-up peppery sauce. Legal eagle Cecil and I were soon battling it out. The others were breathing hard and reaching for their wine glasses, but Cecil and I were enjoying a bit of light-hearted banter. At least we were both trying to give the impression of light-hearted banter.

"You can see what Mom means," I said, forking a good dollop of *muc* into my mouth, smiling happily as the food scalded my throat.

"Means about what?" Cecil said, trying to smile hard himself.

"About Mrs. Ng's food being a bit bland."

"But this is very tasty," Cecil said, drinking more than he should.

"Yeah, yeah," I said, "it's a subtle blend of herbs and spices, but it's got no real fire. I like food with a bit of oomph. Let me fill your glass."

I filled Cecil's glass. I leaned over the table and filled everyone else's glass. I whispered quietly to the scullion-bot, "Get a couple of more bottles, whip the corks out. Bring me a mineral water while you're at it."

I only took only the smallest sips of my mineral water. Some people think you can quench hot food by swilling wine or beer or water around in your mouth. Wrong! The liquid just ensures maximum penetration. It picks up the active ingredients and it bathes, it soaks, it marinates your taste buds. I knew this, but no one else around the table had the slightest clue.

By the time we had fought our way through the meal, sweat was dripping from Iolanthe's nose. Mom had to use her handkerchief half a dozen times. My throat and gullet were like the insides of a volcano and I reckon everybody else's were worse. And they were all pissed as newts. I thought it was time to strike.

"It's good about our boarder, isn't it?" I said to Cecil.

Cecil's eyes were a bit glazed and he had to reach for his wine glass before he could answer. "Boarder?"

"Yeah, Mom and Dad reckon I need something constructive to do, you know to rehabilitate me. A bit of penance, that sort of thing."

"Well, speaking as your lawyer..." Cecil managed to say, panting.

"....You have only my interests at heart," I said.

"Well, yes of course."

"Hey Mom," I said across the table. "Cecil agrees about the boarder."

"What?" Mom said.

"He reckons it will do me good. Don't you, Cecil?"

"Er... something constructive would certainly be a good thing," Cecil said vaguely.

"What are you talking about?" Dad managed.

"Poor old Mathewmark," I said. "He's coming to stay."

"What!" Mom and Dad said together.

"See, I'm responsible," I said, leaning over and refilling their glasses. "So I've got to do the right thing."

"What right thing?" Dad said.

"Look after Mathewmark," I said. "While he's staying with us. Mr. Abdel-Malek was most impressed with my generous offer."

There was a shocked silence, and then a babble of voices. Finally Mom gasped, "You've... you've been talking to Mr. Abdel-Malek... you're not meant to..."

Cecil cut in with, "Speaking as your lawyer, Amanda, I must advise you not to directly approach the judiciary. If any communication is required, you should first consult—"

"Oh, it's all gone through the proper channels," I said. "I wouldn't do anything as unethical as try to chat up Mr. Abdel-Malek in person. I mean that would be a gross violation of the doctrine of the separation of powers and would have a lamentable effect on the impartiality of the wisdom of Solomon and call into question etcetera etcetera. But I don't have to tell you lawyer types that, do I?"

Gosh it's good to be stone cold sober when everybody else is as drunk as a skunk. I gave Cecil a friendly pat on his thigh under the table. I slipped my shoe off and ran my instep up and down his calf a few times. And I laid a mighty rave upon the drunks. By the time I'd driven home the fact that Mr. Abdel-Malek was in favor of my plan, and convinced them that I'd only been communicating with the Magistrate by certified e-transmissions via the Clerk of Court, and that I wasn't going to be arrested for trying to pervert the course of justice, by the time I'd convinced them of all that, they'd pretty much accepted that there was nothing they could do to stop Mathewmark coming to live with us.

"I must say," Cecil said to my parents, when we were all wobbling off to get a bit more comfortable and drink a lot of coffee, "it is very good of you both to take these steps for Amanda's rehabilitation. Speaking as her lawyer..."

"I think I'll pass on coffee," I said.

I left them all to it. I went up to my room and really did send a quick official e-transmission to the Clerk of Courts. For the attention of his honor Mr. Abdel-Malek....

27: MATHEWMARK

"This is for the pecs," Tony told me, leading me to one of the gleaming Tools of Frivolity in the hospital recovery "jim." I had never seen so much shiny metal and leather, including the fancy harnesses the draughthorses wear on Jagannatha Day parade. He made me lie down on a firm bench and grip a short jutting bar of metal in each hand. They seemed to be stuck to the wall, but when I gave one of them a shove it moved upward only slightly, as if it weighed as much as a bag of potatoes.

"What are 'pecs,' Tony?"

"Those muscles on your chest between your nipples and your collarbone. Yours are in better shape than most I see here, you must have done some heavy workouts in your time."

I didn't know what that meant, so I said, "Working outdoors and inside in the sheds, it builds a lad's strength for righteousness, so my pastor says. What should I do with these bars?" I tried to pull them down to my chest, but they wouldn't budge.

"Hang on, old son, let's set the resistance." He pressed some buttons, and the number 20 glowed into cool blue life above my head, between the bars. "Now, just press up slowly, elbows out here to start, that's it, and straighten your arms. Terrific. Okay, let's have three sets of ten." He reset the number to 25 and left me pushing at the suddenly heavier bars while he wandered off to another part of the "jim."

I was sweating a bit, but not as much as if I'd been mucking out the milking shed. And the smell of the air was sweeter too. But as I pumped my arms up and down, and felt the sweat slowly run into my armpits, I was suddenly sick with longing for the old sheds, for the warm smell of cow shit and the cackling of hens and the darting sight of our plump tom cat after a mouse or rat in the straw. Good old Kevin, I wondered if he was missing me. I got to ten and rested for a moment, as Tony had told me to do, and a powerful yearning to see my dear old friend Ebeeneezer rushed over me. My eyes prickled, as if sweat had run down from my forehead, which was also true. Nearly in tears, I remembered the clean green and brown of the sorghum fields and trusty Ebeeneezer plodding along at my side, or pulling the cart in his harness up in front as the dust puffed from the rutted road.

When I'd finished my set of thirty exercises, I lay there on my back for a moment with my burning eyes shut. A rhythmic banging thudded away in the room, some Outsider's idea of music I suppose, and it made my heart beat faster, or maybe that was just the exertion. I was terribly homesick, lost in this awful place. It might have been better if I could have spoken to Amanda, but she hadn't been allowed to visit the hospital since the operation.

"Oy, come along, you slacker," Tony yelled in a jolly tone, "let's hop on the treadmill and show me some cardiovascular effort."

I didn't understand that, either. Pecs and lats and abs and quads, strange names for all the bits of the body I never knew had special names. And now this cardy-something. I mooched over to his new Instrument of Satanic Torture, thinking how shocked Auntie McWeezle would be if she saw me here in this "jim." Not to mention old man Legrand—he'd be sure it was a fit and suitable place for a sinner like me.

"Jump up, Mathewmark. That's it, pop your feet into the retainers, and just look straight ahead for a mo. I'll give you something nice and woodsy, sort of just like home, eh?" He slipped a pair of light gloves over my fingers, and the curved plastic bar in front of my eyes shot out twin beams of light that seemed to search my face for an instant and then—

—locked into my eyes with a soft purple haze that faded, as I blinked, into something that just could not be. I tensed up, quite scared, because it was as if Tony had picked me up and thrown me without warning into another part of the world. The hospital "jim" was gone. I stood in a clearing halfway up a hill under a pale sunny sky streaked with light clouds. A dozen shades of green were grasses, and trees with broad branches and leafy twigs tossing in a light wind, and low shrubs growing between the trees, and vines with pink flowers in the shape of trumpets... But I couldn't smell any of their fragrances, and the light breeze in my face was blowing from the wrong direction.

I shook my head in disbelief, remembering the dream where Amanda and I had flown into the heavens like birds or bats or angels. Nothing in that dream had made more sense than any other dream, nothing had held still long enough to catch hold of it. Yet it still seemed so real, in some foolish way—as real as this place Tony had sent me to.

A bright yellow arrow appeared in the middle of the air, at about shoulder height, pointing up the hill. I opened my mouth to protest, and then found myself laughing. This was just so ridiculous. Tony's voice said in my ear, "Come on sport, follow the arrow. Just a light jog to start with, up the hill, and then let yourself ease into a run. Okay?"

I swung my head around left and then right, but he wasn't there. No other human was. The clearing in the woods stayed put, though. I looked down at myself. I was wearing a skin-tight garment of blue and black, and my feet were bound in those pliable shoes Amanda had called "grippo sneakers." I raised my left foot, and it felt slightly heavy but not restrained. The yellow light was blinking and jerking forward beckoningly. Oh, why not? Everything here was as crazy as everything else—let's go for a run through a wood in the middle of a hospital building.

I started to lope up the hill, and a small animal started from cover and dashed across the path. I followed it with my gaze as I picked up speed, a rabbit with laid-back ears and white flag. The sun was at my back, out of my eyes, and comfortably warm. I started to run for the pure pleasure of it, something we rarely had a chance to do in the Valley once childhood games were behind us. The refreshing air in my face flowed faster as my speed picked up. The ground rolled along beneath my feet, and my arms swung easily back and forth at my sides, at waist height.

When I reached the top of the hill, the path curved down in a gentle loop and vanished between trees. A bird or two lifted from branches and flew past me, caroling. A glint of water shone to the east, down through scrub. Suddenly I was tired of the path. I swung away to investigate the creek down below-

And nearly tumbled over. My feet felt as if they'd got stuck in heavy mud, although I couldn't see any.

"Sorry, Mathewmark," Tony said in my ear, "you'll have to stay on the track. The program's adaptable up to a point, but it has its limits. Here, I reckon you've done enough exercise for one morning, let's call it a day shall we?"

The wooded hill faded back into purple haze, and then I was blinking at the white light of the "jim." Tony was bent down undoing the strips that held my feet. I shook my head, struck by vertigo, and felt for a moment as if I was about to throw up. The breeze was coming from a vent in front of me, ebbing away now that I had stopped running in place.

"Oh-oh," Tony said, glancing at my sweating face. "Virt sickness. You'll get over it soon enough, I suppose the learning curve is a bit steeper if you get into this as an adult. Wait until you try skiing down the erupting mountains of Io! Come on, lean on my arm, we'll whiz through some quick cool-down exercises and then we'll get back to your room for a good hot shower and some lunch, eh?"

The prospect of lunch cheered me up. Odd heathen menu they provided here, certainly, but wonderfully tasty. "Hospital food," Di the new orderly had said enviously the second day after I woke up. "Wish the menu in the staff caf was as good. I don't suppose you feel well enough to try that chocolate pudding?" she had added hopefully. I shook my head, the cable tugging, and she took the bowl with an appreciative smile, dipping the creamy stuff into her mouth with happy smacking sounds of her lips. "I sometimes think it would be worth having a bad accident," she told me confidentially, "just to get a rest up for a few days and work myself through this yummy menu."

That had been a reminder of Valley custom, in its way, because the old biddies tell us that the way to regain health is to eat wisely and well. The difference was in the kinds of food they provided here. No purgatives and spring water. Something called pizza, for example—crusty and hot, with a dozen delicious toppings of tomato and spicy meats and tiny sliced mushrooms and many rich runny cheeses, the bread soft and light inside. I couldn't make up my mind what I liked more: something called *coq au vin*, which is a chicken in wine, with crisp green beans and small roasted potatoes, or *saltimbocca*, which Di the orderly told me meant "jump in the mouth," beaten meat of baby calf under a layer of fine swine's bacon, smothered in creams and butter and herbs, with a tasty salad tossed lightly in oil and vinegar and still more herbs, and tangy garlic, or fresh trout and fried potatoes. That was the first and last time I gave up my sweet to a member of the staff. I looked forward every day to the *profiteroles*, which contained that chocolate stuff Amanda had given me in the Valley, and ice creams and pears in brandy and other treats I had never even heard of at home, famous as it was in the Valley for wholesome scones and cider.

"Mind and body are one," Dr. Janice told me when she came by on rounds to visit me and check that the wound in my head was healing properly. "A sound mind in a sound body, I'm sure they must teach that old truth in your village?" She seemed pleased to see me tucking into my trout, laying open the back of the fish with a knife and taking out the bones in much the same way she must have gone into my poor head. She tapped my skull, and stepped back, looking pleased. "No pain, I hope?"

"No, thank you, doctor." I could scarcely believe it, but it was so. If this sort of damage had befallen some poor soul in the Valley, I don't think our herbal remedies would have prevented him from yowling in pain for many a day until, very likely, he passed away from a miasma or a gangrene. They told us this was the way the God of our Choice intended matters for us, in the vale of tears. I was starting to wonder if that was absolutely true, or whether maybe some of the old men and biddies might have slipped up in their translations and teachings from the wisdom of the ancients. Old man Legrand would have gone crimson in the face if he'd known what was happening to me, he'd have screamed and hollered that all this was the work of the fiend. Once, I'd have agreed without hesitation, and might still, except that it meant I'd be the one lowered in the casket into consecrated ground. One day the end will come to us all, and if we've lived lives of virtue and self-sacrifice we will be raised up in glory—but I'd rather put it off for a while yet.

And that thought, of course, made me feel guilty and wicked. It is the way of polluters and sinners to seek only personal advantage, rather than buckling down to the hard choices of self-denial. Even if you must perish in defending what is right.

Then again, it suddenly struck me that old man Legrand hadn't actually faced that choice himself, not life versus death. There he was, strutting about in all his pomposity, keeping his eye jealously on Sweetcharity, but he'd never looked death in the face as I had. Or if the choice had lain before him, he too must have chosen life. Either way, I figured I was just as well placed as him to cling to hope and be grateful to those who had plucked me back from the edge of doom and a life of simpleness with only half a brain. I shuddered, and turned for comfort to my bowl of warm apricot tart with a hint of lemon and a dollop of thick cream.

I pinged Tony.

"Do you think I could make a telephone call now to Amanda?"

"Don't see why not, old son. I'll fetch in a hard phone as soon as I can find one. Failing that, you'll have to go down to the lobby." A little while later he returned with a frustrated expression, holding a small machine. "Seems to be a lock on her implant. Must be from the court case. Or maybe her olds just want her grounded. Either way, you'll have to call the Kolby-McAllisters at home and ask for her. They're probably still at work, but here's the phone. I've keyed their number, just push 5 and leave a message if the call isn't forwarded."

As usual, I didn't have a clue what he was talking about, but I took the wafer from his beefy hands and examined it. The same kind of dot of light that had speared purple haze into my eyes in the "jim." A set of oblong pads with single numbers. As Tony tidied away the wreckage on my table, I touched the 5. Twin beams of light leaped into my eyes.

I was sitting in a small charming room facing a large gilt-edged mirror. I couldn't see my own reflection, though. A voice said in my right ear, "I'm sorry, Mr. Kolby and Ms. McAllister are not available to take your call just at the moment. Would you like to leave a message, speak to the housekeeper, or option?"

I moved my mouth and no words came out. I swallowed hard.

"Um, excuse me, could I please speak to Amanda?"

"I'm sorry, Miss Amanda Kolby-McAllister is not taking calls this month. You may leave a message for her attention. Warning: this message will be screened by NannyWatch."

I'd got to my feet, still holding the wafer, and looked around me. The small room was empty, apart from my comfortable chair and the big mirror. There were no doors or windows, no way out or in. I was starting to feel claustrophobic. I was also feeling fed up and even a bit angry. After all this, she wouldn't even *talk* to me? Ha, so much for that stupid dream. Or was it her parents who wouldn't *let* me talk to her? They must be feeling pretty annoyed at her for all she'd done. After all, her prank had got that Vikram kid killed and almost killed me. Not that I was trying to dump the blame on her. I'd gone down the vent because I couldn't deny my sinful curiosity. But it was all so damned *annoying*. I felt the frustration rise in me, boil over. I *wanted* to talk to her, and I wanted to talk to her *now*. Why should some stupid—

The mirror shimmered, and Amanda was gazing out at me, looking completely astonished. She was wearing something soft and slinky, and she had some kind of fiddle tucked up under her chin and a bow in her right hand. She gaped at me.

"Mathewmark!"

"Uh, they just told me I wasn't allowed—"

"How did you break the lock on my implant phone?"

"Your—? I don't have a clue. Tony gave me this portable phone and I was talking to someone I couldn't see at your place and they said you weren't permitted to—"

"Yes, yes, but you've reactivated my implant! Oh my god!" She looked thunderstruck, and the fiddle bow waved foolishly in her hand, completely forgotten. "This is the same thing that happened when we went into vee together before your operation."

Everything swirled and wavered around me. No, surely it had been a dream!

"We went flying," I said in a very small voice.

"Well, not literally," Amanda said. "In the sim. Somehow your connect to the hospital neural net let me do a node-to-node right into your head. Is that's what's happening now?"

"Amanda, you might as well be asking Ebeeneezer. Do you mean this new part of my brain is a sort of telephone?"

"Sure looks like it." The girl was flushed with excitement. She was about to jump out of her skin. "Hey, this is terrific, Mathewmark! This is so glumpzoid! Maybe we'll be the new Mall gods after all, my hayseed friend. Listen." She paused, and I could see her thinking very fast. "Yes, why the hell not tell you? Mathewmark, you're coming to stay with me and my folks for a while."

I could feel her excitement like a snake bite, first a jolt and then paralysis. And my homesickness rushed back, bitter and sorrowful.

"Amanda, I just want to go home. I want to go back to the Valley and see my brother and Mom and Dad and Auntie McWeezle and, and Ebeeneezer—"

She put down her fiddle as if she'd just noticed it in her hand. Was that sympathy in her eyes? Hard to tell with the wild girl.

"Could be a bit hard to arrange just now," she said. "But look, here's the next best thing. I'm coming over to get you and bring you home with me. Mom and Dad have already agreed, I talked them into it. And I've just thought of a way we can *both* go back to visit the Valley."

"You can't," I said wretchedly. "Tony said you're grounded. And I can't, because old man Legrand says I'm a blight of the fiend."

"Old man Legrand and his wimpy grand-daughter," snorted Amanda. "We'll set them straight. We'll drop in and give them what they deserve."

"Not Sweetcharity," I objected. "That would be unfair. She hasn't done any—"

"Oh, all right, I'll let the princess of cow-droppings off the list." She was grinning and giggling with delight at her own plan, whatever it was. Maybe she really was a wicked force for ruination. "Okay, hang fire, yokel-man. I'll be at the hospital as soon as I can arrange for a cab."

"How *can* we go back to the Valley?" I yelped in frustration, expecting her to vanish back into the mirror. "They won't let us through the Gatehouse."

"Ah hah," Amanda said, and then she really did fade away into the silvery glass, leaving only her grinning mouth. "Ever heard of... liar bees?"

28: MATHEWMARK

"It's like looking through a knot-hole," I said.

"What's a knot-hole?" Amanda said.

"A hole in a bit of wood," I said. "You get them in doors and walls. If you want to spy on somebody, you can look through a knot-hole."

"Here they just use NannyWatch," Amanda said.

"It doesn't seem right," I said. "Hovering in space, looking at people."

"Oh for pity's sake, Mathewmark. Do you want to revisit your Valley or not? It's your home after all. It's where you grew up."

She was right, of course. There were times when I felt so homesick I could cry. Did cry. And they had gone and shut me out, for no reason at all. Or for the stupid, halfwit reason that they wanted me to be a stupid halfwit. I had a right to go back. Even if I went back as a liar bee.

Amanda pulled a box from under her bed. It had Fleetfoot Grippo Sneakers written on it, but there were no shoes inside. Just two liar bees. Amanda took one out and handed it to me.

"Go on, Mathewmark. It won't bite."

Gingerly I held the thing in the palm of my hand. It was only a little bigger than a normal bee, but ten times as heavy.

"There you are," said Amanda, "Satan's little helper. That's the one I used when I was tormenting that lunatic with the whip."

The temptation was immense. The temptation was delicious. "Teach me how to drive it," I said. "I want to torment Legrand as well."

"Atta boy," Amanda said. "Sit down in front of that console. Grab hold of that joystick."

"Looks a bit clunky," I said. "What happened to the wafer with the beams of light that let us go off to nevernever land?"

"Getting choosy already. Tut-tut." Amanda wagged her finger at me. "You're right, this sucks. Almost twentieth century technology. One of Dad's old machines, I found it in the attic. But it doesn't have a NannyWatch chip."

She was grinning like a thief.

"You mean it can't spy on us?"

"Correct." She flipped a button, and the screen turned into a picture. "But luckily there's nothing stopping us from spying on everyone else."

* * * *

It was late afternoon by the time we got the picture on the screen to show the grey cliffs of the bluff through the liar bee's eyes. It was funny looking at the Valley walls from the outside. All my life I'd seen them from the inside. It was like using two mirrors to see the back of your head.

"Okay," said Amanda, "take it up and over. This is a damn sight easier than riding the muon plant's thermals, I'll tell you."

In response to my hands on the joystick, the bee soared up the side of the bluff, and then like a diver jumping out of the tree at the old swimming hole, we were over the top. Suddenly the whole Valley was below us. But in miniature, like a map.

"Whoa there," Amanda said. "Slow down. Float around a bit. There's no hurry."

So for half an hour I made the bee fly slowly across the landscape. I could identify everything: each cottage, each village, each farm, each twist and turn of every track. High up in the sky I circled our place. The apple orchard was in blossom—the vegetable patch was in need of weeding. A mule cart was approaching from the west.

"Hey," I said to Amanda. "I think that's our cart. That must be Ebeeneezer. And... and... I think that's Lukenjon driving."

"Well, take the bee down. Let's have a chat with him."

Suddenly I was a terrible jumble of emotions. I wanted so much to see my brother again, to talk to him, to tell him all the stuff that had happened to me since that night when I'd disappeared down the vent, to ask him how things were in the Valley, to get all the gossip. I wanted to talk to him so much. But I didn't want to appear as a liar bee. I hung back.

"I can't," I said to Amanda. "I'll just watch from a distance."

For the next twenty minutes we watched Lukenjon. He arrived at our farm, unhitched Ebeeneezer, brushed him down and turned him loose in the lower forty. We watched him splash his hands and face at the pump and disappear through the front door. Smoke rose from the chimney. I felt my mouth suddenly water at the sight. There would be food on the table. Maybe flapjacks and honey and cream from our cow.

"Fly the bee in the door," Amanda said. "Or through a window."

"I can't," I said. "I can't." And I let go of the joy stick and buried my face in my hands.

"Hell, we'll crash the thing," Amanda said, suddenly brisk and in command. "Shove over, Mathewmark. I'll fly it for a bit. We'll go and see the loony with the whip."

She gave my chair a push and slid hers in front of the screen. For a minute I sat with my face covered, mind buzzing with a mix of emotions. When I looked up again, the screen showed the track that leads to the Legrand farm. Amanda had the bee zooming along a few meters above the ground, trees flashing past beside and above it.

"This is the way, isn't it?" she said.

"Yes," I said. "Turn right at the next fork and then go up the side track by the flowering gum."

"What's a flowering gum?"

"A tree."

"There are quite a few of those around," Amanda said. But she didn't actually need any further directions. She flew the bee straight up to Legrand's cabin. My heart was in my mouth. There was Sweetcharity—looking prettier than I'd ever seen her—hanging out the washing.

"Check the unders!" Amanda yelled. "What winners!"

Old Man Legrand's longjohns were hanging upside down from the line. And, indeed, they were a sorry sight: yellow and baggy and much patched.

"They're a work of art," Amanda said. "You could put them in an exhibition. *Lingerie de Clodhopper*. Here, Mathewmark, I'll fly the bee, you do the voice. Just talk into the overhead mike."

"I can't," I said.

"Yes, you can," said Amanda. "She's your beloved, the apple of your eye. Coo some sweet nothings into her shell-like ears. The mike's on."

The bee closed in. Sweetcharity didn't look up at the insect, just brushed the air ineffectually with one hand. In the other hand she held a wet, embroidered scarf. Sweetcharity took a wooden peg from her mouth and secured the scarf to the line. Amanda dug me in the ribs. "Say something," she whispered.

"Hello, Sweetcharity," I said. "Don't be scared."

Sweetcharity screamed, dropped the wicker washing basket and ran, still screaming, into the house.

"What a cry-baby," Amanda said. "After her!"

With a few quick flicks of the joystick Amanda had the bee zooming after Sweetcharity. But as the bee made its run under the veranda eves towards the door, the door banged shut.

"Ouch," I yelped. I felt for a moment as if I'd smacked my nose into the wall.

In front of us the screen was blank.

"Hell," said Amanda. "We've crashed. I'd better run a diagnostic."

She quickly began ordering the computer to do things in words I couldn't understand. At the same time her left hand did complicated things with the joystick and her right hand pressed buttons on the keyboard. The computer suddenly spoke, sounding cross.

"All self-repairing circuits are currently in full operational mode. Please do not confuse the bee with irrelevant commands."

"Smartass," Amanda said, sitting back and folding her arms.

"I try to please," said the computer.

Amanda said to me, "The bee will be up and running in a few minutes. We've just given it a bit of a jolt."

I was still rubbing my nose. It was as if I'd become linked for a moment to the liar bee. "We scared poor Sweetcharity out of her wits."

"I don't think she had many wits to start with," Amanda said. "What we are going to need is one of these knot-hole things."

"Why?"

"To get the bee into the house, lamebrain."

I started to say, "Perhaps if we—"

But I was cut short. The screen was suddenly showing a vivid picture of the Legrand veranda planks, and the computer announced, "All systems go."

"Beauty," said Amanda and grabbed the joystick again. "No need for a knot hole, we'll just crawl under the door. God, these old hovels must be draughty, look at that."

I jerked up in my own seat, and felt my shoulder-blades pulled back, as if I had buzzing wings. I was starting to lose control of my imagination.

In a flash the bee was under the door and hovering in mid-air. The Legrands' kitchen was much as I'd remembered it: a bleak place with none of the warmth that someone like Auntie McWeezle brought to her kitchen. Where were the gleaming copper kettles, the shelves of brightly colored preserved fruit in jars, the red and white checked table cloths? There were no strings of onions or smoked sausages hanging from hooks. Just a smoky stove at one end of the room and a big wooden table in the middle of the room. The table was none too clean, but the small plastic box, the computer, that sat on the table was shiny and new.

"Look at that!" I said to Amanda.

"Look at *him*," Amanda said, "he's hooked. Where the hell did he get his hands on a notepad? And where's the juice coming from? It doesn't look like a solar-powered model."

Behind the computer, old man Legrand was crouched in a broken chair. He was madly tapping keys, yelling commands, swearing at the screen. Sweetcharity stood behind him, trying to get his attention. She looked wild and beautiful and a little desperate.

"Grandpa, Grandpa," she said, tugging at his shoulder. "I've been chased by a liar bee."

"Not now, Sweetcharity," old man Legrand said, shrugging off her hand. "I'm busy."

"A liar bee, Grandpa. The devil's familiar! It spoke to me."

"Fifty thousand on red!" yelled old man Legrand.

"Fifty thousand on red confirmed," said the computer.

"It chased me!" yelled Sweetcharity.

"Be quiet, Sweetcharity. The wheel's in spin. Come on, come on, you little spinner of dreams. Stop on red. Stop on red." The computer uttered a triumphant trumpet blast, and he lurched back in his chair with a gleeful expression, and flung up his arms. "I've won, I've won! I've doubled my money!"

"Oh Grandpa, it's bewitched you," said Sweetcharity. "The infernal box, it's taken your soul."

"There'll be no blasphemy in my house," roared Legrand. "Don't talk to me of stolen souls, you young hussy!"

"The Outsiders, they've bought your birthright for a box of dice!"

"Place your bets, ladies and gentlemen, place your bets," said the computer.

"A hundred thousand on red," yelled Legrand.

"One hundred thousand on red confirmed," said the computer.

"Oh Grandpa, look!" shrieked Sweetcharity. "It's come inside. It's coming to get us. The bee!"

"Be quiet," cried Legrand.

Amanda spoke into the mike in a cool sexy voice. "Actually this throw will land on black, it could not be otherwise."

"Who said that? Who said that?" yelled Legrand.

"The great laws of chance said that," Amanda said.

Legrand looked around wildly. Sweetcharity pointed straight at the bee's eyes. On the screen in Amanda's bedroom, she seemed to be looking straight into my eyes. "There! It's there, Grandpa."

"Last bets, ladies and gentleman," said the computer. "Last bets on throw number five hundred and forty-two of the great mid-week, on-line Gamble-a-Thon."

"Black," Amanda said. "The ball will land on black."

"Change my bet," Legrand yelled at the computer. "Change it to a hundred thousand on black."

"Change of bet confirmed," said the computer.

"It's a liar bee, Grandpa. "It lies. It always lies," Sweetcharity said, looking wild and crazed. "The ball will land on red."

"Change my bet," yelled Legrand. "Change it back to red."

"No further changes permissible," said the computer. "The wheel is in spin."

"Let's watch this," Amanda whispered to me and maneuvered the bee so that we could watch the computer over Legrand's shoulder. On Legrand's screen was a spinning wheel. It was divided into black and red segments, each carrying a white number. A small white ball appeared to be rolling around the wheel at a much slower speed.

"What's that?" I whispered to Amanda.

"Mid-week roulette," Amanda said. "A mugs' game."

The spinning wheel was slowing, the ball was almost stopped. It had stopped. It was in segment number twenty-one. A red segment.

"Ha ha ha, he he he, never believe a liar bee," chanted Amanda into the mike.

"Oh Grandpa, we're ruined," sobbed Amanda.

"Foul fiend of hell!" yelled Legrand.

"Player Legrand, your current credit has been exhausted," said the computer smoothly. "But we at Mid-Week Roulette Limited are happy to offer you further credit in recognition of your loyalty to our company. Should you care to accept this offer, all you need do is place a further bet on the great wheel of fortune. May the luck be with you, Player Legrand."

"A hundred thousand on twenty-two," yelled Legrand.

"Grandpa!"

"Be quiet, Sweetcharity. I know it in my bones. Twenty-two is the winner!"

"He's just betting on one number?" I whispered to Amanda.

"Better odds," Amanda said. "He'll really clean up big time if the ball lands on twenty-two."

I looked at the wheel. There were a total of twenty-four black and red segments and two green ones. "What are the green ones worth?" I whispered.

"Nothing, everybody loses their dough on the green."

"The man's mad," I said.

"No kidding," Amanda said. Then she spoke into the mike, "Twenty-two is a wise choice, Player Legrand. I congratulate you on your gambling wisdom."

"Shut up, you," muttered Legrand, but he sounded secretly pleased.

"Grandpa!" said Sweetcharity. "It lies. It's a liar bee. It lied last time, it's lying now."

Legrand turned his head, craning to look at the bee. The man's face was flushed, his eyes sparkling with greed. But there was doubt in his expression. "Speak true, or I'll smite you back to hell!"

"Twenty-two. True as true," chanted Amanda.

"It lies," wailed Sweetcharity.

"Last bets," said the computer.

Legrand clenched his fists. Sweat ran down his face. He spun to face the computer. "Change that to twenty-four."

"Twenty-four confirmed," said the computer in its level tones.

"Bad choice," said Amanda into the mike.

"The wheel is in spin," said the computer. Everybody watched the ball. Legrand gripped the edge of the table. Sweetcharity stood aghast, her eyes on the screen like a mouse watching a snake. Amanda and I were equally fascinated.

"It'll be bloody funny if it does land on twenty-two," she whispered to me.

Suddenly I wasn't there in her bedroom, not sitting beside her watching the screen. I wasn't even connected in some crazy way, as I had been for a moment or two, with the liar bee. I'd jumped right into the distant whirling roulette wheel. In fact the wheel wasn't even real, you couldn't have touched it with your fingers, it was a sim. I could feel myself spinning, each clicking numbered space spinning at my fingertips as the simulated ball leapt and flew and jumped again in the simulated roulette bowl. I was slowing the wheel, slowing *with* the wheel. I knew exactly where the white ball was in its random flight, and exactly where each slot stood on the wheel that was me. At exactly the right moment I... stopped spinning.

The ball came to rest firmly in the number twenty-two segment.

"Ha ha ha, he he he, always believe the liar bee!"

I glanced at Amanda, shocked and slightly ashamed of myself. She was laughing her head off, eyes bright with pleasure at old man Legrand's come-uppance. She didn't look at me. I realized she didn't know it was my doing.

"Ye vermin from hell, ye flying plague-carrier, ye—"

Legrand was crazed, spitting curses, spitting spit. He hurled himself out of the broken chair which tipped over and went skidding across the room. He flung himself at the wall. Only one thing decorated his dreary kitchen, and a grim decoration at that. It was his whip, hanging from a nail. Within seconds he was flailing the air, cursing and yelling. The tip caught a pewter mug and sent it crashing down, followed by a stained saucepan. Sweetcharity ducked under the table without hesitation. I reckoned she'd had to do that a few times before.

"Time to skedaddle," Amanda said to me and started maneuvering the bee towards the gap under the door. She never made it. There was violent crack and everything on our screen went blank again. I felt the shock go through me. My ears rang.

"Check the self-repairing circuits again, will you," Amanda said to her computer.

"Your bee is totally destroyed," said the computer. "No repair possible."

"Ah well," said Amanda. "You win some, you lose some. You can switch yourself off now." Then she turned to me and said, "It's lucky we've got another bee, Mathewmark. It just might be your salvation."

"What do you mean?" I said. I was moving my jaw carefully. I'd just been king-hit by one of the big kids in the schoolhouse playground. No, that was years ago.

"Well, if it's that madman who's convincing all the other Elders to keep you out of the Valley, and if he's gone and fallen into the secret Outsider vice of gambling—" She paused.

"Amanda." I was feeling very weird and floaty.

"—we've got the makings of a nice little blackmail scam."

I fainted.

When I woke up, Amanda was holding a cold wet face cloth to my forehead, looking anxious.

"Don't worry, Mathewmark, he won't know it was us flying the bee. Anyway, it's his own fault, the old hypocrite."

"Whoa," I said, and sat up. I'd fallen sideways off the chair onto the bed, it looked like, so nothing was broken or even bent out of shape. I put my dazed head in my hands, clutching the cold face cloth. "Listen, there's something I need to tell you about the chip they stuck in me. And, and the liar bee."

29: AMANDA

When I got back from class the next day, Mathewmark was zoned out in front of the vee, looking bored and irritable.

"Come on," I told him, "I have the answer to your blues. And mine. The Mall."

" 'Maul'?" said that amazingly wired hayseed. "Last year Tobius Groomsgulch was mauled by old man Grout's bull when he couldn't scramble over the fence fast enough."

"What was he doing, collecting cow crap or something?" I said. "To spread on the turnips? You nerds probably eat turnips, don't you," I said with a shudder. Actually I've never eaten turnips and don't know what they are, but they sound nasty.

"He was taking a short cut across the paddock to bring Auntie Mc-Weezle her spring seedlings," Mathewmark said. "Every spring we—"

"Anyway," I said, "I didn't say 'maul.' I said 'mall.' You now, m-a-double-l. We've been putting this off long enough. Magistrate Abdel-Malek says you're supposed to get out and mingle, so I'm the bunny who gets delegated."

"I don't know what an m-a-double-l is, Amanda." The boy looked so crestfallen I took pity on him.

"Come here, dopey. We've got to dress you right, and mess up your hair. If you hit the lights in that outfit, everyone will kill themselves laughing."

Myrtle McWeezle had brought him a big suitcase of really shocking clothes, and left it behind when she returned to the Valley. Obviously they spin all their fabrics by hand in that awful place. At least Mathewmark didn't wear baggy yellow longjohns, because I'd made Mom buy him a dozen pairs of boxers and some reasonable yellow and purple striped leggings. His hair was still way too long, and just its normal color. I thought bright pink would be triff, but he backed off with a scary glint in his eye when I suggested it.

I sent Mathewmark down to talk with Mrs. Ng for ten minutes while I got ready. I hadn't been back to the Mall since poor Vik's death, and I wanted to hit them between the eyes.

"Come on, then," I said, coming down the stairs, "it's the shank of the afternoon, let's hit the Mall."

"You still haven't told me what it is."

"Don't be whiny, it's not attractive." Not that he was. Whiny I mean—actually, Mathewmark *is* quite attractive, in exactly the same rough-spun way his clothes aren't. If you see what I mean.

He looked up from the table and wiped a smear of chocolate cake off his mouth. "You look... interesting."

I pirouetted on my heels, and took a bow. Nothing like some primary colors blended with rowdy pastels to cheer you up, I always say. A bit of fake fur, a touch of gleaming plastic, something woven, a bit of clinking chain, couple of strands of optic fiber and mirrors— Not that anyone would notice, they'd all be smirking and poking faces at each other when they caught sight of nature boy in his woolen vest and leather boots and straggly hair. I took a deep breath to give myself courage, shouted goodbye to Mrs. Ng in the kitchen, and dragged Mathewmark out to the waiting cab.

Our metro enclave is way bigger than anything the farm boy had ever seen, outside of vee. Not that it's disgustingly huge and sprawly and filled with poor people like most of the cities. But we do have some sights to make you proud to be a metro citizen. True, half the sights are computer-generated holograms patched over old retrofitted buildings, and a quarter of the rest are flexi-facades that shift and change as the polling indicates the way the mood of the metro is altering, but the most awesome, I reckon, is the Mall.

The cab hummed down Spencer to the river, crossed at the bridge, and turned past the Casino which had all its lights blazing and cavorting despite the afternoon sun. Mathewmark gawked at it as we passed with his jaw dropping, watching a huge cowboy riding a bucking bronco.

"That's the biggest man I've ever seen," he told me seriously.

"It's a hologram, you dodo. Like, a vee thing. A sim. You know, it's not actually there."

"All right," he said irritably, "I get it. Oh, my." And his jaw dropped again.

The cab slid us up the sloped drive and into the Mall's main court parking space. Towers of sugary light reached above us into the clouds. It's funny, you don't actually see the hologram towers until you're right there, inside the projection perimeter, but they look so impressive and tall and glitzy and glumpzoid that you instantly forget the Mall's basically a huge three-dimensional virtual reality projection. The cab recorded my credit, and let us out on the gold-paved pavement.

"I've never seen trees like that," Mathewmark said. "What are they?"

"They're trees, what else do you need to know?" Something came back from a program I'd seen about Los Angeles, before the megaquake. "Palms. They're palm trees."

"They'... wonderful." The farmboy was wandering over to them in a fit of admiration. He reached out to stroke the bark, and literally got a shock when the protective screen hit him with a stinging electric spark.

"No touching, sir," the automatics said coolly. "Please stay behind the yellow line. If you follow the path, you will find excellent shopping opportunities for the most discerning tastes at the House of Mango Eatarium and Clothery. For a flattering make-over, do try the Hair Goes There on level four—"

I dragged him away. "Don't *gawk*, for heaven's sake," I told him in a whisper. "You look like a goose."

He blinked, and kept gawking. "This is the Mall?"

"It's the centre of the social universe," I said. "And because of you I haven't been able to come here for nearly a month."

"I see." Mathewmark pushed his hands into his baggy trouser pockets and glanced sidelong at me. "Nothing to do with what you and your friend Vikram got up to in the Valley, I suppose."

I flushed, I could feel my face going bright red. I wanted to shout something rude and hurtful at him, and opened my mouth to do so, then closed it again. He was absolutely right, of course. He was partly to blame for Vik's horrible death, but he hadn't known what he was doing. The poor farmboy didn't have a clue what a risk he was taking when he stepped into that dark vent and started down the hand-holds. We knew, though, Vikram and me, we knew and we didn't care. We were wild thrillseekers, weren't we, out for an excellent adventure that would make us Mall gods. I trudged along under the brilliant lights, hardly hearing the thumping music from a hundred exciting stores. I couldn't look Mathewmark in the eye. But then I pulled myself together. What the hell, that was then and this was now, and you can't put the toothpaste back in the tube.

I felt Mathewmark's hand touch my shoulder. "I'm sorry, Amanda," he started to say, "that was harsh—" but a shrill yell from overhead cut him off. I raised my eyes to the mezzanine.

"Manda, you're back!" cried Tomasina Gainotti, waving frantically. "Without your wings, but with a new angel."

Juliet Burkenstock stood beside her, drinking a milkshake made of something that seemed to fizz and sparkle. Must be new since my last visit. She was dressed like some old twentieth TV goth character. Tomasina, I saw now, was doing Buffy the Vampire Slayer, not the Kristy Swanson movie, the Sarah Michelle Geller version. She waved her pointed bamboo stake. I tried not to give any indication that I'd seen them. They were the boring try-hards of the Mall. I let my eyes glide this way and that, checking for Steve and Bessie. Couldn't see anyone. Itzhak Posner had come out to the railing now, blinking owlishly behind his glasses, doing Giles the Watcher. He had a pile of old books under his arm, suitable for a librarian of the occult. He was way too short for the role, and just looked more of a jerk than usual. I don't know why they didn't get him fixed with growth hormone, I suppose it's the same prohibition against genome medicine that leaves him with myopic eyes.

"Amanda, your friends are trying to catch your attention," Mathewmark said, tugging at my arm.

"Don't look at them." I hissed between my teeth. "They're dweebs. They're dorks. They're losers and try-hards."

Mathewmark made a strange noise in the back of his throat, but when I glanced at him suspiciously he was just staring at his feet looking miserable. "Come on," I said, "we'll take the shaft up to the 18th level, that's where the dreadest kids hang." Or so I'd heard.

He trotted along after me, hardly rubbernecking at the stores with their pouting mannequin bots and tempting aromas, and followed me into the elevator without a word. Then, as the doors closed, as we started to accelerate upward in a smooth rush, he freaked, to the alarm of the others who had been standing there gazing politely into infinity.

"Oh no, this is a vent," he yelled. He clutched at my arm, and his eyes were wild. "This is one of those devilish tunnels into the bowels of the—"

He slapped his hand against his patched skull. A jangling alarm burst out, and the elevator slammed to a stop. The other three people in the compartment cried out in dismay as the light went off.

It came on again almost instantly, but Mathewmark gave a howl like a dog and plunged against the closed doors. They slid open with a grinding noise, and I saw that we had stopped halfway between floor and ceiling on the fifth floor. Mathewmark crouched, twisted, threw himself through the narrow space and rolled away from the shaft on the burnt-orange carpet. People turned and stared. I squatted in the narrow half-opened doorway, peering down. The floor of the elevator was a good meter higher than it should have been. One of the men inside with me was pushing buttons and speaking firmly to the elevator computer, but nothing was happening. If I tried to jump out now and the compartment started to go up again, I could get mangled. Oh, what the hell. I jumped out, landed on my toes, sprang forward too hard, tumbled over and grazed my hands on the orange carpet.

Behind me, I heard a bang. The elevator doors slammed shut. With a distant hum, it rushed away toward the top of the Mall. That wasn't the only noise. Bells were now ringing everywhere, fire alarms and door buzzers and who knows what else. Piped music was booming away, sitars competing with waltzes, and a ghastly wailing of bagpipes from the Scotch Finger. Lights were going on and off in all the stores and bistros, and a waiter came running out with his moustache on fire and a blazing pancake on a silver tray in one hand. "The machines are going mad," he screamed. "It's the revolt of the robots!"

Mathewmark lay on his back, rigid, eyes rolled back. I crouched over him, slapped him gently on the other side of the face from his implant wound. He was breathing harshly. A woman ran past clutching five silk dresses with tags still on them, and trod on his hand. It made no difference, he just lay there having a fit or whatever it was. I tried to make him sit up. A siren started to hoot, and lights were strobing weirdly, all the vees in all the store windows going nuts, as if they were connected somehow. They flashed lurid red all at the same time, then it was pitch dark for an instant and I heard people moan in fear, then it was bright electric blue, and then dazzling grassy green.

"Come on, wake up, Mathewmark, we have to get out of here!"

He groaned, but it didn't sound like pain, not physical hurt. It sounded like he was trapped by the fiends of hell. He opened his eyes and looked at me.

Something completely terrifying happened.

We were falling in the blue flickering ventilation shaft. Our fingers stretched out to find the rung in the side of the shaft, but we couldn't reach them. Everything smeared. We were looking over the edge of a metal barrier in the flashing darkness. Something roared and rushed. Somebody jumped out into the darkness, flung a black mesh. Another body flew in the dark. We hesitated only an instant, and went over into the darkness as well. Our hands were outstretched. Our legs were flailing in the gusty stale air. We hit something with a foot, a body flew past, smashed and screamed, screaming everywhere, and then our fingers were caught, and the jolting started, smashing and smashing and smash—

I kicked away from him. The Mall was in a kind of electronic meltdown. People were running in every direction, and the elevators were opening and closing, doors banging, hard phones ringing...

"Stop it," I yelled to Mathewmark. "Stop it right now!"

All the virtual displays in all the store windows within eye-sight changed. There was Ebeeneezer, in the window of the fashion shop the woman had stolen her silk dresses from. He nodded his old grey head in the green grass. Auntie McWeezle was trapped in the window of the

Scotch Finger, holding out a plate of steaming scones while Jed Cawthorne pilfered a handful of them from her stove and stuffed them in his shirt. I looked around wildly, unable to believe my eyes. Something was morphing all the vee displays in the Mall, turning them into pictures from Mathewmark's confused and frightened mind. The elevator came past again, stopped, flung open its doors. Luckily there was now nobody inside. Its vee display stopped presenting the elegant polished timber it usually showed. Old man Legrand crouched inside the elevator, or seemed to, bent over his wicked computer. We couldn't hear anything he said, but it was obvious he was playing on the virtual casino again. As we watched, goatish horns grew out from his forehead, and his eyes went red.

"Something wrong with this young fellow?" A middle-aged man bent down over us, opening a bag with professional calm, not letting these mad hallucinations trouble him. "I'm the staff doctor from the health club," he said, running a scanner around Mathewmark's head. "My goodness."

"Yes," I said, "he's had a kind of fit."

"He's been in surgery recently? Something serious done to his head?"

"Implant," I said. "At the Neurological Hospital. His name's Mathewmark Fisher, you should be able to find his emergency records there." Thank heavens doctors can do that immediately if it's an emergency, patch into your health records on the phone-net. I sat back on my heels, swaying a bit, as the doctor rolled up Mathewmark's sleeve and fired in some medicine. Ebeeneezer, munching in the window, made a noise like a strangled chicken and blinked out. So did the other scenes of Valley life. Mathewmark's eyes were shut, and his breathing had gone back to normal.

"He'll be all right," the doctor told me. "We'll get him back to hospital. You'd better come along in the ambulance."

People were talking in small shocked groups. The elevators seemed to have gone back to normal, but I don't think anyone dared to use one just for the moment. After a while, a medical team came up the stairwell with a gurney, splashing through the puddles of fire retardant that had sprayed parts of the Mall. We took Mathewmark down in the elevator once an engineer assured the doctor that it was back to full and reliable functioning capacity. The ambulance had driven in to the lower court, light rotating, and as I walked beside the gurney, with Mathewmark tucked on top under a silvery blanket, I glanced up again at the mezzanine. Elizabeth Wing was staring down with what seemed to be a mixture of envy and bitterness.

I'd done it again. Maybe I wasn't destined to be a Mall god, but I'd certainly managed to impress those try-hards.

30: MATHEWMARK

"Frankly you are a bit of a mystery to us," Dr. Janice said.

"You mean you've made a hash of my implant," I said.

"Well, I wouldn't put it quite like that."

"But look," I said. "Machines and virtual reality sims and midweek roulette wheels—they're not meant to be directly influenced by human thought? I mean, by someone's implant?"

"Well, not quite in the way that you seem to be able to influence them," the doctor said. "Of course your implant is connected to the net by radio, so it's not out of the question."

"I don't exactly *try* to influence them," I said. "It just happens."

"That's the problem," Dr. Janice said. "Quite frankly, we feel it would be better if you were in an environment where there weren't any of society's more complex inventions on hand for you to destroy. The bill for the damage to the Mall is likely to be half this hospital's annual budget. Our lawyers are working on a possible defense at the moment, but it was this hospital that inserted your implant and if liability is proved..."

"You want me to go back to the Valley?" I said hopefully.

"It would make things simpler."

"The Elders said they won't have me back."

"Isn't there any way they can be persuaded?"

"Well, Amanda does have a plan."

"Oh dear, that Kolby-McAllister girl," Dr. Janice said.

"She's your best hope," I said. "She's *my* best hope. There's nothing I want more than to go back home."

They kept me in hospital overnight, for observation, but let me return to Amanda's place the next day. I can't say Amanda's parents were all that glad to have me back. Apparently there had been a lot of publicity about the Mall meltdown. It seemed to have done Amanda's reputation a world of good, at least she said it had. But the publicity hadn't been quite so pleasant for her respectable parents. Nevertheless, they struggled to make me welcome again—but looked very relieved when I said I thought I'd be able to return to the Valley soon.

I still didn't know what Amanda's foolproof plan was, but I soon found out. By the next afternoon Amanda and I were piloting the second bee to the Valley. We made straight for old man Legrand's cabin. Once there, we did a quiet circuit. All seemed rather still. The door was open, so we wafted the bee inside and had it settle on the dusty shelf above the cold stove. There in front of us was the Legrands' kitchen table and there was Legrand. He was collapsed in front of the little computer. Nothing seemed to be happening. I made sure the mike was off and said to Amanda, "Do you think he's dead?"

"No," said Amanda. "I think he's run out of credit."

As we watched, Legrand raised his head and croaked at the little computer, "Just twenty thousand, that's all I ask."

"Credit expired," said the computer pleasantly.

"Ten thousand?"

"Credit expired."

"Five thousand? Five miserable thousand. Just to get me back on my feet again. I've got a winning streak coming, I know it in my bones. Five thousand? Three?"

"Credit can only be granted against security," said the computer. "Please list your assets."

"I live in the Valley of the God of our Choice, Inc.," whined Legrand. "I've only got a small farm, but it must be worth a few thousand."

"Real estate in the Valley cannot be alienated," explained the computer helpfully. "Your farm is not a recognized asset."

"It's all I've got."

"Credit denied."

"I'll get you permission again," Legrand said. "You can build another tunnel."

"The MagLev Authority requires no new tunnels under the Valley. Your services as a confidential consultant have been terminated."

"Oh, God of my choice, what am I to do?"

"There I cannot help you, sir," said the computer. "And I must warn you that the batteries are running low. Any further communication will require vigorous pedaling."

I was putting two and two together, shocked by the elder's shameless ways. "That's how the tunnelers got permission in the first place," I said to Amanda, shaking my head in disbelief. "They went and bribed Legrand. They got him to persuade all the other Elders."

"Looks like it," Amanda said. "Normal business practice, I would have thought."

"They must have slipped him the computer at one of those Gatehouse meetings," I said.

Amanda nodded, grinning. Nothing shocks that girl. "And once they got him hooked on midweek roulette, they could get him to do anything they liked. Okay, let's have a chat to him." Amanda switched the mike back on and said, "Ah good afternoon, Mr. Legrand, perhaps I can be of assistance."

Legrand lifted his head and looked around. "Who said that?" he growled.

"I am your friendly liar bee," Amanda said. "And I hold the keys to your salvation."

"I'll swat you like I swatted your foul companion," Legrand said. "There wasn't much left of that damn fiend—"

Legrand glanced at his whip hanging on the wall, but made no attempt to grab it. His voice was hoarse and feeble. All the fight seemed to have gone out of him. He was just going through the motions.

"I can arrange credit," Amanda said.

"Credit?" Legrand said. Small sparks of hope glinted in his bloodshot eyes.

"And with credit," Amanda said, "the wheel will spin for you again. You could win millions, billions, trillions..."

"And I'd have to make a pact with the devil, would I not?" Legrand whispered.

"Better the devil you know than the Maglev Authority," Amanda said.

"You're a fiend from polluters' hell," Legrand mumbled.

"I'm a source of credit," Amanda said.

"And what do you want in payment for this credit?"

"The return of Mathewmark, son of this Valley."

"That young lecher, always whispering his vile blandishments into the ears of Sweetcharity..."

"Be that as it may," Amanda said.

"The fleshpots of the Outside are welcome to his presence."

"It is in the fleshpots of the Outside that the offices of Midweek Roulette can be found," Amanda said. "Even as we speak, the wheel is spinning, fortunes are being made, Lady Luck is smiling. But she is not smiling for thee, Elder Legrand."

Old man Legrand lay his head upon the table again and closed his eyes. We watched in silence. The muscles of his face twitched and clenched. Rage and despair and greed showed on his sightless face. He opened his eyes and looked up.

"And all you want, bee from hell, is the return of Mathewmark?"

"It's a deal."

"It's a deal for fifty thousand," Legrand said from between clenched teeth.

"It's a deal for fifty," Amanda said.

"Thousand?"

"Fifty. Full stop."

"Begone. Before I crush ye."

"All you have to do," Amanda said slowly, "is bet on the numbers I tell you to. Fifty will soon multiply."

"Begone."

"I just might do that," Amanda said with a sigh. "And then you'll never get credit... ever."

"All right," Legrand said at last, "But the fifty had better multiply and multiply fast."

"You are going to need recharged batteries," Amanda said. "Start pedaling, old man."

But Legrand made no move to pedal anything. He rose and made his way to the door of the cabin. Voice suddenly back to full strength, he yelled, "Sweetcharity! Get in here. Bring the contraption. Now!"

Amanda switched off the mike. "What a ratbag," she said to me. "He's going to make that poor drip of a girl recharge the batteries."

Half a minute later, Sweetcharity backed through the cabin door, lugging a thing that looked like a foot-operated butter churn. Amanda almost choked laughing. "They must have given him an old-fashioning wiring diagram to build that heap of crap," she said. "It's like something out of the middle ages! What'd he use, a soldering iron?"

"He might have found it in the basement of our Museum of Wicked Ways," I said. "We have an old automobile in there that still runs, we start it up once a year on All Hallows Night during the bon-fire and drive it around the sports oval while all the little kids throw mud balls at it. Anyway, we did until a couple of years ago and then we ran out of gasoline. I never got a chance to drive it."

Sweetcharity heaved the thing into place, looking ready to burst into tears.

"Connect her up, girl," Legrand said. "And look smart about it."

"Oh Grandpa," Sweetcharity said. "No good will come of it."

"Connect her up and get pedaling!"

I watched with increasing rage as my own beloved Sweetcharity attached wires to the computer and climbed onto the modified butter churn and started pedaling. Amanda was giving soft verbal instructions to our own computer. The screen flashed up a message. "There," she said with satisfaction, "credit transfer complete. The damn fool now has fifty to play with."

"He'll just lose it," I said.

"No he won't," Amanda said. "You've got to make sure the ball stops in the right segment."

"But—"

"No buts, Mathewmark. You've done it before. Do it again."

"I wasn't *trying* before."

"You weren't exactly 'trying' in the Mall, but you practically fused the whole shebang."

"I'll give it a go," I said.

Amanda flicked the mike back on. "OK, Sweetcharity, hop off that thing. Legrand, get ready to play."

"A liar bee!" screamed Sweetcharity.

"Never you mind about no liar bee," yelled Legrand. "Lady Luck is smiling on me."

"Bet on number twenty-one," Amanda said.

"Don't do it," Sweetcharity pleaded. "The liar bee lies!"

But Legrand took no notice and placed his bet. Amanda maneuvered the bee off the shelf and positioned it in the air where we could see the roulette wheel.

"No more bets," said Legrand's computer. "The wheel is in spin."

"OK, Mathewmark," Amanda whispered to me. "Do it."

I concentrated like hell. I brought all my thoughts to bear on the spinning wheel, the trundling ball. Nothing happened. The wheel began slowing. I tried with all my might to recreate what I had felt before, I tried to become the wheel, to be the wheel. But all I was doing was sitting in Amanda's room, tensing every muscle in my body, looking at the roulette wheel on the screen through half-closed eyes. "It's no good," I muttered.

"You're trying too hard," Amanda said. "I'll take your conscious mind off the task."

Suddenly she grabbed me under the armpits with both hands, tickling me fit to bust. I collapsed in hopeless giggles. I collapsed into the wheel. I was the wheel, and the wheel was me. And I was almost stopped. The ball was clacking towards its resting place on number ten. Without any deliberate thought I eased the wheel, I eased myself, to a halt. The ball clicked into number twenty-one.

And then I was back in Amanda's room, watching old man Legrand slathering at the mouth and rubbing his hands together as he prepared to place his next bet.

"Well, that's how it's done," Amanda said. "Don't try too hard. If you do I'll tickle you again."

Within half an hour we had Legrand's stake up to fifty thousand. "Righto, Legrand, I'm off now," Amanda said. "Just do what you promised or I'll never come back."

"Don't, don't come back," Sweetcharity said.

"Come back!" yelled Legrand. "Just one more spin of the wheel, just one more spin—"

But we heard no more, Amanda had taken the bee out of the door and was setting a course for home.

"I'm not sure he'll convince the Elders to let me back," I said.

"Of course, he will," Amanda said. "He'll lose that fifty thousand in two days flat. Then he'll want more credit, but he'll know the liar bee won't play ball until he's got you back in the Valley. He'll be desperate. I reckon the invitation to return will rock up on about Friday."

It actually rocked up on Thursday. The Elders of the Valley of God of their Choices, Inc had sought wisdom from the divinities and spirits of their choice and it had been revealed to them that the prodigal son Mathewmark Fisher should return to the Valley of his birth... On and on it went in Legrand's increasingly desperate handwriting.

"They want me back," I said to Amanda. "They say they think my presence will prevent a great pestilence."

"Mumbo jumbo," said Amanda. "But I'm glad for your sake, Mathewmark," and she kissed me. It was a nice kiss.

"I'll miss you," I said.

"No you won't," Amanda said.

"Yes I will," I said. "I'll wonder what you are up to, how things are going on the outside."

"Then I'll tell you," Amanda said.

"How?" I said.

"You've got a telephone in your head, dumbo. We can yack to each other any time we like."

31: AMANDA

Official Communication To the Clerk of Court

Dear Sir/Madam

Could you please place this message in the registered Public Database of communications with the court. Could you please forward a copy to Mr. Abdel-Malek.

Dear Magistrate,

As I am sure you know, Mathewmark has been allowed to return to his Valley. I reckon I played a small part in making the Elders change their minds and come to their senses. But when Mathewmark has gone, I'll be confined to home and school again. This doesn't seem fair. Have you got any more hayseeds who need showing around? If so, I'd like to offer my services. Yours sincerely Amanda Kolby-McAllister

PS. If I go to the Gatehouse with Mathewmark, I'll be in breach of the court's orders on my way home. Is this all right?

Official Communication

Magistrate Abdel-Malek to Ms. Amanda Kolby-McAllister

For inclusion in the Public Database

Dear Ms. Kolby-McAllister,

As the supervising Magistrate I deem it my duty to accompany Mr. Mathewmark Fisher to the Gatehouse to insure that his re-entry to the Valley of the God of his Choice proceeds smoothly. As his court appointed mentor you may also accompany Mr. Fisher. I will insure that your return home is not in breach of court orders. I shall call for you both in my autoglide at 0900 hours tomorrow.

Yours sincerely M.K. Abdel-Malek

* * * *

"We've got a lift," I said to Mathewmark. "Mr. Abdel-Malek himself."

"He might want to ask us questions," Mathewmark said. "You know, about the liar bees. About how we blackmailed old man Legrand. About how I fixed the roulette wheel." He looked panicked.

"I don't think he will," I said. "I reckon Mr. Abdel-Malek knows when not to ask questions. Anyway, I'll take Strad the Lad. That'll shut him up."

* * * *

They're wafted around in pretty plush autoglides, these Magistrates. Big as a limo, and the acoustics were brill. All the way out to the Gatehouse I played the Tchaik, which is shockingly tricky but I wanted to impress Mr. Abdel-Malek. I started to crunch, as usual, the uneven tones setting my teeth on edge, and I brought the bow down too hard. There's nothing airy and ethereal about a violin bow, however it might look to the audience. It's a hammer, remember? The E string broke.

I felt like bursting into tears, but nobody said anything nasty. Nobody said anything at all, in fact. I packed Strad the Lad away. Mr. Abdel-Malek sat with his eyes closed and didn't open them until the autoglide soundlessly lowered itself to the ground in front of the Gatehouse. Mathewmark had blinked once at the horrid screech as the string went, and then had gone back to his non-stop rubber-necking through the view-paneling. Was he pleased to be leaving the Outside? Was he secretly sorry that he'd never be returning? Did he half-wish he could have stayed longer on the Outside, seen more, experienced more? Or was he full of excitement at returning to his beloved Valley? All of the above, I reckoned.

The three of us walked across the forecourt to the Gatehouse. It was a grim stone building with no windows facing the Outside. On both sides high stone walls stretched between the Gatehouse and the cliffs forming the Valley. The door was huge, solid wood studded with nails. As we approached it, it creaked slowly upwards like an old portcullis. Talk about quaint. We entered a large room, well-lit by glazed windows on the Valley side. Outside, in the sunlight, I could see Ebeeneezer standing patiently with his cart. In the room, a huge wooden table stretched out between us and the reception committee. I recognized Auntie McWeezle, of course, and Lukenjon and old man Legrand. The others I didn't know, I reckoned they must be Elders. I don't think Mathewmark's parents were there, probably they disapproved. Old man Legrand had a parchment document in his hands.

"Mathewmark Fisher," Legrand said, reading from the parchment like some croaking old prophet, "the Elders, in their mercy and their wisdom have permitted you to re-enter the Valley despite the machinery of the devil that resides in your foolish and sinful young head—"

"It's no more foolish or sinful than a roulette wheel," I said in a conversational tone.

Legrand stopped talking, pole-axed. One or two of the others blinked, glanced at me in puzzlement. Myrtle McWeezle paid no attention to anything but her beloved nephew. She came quickly forward to her side of the huge table and stood there with her arms extended.

"Auntie," Mathewmark said.

"Mathewmark," Auntie McWeezle said. "Thank the Goddess..."

"Good to see you," Lukenjon called. "I'm sick of doing your work and mine."

"Brother," said Mathewmark, nodding, a huge grin breaking out on his face.

He turned and offered his hand to Mr. Abdel-Malek. He embraced me, pulling me against him for a moment, gave me a chaste kiss, and then let me go without another word. I felt a kind of happy hum inside my head, which I guessed was Mathewmark doing things to my phone again without knowing it. Then he took a huge flying leap onto the table, and in a twinkling was on the floor on the far side, among his own people, embracing, kissing, shaking hands, talking rapidly.

Only Legrand stood apart. He seemed to recover from his pole-axed condition, he cleared his throat and began again in his pompous drone, "These are the solemn conditions and requirements that are placed upon you, Mathewmark—"

"Hey, you." I sidled up to the table and stood directly opposite Legrand. Out of the corner of my mouth I muttered, "I'd dump that infernal computer of yours, if I were you. The liar bee has gone on strike. No more hot tips..."

Legrand looked furtively around to see if anybody else had heard me, but everyone was concentrating on Mathewmark. The Elder fixed me with his crazed eyes.

"You?" he said.

"Buzzzzzz," I said.

Mr. Abdel-Malek stepped in beside me about then and gently took me by the arm. "Time to go, Amanda." Deep inside my head, I still felt Mathewmark's warm, happy humming. For some reason that made me think of poor dead Vikram, who wasn't there because of our stupid prank. I thought of Vikram's tiny clone twin brother, growing in a tank in a hospital. At least Mathewmark was alive and happy and about to go home with his family. I gave the Magistrate a kind of determined grin, feeling my eyes prickle, and he led me back through the big gateway into the bright daylight of the Outside.

AFTERWORD

I met Rory Barnes in 1964; he and a number of fellow students would become friends and live together singly or in couples in various houses, on and off, for years after. Rory was majoring in Philosophy, with side dishes of English Lit and Politics; his murderously witty and good looking girlfriend was Helene Barnes, no relation. A mutual friend was Jean Bedford, later a notable Australian writer. There were others, a merry crew. I was a couple of years ahead of them at Monash University (for many years now an international hotbed of genetic engineering, but then a murk of red mud still under construction), but found their laidback intelligence and mirth irresistible. In 1965 we all moved into an old farm house, nicknamed the Vatican (not my coinage, although I'd spent two years in a Catholic monastery before university) a mile or so from campus, and lived there that year even after we managed to burn several rooms, including the kitchen, into uselessness.

There was the war in Vietnam, and the draft. None of us was caught in it, but we all played our small dissident parts. It was, of course, the best and worst of times. It is against this seething background of the twentieth century that the tangential history of the Broderick & Barnes collaborations began,

My first collection of short stories came out in that year of the Vatican, but my pals followed different trajectories until Rory and Jean had their first novels in print years later. In fact, although Rory's first novel was written in the early 1970s it wasn't until 1983 that a transformed version of it, science-fictionized by me as *Valencies*, appeared from the University of Queensland Press. (Jean's first book was a tender, poignant short story collection, *Country Girl Again*, in 1979, and her notable novel about the sister of bushranger Ned Kelly, *Sister Kate*, was published in 1987.)

Years after *Valencies*, I wrote a radio drama, *Zones*, for the Australian Broadcasting Corporation, and decided it would make a good spine for a Young Adult novel. I couldn't get it to gel, though, and invited Rory (who by then was living in Adelaide, South Australia, 450 miles away from my place in Melbourne, Victoria) to join the fun. And it *was* fun; the story opened out, a new voice joined the narration, the plot thickened, our new ending curled back satisfyingly to the beginning. It was bought by HarperCollins Australia, in 1997, for their Moonstone imprint—and ever since has been listed witlessly in some places as *Zones (Moonstone)*, as if that's the title

In both *Zones* and the next Broderick&Barnes collaboration, *Stuck in Fast Forward* (HarperCollins Australia 1999) which eventually grew up to become *The Hunger of Time (E-Reads 2004),* we spent some days working on the same computer at Rory's and his wife Annie's place in Adelaide. If one author got restless and abandoned the keyboard in mid sentence, the other might sit down and keep going, having first edited the existing text on the screen. And, of course, with our long-distance novels we've been able to bat stuff back and forth by email between Adelaide and Melbourne or San Antonio as often as we like. The real trick to joint authorship is to accept that the final version will be something completely different from the novel you'd have written alone. Control freaks need not apply. The rewards of working together are easily stated: you get twice the inventiveness when it comes to twists and turns in the plot and you have characters who are the products of two different minds. In some ways, the interaction between characters in a jointly written novel mirrors the interaction between the authors. And it's enjoyable working with another person on something usually as solitary and even lonely as writing.

Here's what happened with the novel that briefly had the working title *Hell's Teeth*, now the more salient *The Valley of the God of Our Choice, Inc.* Various of the States that comprise the Commonwealth of Australia hold annual or biennial Writers' Festivals, always well attended under a raging summer sun. Probably the most famous internationally is the Adelaide Writers' Festival. Not to be outdone, science and philosophy took up the challenge, and the inaugural Adelaide Festival of Ideas was held, unusually, in early July 1999, the middle of cold rainy winter in Australia. (It's now more sensibly convened in October.) I was an invited guest, dining with the brilliant polymathic cosmologist and lucid science writer Professor Paul Davies, the equally fecund mind scientist Professor Allan Snyder, and plenty of other science groupies like me.

Staying again with Rory and Annie, I thought it would be jolly to start another co-authored novel, so we began one that quickly died, *Chatterbots*, then settled on our idea of a future in which extremely high technology ruled the roost everywhere except in enclaves of fundamentalists of a cultish kind. We plotted sections during brisk walks through the parks and elegant streets of Adelaide, churches of the God of various choices on many corners, then wrote chapters in the accustomed hot-word processor manner. *Hell's Teeth* was started on July 14, 1999. By the 19th, back in Melbourne, I made a calendar note that we had 30,000 words drafted. Of course by this time we were swapping ideas and chapters by email. On August 14, the first draft was done; by the 19th it was edited and ready for submission.

* * * *

It's possible to write a novel in a month, but it takes way longer than that to submit it to a publisher (even one who's published several of your previous books) and get an answer. Months crawled by. On April 6, 2000, HarperCollins Australia declined the book. We'd lost hope by then and submitted it in parallel to Penguin; they rejected it by the 11th. On the 17th we sent it to Hodder; at that point my records get too confusing to follow, but that press, too, declined our story.

Why? If you've now read *The Valley of the God of Our Choice, Inc.*, you'll know that it's a sprightly, entertaining tale with more than a few moments of action, danger, romance, and humor. I suspect in part that we were undermined by a tectonic shift from science fiction to fantasy in Australian genre fiction-marketing, which has since consolidated into an empire of gigantic trilogies mostly by skilled women writers whose work is now read in the millions around the world. It wasn't that Aussies stopped reading or watching science fiction, but when they chose to do so it was easiest to pick up an imported US or British novel or reliable franchise confection (*Star Wars, Star Trek*, that sort of thing). Meanwhile, publishers such as HarperCollins found that their profits were so greatly enhanced with fantasy fiction that it would be foolish to buy more sf when for the same investment they could sell hundreds of thousands of fat fantasies.

Rather than beat a dozen more dead horses, I decided to revisit this novel, recast it as a more ambitious and serious adult work, introduce new characters and background, carry the narrative forward… all the way to the literal end of the world, in fact. That became *Transcension*, which a couple of years later in the US Tor published under my name alone (rather unfairly to Rory, whose input makes up nearly a quarter of the novel, as is acknowledged obliquely in the book's dedication). It won the Aurealis award for the best Aussie sf novel of 2002.

Still, it seemed to baffle many American readers. Granted, more than any other genre of fiction, science fiction in many respects transcends national boundaries, even language boundaries. But under the surface, distinctive tones and elements set Aussie voices apart. Our fiction shares a kind of relaxed, mocking tone toward authority—what Australians call a "larrikin" attitude. Even when we're writing about massive brain damage and its cybernetic repair, or the end of the world, we remain a bit facetious, a bit ironic, a bit playful.

That's true also, inevitably, of *The Valley of the God of Our Choice, Inc.* The mood is a little like that of the joke by famous British comic Bob Monkhouse: "I want to die like my father, peacefully in his sleep, not screaming and terrified, like his passengers." Rory caught that mood of macabre black humor in a reminiscence about the transition from this book to *Transcension*:

I was once in conversation with Peter Corris [the crime novelist husband of our long-ago housemate Jean Bedford] about the way the decades seemed to flash by with ever increasing speed. He instantly came back with this witticism.

But at my back I always hear
Time's winged chariot changing gear.

Some years later I relayed this to you and more years later you used the quote at the beginning of *Transcension*, attributing it appropriately to Corris. Some in-house lawyer at Tor wanted to know if we had got Corris's permission to quote him. No, we hadn't, but would. You wrote to Corris seeking this favor. Peter, inexplicably, denied authorship of the quip and insisted that if I had some recollection of it occurring in a conversation, then I must have said it. This was duly relayed to the lawyer. Fine, said the lawyer, is Mr. Barnes happy to have his name on the quote? No, certainly not—Mr. Barnes is one of the authors of the book, you can't quote yourself in an epigraph. You pointed out that it was only the last two words that were in contention, all the rest was pure Andrew Marvell. Oh, well, said the lawyer, if the quote has two authors, both of them need to give permission. Have you approached Mr. Marvell? No, no, we replied, don't worry about Mr. Marvell, we have reason to believe he's dead. Oh well, in that case you must approach his estate, do you know the name of his literary executor? Don't worry about Mr. Marvell's literary executor, we've reason to believe he's dead as well.

I thought this was hilarious and fell off my chair. But in the event we took the softer, kinder path and the epigraph's attribution, as published, read:

Apologies to Andrew Marvell
(1621-1678)

Time's chariot is still accelerating. These days we call it the impending Singularity (or sometimes the Spike). But occasionally we can recover a moment of the past, that simpler time. This has been such a moment. We hope you kicked back and enjoyed it. Or if you're the kind of irritating reader, like me, who goes straight to the Afterword first, well, hop back right now to the start and chow down.

—Damien Broderick,
January 2014